# FOAM

*on the*

# CREST

*of*

# WAVES

# FOAM on the CREST of WAVES

*a novel*

silke stein

This is a work of fiction. Names, characters, places, and incidents
either are the product of the author's imagination
or are used fictitiously, and any resemblance to actual persons,
living or dead, businesses/companies, events, or locales
is entirely coincidental.

Text copyright © 2018 by Silke Stein
All rights reserved.

Published by Caper Books

No part of this book may be reproduced, or stored in a retrieval
system, or transmitted in any form or by any means, electronic,
mechanical, photocopying, recording, or otherwise,
without express written permission of the author.

FOR RANDALL

# PROLOGUE

*M*ommy must rest now, to gather strength. Later she will be able to help me haul her into the dinghy. Her funny bone points toward the sky while the gunwale rubs against the soft flesh on the inside of her elbow. I clasp her cold hand with both of mine; the ocean wants to play tug of war. Her fingers are wet and slippery like bull kelp leaves — I fear they will escape my small palms any moment.

    She watches the clouds rushing across the sun. I gaze at her white face. Water splashes over her eyeballs, nose and mouth. My lips are salty too. From tears, or sweat, or from the whitecaps' froth, I can't tell them apart.

    The wind is stronger now. I feel its force. Waves pound against the thin hull of my small vessel.

The sea gurgles and foams all around us. Sea foam.

I hear a low rumbling and peer at the horizon. Far out in the west, a container ship goes by. Too far to spot us. The jagged rocks of the shoreline to my right show no interest either. The cliff tops are empty. Nobody lives on this part of the coast. Nobody will look out the window and see our struggle. No one knows I'm here.

I cower in the dinghy, still clasping her white hand. How cold can skin get? Hers seems colder than the icy water. I want to jump overboard and hug her, warm her, and bring her ashore. I can swim as well as a dolphin, but my wetsuit lies in the trunk of our car, which is parked behind the boathouse.

My arms are numbed by the chill, and tired because of the ocean's nasty pulling. I claw my fingers into the cuff of her sleeve. The rubber stretches. Her arm twists and I let it go. It bumps against the boat's side and flops into the water.

I bend over the gunwale, reach down and seize the hood of the wetsuit top, which is floundering around her neck.

I try to lift her head. Ocean spray pelts my face.

My hair hangs down into the water and mingles with hers. Long red locks, swirling — like in the mermaid painting on my bedroom wall, like in the pictures of the lovely book she made for my sixth birthday two years ago.

"Please," I shout, jerking her neck, "you have to help me!" Her chin pokes up. Water runs into her nostrils.

She must be too exhausted to move — or to speak.

We are face to face. Her clear blue eyes stare without seeing me.

I yank the hood again.

Her body shifts sideways.

The dinghy thumps against her. I wince and let go of the hood. The hull strikes her a second time. Right on the forehead, where the Band-Aid was. The cut stopped bleeding a while ago.

She floats, looking skyward again, unmoved, enduring the pain in silence while the water gushes over her face. Her beautiful face. Oh, if only I hadn't come. "Stay in your room, Abbie, until I get you!" she had said. I didn't obey.

I try to grab her shoulder, but I can't get ahold of the slippery rubber. I try to seize her hair, but it swirls out of reach. I paddle with my hands, attempting to move the boat closer, but the sea tosses her farther and farther away — away from me.

"Mommy," I scream. "Don't leave me!" A wave leaps at my face. I blink and cough out water, and when I look for her again, she's gone.

# One

## ABALONE
### FRIDAY AFTERNOON

The eelgrass sways. Kelp curtains shelter me. I sit among the leafy pillars of the serene temple, looking up at the shimmering roof of azure. Streamers of sunlight dance through the moving water. Floating algae touch my arms like loving sisters. The current's supple melodies wave by my ears.

Down here, we don't use words. Yet they lie in wait, in the niches of my brain, ready to crawl out and gather, unbidden, unwanted, whenever I try to forget them and become one with the world I love. How can I describe the peace surrounding me with blunt expressions that tarnish its beauty?

How can I praise the soothing cool, the colors of the anemones, my finned companions, without employing the only language I know?

During the last seven years, I have mastered silence — learned to ignore my tongue, as I could not rid myself of it. I never speak to the Props; however, I have no choice but to think their thoughts. That is, until I meet my people. They will teach me their ways and words, and call me by my true name.

Abalone Macklintock — I drag this tag around like an anvil chained to my ankle, though not for much longer. Soon, I'll be able to leave everything on land behind when the indigo gates finally open and my new life begins.

I stretch out my limbs, and my fin brushes past a holdfast next to me. It doesn't budge. Oh, to grab onto the ocean floor like the bull kelp with its tasseled anchors — to never let go again, to never leave this place. I suppress the urge to sigh. I still have about three more minutes before I'll need air.

Across from me, by the fissured rocks, the slender kelp stems part, and a small face appears. The diving sunrays reflect off smooth, speckled fur, turning the forehead and shoulders silvery white. It's a young one, maybe six or seven months old. Yet, it moves without the natural gaiety of a harbor seal pup. Dark eyes stare at me, mirroring my mood.

Contrary to mine, though, its unhappiness is curable, its predicament obvious: it wears a necklace — and not a pretty one. Choked by a Prop-made device, ensnared by people who do not care that what they do brings pain to others, the little seal is facing death by slow suffocation.

It lingers close to me, only a few yards away.

Holding its gaze, I hope understanding and compassion will show in my eyes. No words could ever soothe this suffering.

My knees bend; a quick dolphin kick propels me forward, and I thrust my fingers into the thick bright-green mesh tangled around the creature's throat. It trembles but doesn't attempt to bolt. I yank at the nylon netting, to no avail. Some of the strings are already embedded in the blubber.

I grab the small diving knife hanging from my weight belt. Usually it is employed to harvest kelp blades and stipe, but now it will give life. The seal keeps still as I fix its body with my thighs and start cutting the twisted ropes. I have to be quick; I don't feel the need to breathe yet, but I know with the physical effort it can't be much longer. With every string coming off, I envy the seal more, and long to slash my own ties to the world I have to return to. The seal's head pushes against my belly as the knife slides over its wounded skin. Carefully, I sever the last tightly wrapped cord.

I loosen my thigh hold and the seal zips upward, its belly grazing my face. Above my head, it performs a series of loops and rolls as if wanting to confirm its liberation. I wave my hand farewell, but it darts back to me, nuzzles my shoulder and then thanks me with the ultimate proof of seal affection, the nose touch, before it vanishes into the emerald wilderness of the kelp forest.

Flooded with joy, I dash to the surface for air. Soon I will be free as well. When I'm fifteen, the ocean will take me away.

# Two

## JEREMY
### FRIDAY AFTERNOON

Here she comes, Jeremy thought, wishing his collector's chests were big enough to hide inside. Tessa Pullman prowled through the aisles.

Her smokey eyes firmly focused on him, she dished out greetings to fellow exhibitors along the way, oozing cheer out of every opening in her lime-green lace tunic. Her boot-cut yoga pants hugged her thighs; she had put on a couple of pounds since he last saw her.

"They should ban you from coming here," she said, planting herself in front of him. Her matte pink lips puckered into a fake pout as she glanced over the items piled up on the table between them.

"Your daughter's creations are too awesome. Nobody will want to buy ours."

Jeremy managed a half-smile.

"Hi, Tessa."

"Has Abalone been talking lately?" She tossed her hair over her shoulder, trapping him in a cloud of vanilla and musk. Apparently Tessa thought a few intoxicated nights together entitled her to a lifetime supply of private information. He had learned his lesson during the last three years.

"Not as much as we would like." Jeremy winced, hearing the blatant lie leave his lips. Not as much. Abbie hadn't spoken at all.

"That must be so tough for you." Her face displayed adequate compassion. "But her pieces are wonderful. More amazing every time I see them."

"Yes, I could sell twice as much. She works with precision, though," he said, shuffling from one foot to the other, waiting for the inevitable.

"Just like her father," Tessa said. Her fingertips stroked along the edge of the small sugar maple chest next to her. "Any plans for the evening?"

"Yup, I'm meeting a high school pal in Morro Bay to discuss a business opportunity." In reality, he had an appointment with a bucket of KFC at the local Econo Lodge to watch a recording of San Antonio beating the Heat.

"Too bad," Tessa said and twisted the golden chain of the clumsily wire-wrapped pendant hanging from her neck. "If you feel like having a drink tomorrow —"

"I'll let you know." Jeremy nodded. "Hi, Saralyn, nice to see you," he said, smiling at the spindly teenager who had materialized at his stand unaware of rescuing him from Tessa's advances.

She held out entry forms for the Shard of the Year contest. "Hello, Mr. Macklintock."

"Thanks, Saralyn," Jeremy said and took a form. "Tell your grandmother I'm going for first prize. Abbie has found a giant multi with yellow and orange."

The girl smiled back, exposing her braces. "How does she find all these great pieces?"

"She has Glass Beach right at her doorstep. It's an unfair advantage."

"Yeah, lucky her. And she makes the best stuff ever. I've been saving my money for one of the seahorses. They're so cool. My friend Callie got one in April for her birthday. She never stops bragging about it. I want either a turquoise or a cobalt-blue one. I'm still short, though."

The girl's eyes danced from piece to piece while Tessa observed her from under long dark lashes with growing impatience, obviously contemplating how she could shoo Saralyn to the next table. Being interrupted by this youthful exuberance visibly annoyed her. Or was it the realization that her own goods would never evoke such reactions? Upstaged by a fourteen-year-old. Although, his daughter's jewelry had already outclassed Tessa's when he met her four years ago, after venturing out with twenty-seven pendants, eighteen bracelets and uncertain expectations to his first Sea Glass Festival in Santa Cruz. He ended up, on the evening of the first day, with an empty table and a pile of business cards from gift store owners along the coast, willing to take as much as he could deliver. The unsuspected success and the determined attentions of Tessa Pullman, the ostentatious beauty who exhibited to his left, led to a celebration dinner with too much wine and, before long, swept him into her deluxe ocean-view hotel suite.

"Stop kidding me," she said, when they both lay sprawled on the king size bed, the late night breeze cooling their skin. "I have seen crafts done by children." Neither could she believe that Abbie had designed the logo for Abalone's Own. "You're going to live off child labor." Tessa laughed and poured herself another glass of Pinot Noir. "Wait until she discovers boys." By then he had been drunk enough to tell her what had happened, causing her to get doe-eyed and comfort him with her curves.

"Wow, these mermaid tails are wicked!" Saralyn exclaimed, bending sideways over the table to get closer to the coveted pieces. "You didn't have them last year. I wish I could weave the wire as evenly as she does. They're super cute."

Tessa emitted a muffled snort and snatched a sheet from Saralyn's hand, clearly intending to communicate to the bubbly teenager that it was time for her to end the conversation and resume her duties elsewhere.

Jeremy picked up a tail with aquamarine and another with teal-colored glass and held them out to Saralyn. "Here, have a look," he said. His feelings for Tessa had waned together with the effects of the alcohol, whereas business with the gift stores soon started to flourish. Most of them took a chest or a collector's table too, which made him feel good. They sold now and then, and he was asked to replenish. Some people still understood the value of craftsmanship.

He gradually raised the prices of Abbie's work. Her favorites though, she kept for herself. The walnut chest he had given her last Christmas overflowed with them. Stunning pieces, fit to be worn in the presence of royalty. He secretly stashed away the ones he liked best out of the many Abbie handed over to him. He didn't know what made her reject them. To him, they all looked flawless, sublime. She papered the walls of her studio with layers of drawings. Every week new designs emerged. A year ago she started making sets, necklaces with matching earrings. Wonders of finesse.

Saralyn laid down her entry forms, took the offered tails and cradled them in her palm.

She was almost as tall, yet worlds apart from Abbie's graceful gestures, mournful gemlike eyes — and dormant tongue.

"Oh my goodness," Saralyn blurted, as if to confirm Jeremy's thoughts. "They're so lovely. Adorable. Just awesome!"

Abbie's work had that effect on most people: genuine enchantment, like watching wild horses run. "It's a new style she came up with recently," Jeremy said, smiling. "Let's see what I have left on Sunday afternoon, and maybe we can talk about a discount."

"Fantastic! That would be cool! Thank you, Mr. Macklintock." Saralyn looked like she needed to hug somebody immediately.

Tessa cleared her throat with a simpering cough and moved backward; she had obviously decided to temporarily retreat her forces.

"See you, Jeremy," she muttered and set off toward her tables on the other side of Vet's Hall. The last couple of years, Jeremy had made sure to book a space as far away from her as possible. He knew she would be back, sooner rather than later.

Saralyn placed the tails carefully back in the half-finished display arrangement and reclaimed her forms. "I should get going too. Have a great show."

# Three

## GINA
### FRIDAY AFTERNOON

A light breeze coming from the ocean refreshed the afternoon. Gina gave the tires of her wheelchair a spin and moved closer to the open patio door. She could spend a couple of hours on the deck, just sitting in the sun, doing squat. She looked at her planters. The lavender needed trimming. It's soothing fragrance wafted toward her while Gina gazed across the backyard. The lawn was light brown, like a deer hide — behind it, nothing but bright Pacific blue. Sea and sky melded, no clouds visible above, no whitecaps below. Just seamless, dazzling blue.

Far out on the water drifted a small vessel.

Was it the *Baby Clam*?

She couldn't tell without her binoculars. Her hand reached into the side pocket of the chair. Empty. She must have left them in the living room.

Usually, Abbie stayed much closer to the shore. Where, of course, the height of the cliff face concealed her from Gina's view.

No need to worry, though, the sea was calm today. Gina took her eyes off the boat and examined the herbs. She might cut some basil or parsley for supper after the groceries were packed away.

Gina drove over to her prep zone and lifted the delivery box from her lap onto the wooden counter. What a blessing to have a carpenter as a brother. She couldn't imagine living without all the alterations Jeremy had made: the lowered cabinets and shelves, the knee-high sink, the kitchen island with the stove on her level. Not that it was used much anymore except for boiling water.

Gina unpacked the contents of the clear plastic container: a bunch of organic bananas, five peaches, a pint of blueberries, two pounds of grapes, soy cheese, one liter of almond milk, a mesh bag with bell peppers, green onions, a bag of pine nuts, and half a dozen avocados. She gazed at the selection of groceries on the counter-top — the result of the changes she had made in their life about four years ago, when Abbie got thinner and thinner, only picking at the food Jeremy and Gina served.

First, they had pleaded, then tried to bribe her. They knew better than to threaten. No television for a month. She didn't watch any in the first place. No hanging out with your friends. She hadn't expressed the wish to see Kim or

Gloria since grade three. If you don't eat, you'll lose your boat, your fin, your tools. How could they take away the few things in which she showed interest? No ocean visits. Unthinkable.

Being housebound and in need of purpose, Gina began observing which items weren't rejected and prepared special meals for Abbie accordingly. By then, her beautiful niece already lived as a stranger among them. Finally, Gina took a drastic step to include Jeremy and herself in Abbie's world. With the help of the vegan cookbooks from the Mendocino County Library, she mixed and experimented until she settled on the dishes that met Abbie's approval and provided her with balanced nutrients.

The first winter, Gina found it challenging to give up the comfort of comfort food. The fresh and zesty tastes made her feel raw as well. However, it greatly relieved Jeremy and her to see Abbie empty her plate again.

Gina knew her niece valued her efforts. A brief smile when she got up from the table, a light touch on her cheek, a squeeze of her hand, were Abbie's ways of saying thank you. From time to time, tokens appeared on Gina's night stand. A pretty turban shell. Two purple sea urchins. Drops of sea glass. A volcano-shaped barnacle with a sphere of red inside. Once, a necklace of aqua and teal with an abalone blister pearl as the centerpiece.

Sea glass surrounded Abbie. Lay next to her plate at supper. Spilled out of her pockets when she got dressed. Stuck in the pores of the washing machine. Whenever Gina swept the house, a few mermaids' tears ended up in the dustpan.

"But mermaids don't cry," a ten-year-old Abbie had mumbled once when she still contributed an occasional comment to their conversations.

Gina put soy cheese and almond milk in her lap. As she rolled over to the fridge, she peered at the artifacts attached to its stainless steel front. To a casual onlooker, it was nothing more than the common assortment of keepsakes all happy families pick up along the way — to her brother, though, it was a shrine to former joy.

A time capsule. A memorial.

In the middle hung a large calendar sheet, for the month of August in a year long ago, held in place by two of the beautiful fridge magnets Abbie had molded and painted in second grade, depicting seal pups sleeping among kelp leaves. Her art teacher had called them astounding.

A plethora of snapshots was scattered all over the door's brushed finish. Jeremy lifting Abbie while she dunked orange leather through the hoop of her new basketball stand, both laughing. Father and daughter together on a bench seat in a car of the Skunk Train, a tired Abbie curled up in Jeremy's arms, sucking on her thumb. Abbie on her bicycle coming down Elm Street, lifting the front wheel.

Next to it, a much smaller Abbie dancing on Glass Beach: she had found her first piece of red. With her uncle Ru, *Uncuru* she had called him since being a toddler, both in wetsuits, hers custom-made in size 5T. Gina, Ru and their niece sitting on the front steps of a house painted in sunflower yellow. Abbie and her mother, Fern, wearing identical mermaid costumes. The two couples at the bow of the *True Limpet* before they went diving for abalones.

On the left, fixed with Scotch tape hung a magazine article with a picture of Fern in front of one of her Sequoia paintings, half-hidden by the invitation to a wedding anniversary. A blue-and-gold ribbon for first place in a swimming competition sat at the top right. Five kilometers freestyle. Below it zigzagged a row of white-framed photos from the evening of Abbie's eighth birthday when they all played Go Fish together after supper. Abbie loved using Fern's old Polaroid camera, making the adults pose for her with silly faces. Jeremy had taken every item down for the kitchen renovation and returned each to its exact place afterward. Gina didn't dare touch them.

She glanced at the old calendar again: Abbie's birthday was coming up in six days. Her fifteenth. Usually Gina got a hint in advance about what Abbie needed, apart from the small things that had to be replenished on a regular basis like colored pencils and paper, metal thread and other materials she worked with. So far, Gina had not received any of the little drawings showing a duck nose, wire cutter, or magnifying visor. Abbie didn't need new wetsuits anymore because she fit in her mother's old ones now.

Gina opened the silver door, and the fridge blew its chilly breath at her. She put the milk and cheese on the top shelf and checked the crisper: bundles of spinach, zucchinis, mushrooms, cherry tomatoes.

She thought of her brother as she moved back to the counter. It still wasn't easy for him.

"Raw pizza? You must be joking, Gina," he had burst out one evening while the absent-minded girl at the table chewed on kale salad with a sphinxlike countenance.

Later, after Abbie had retreated to her studio, he and Gina watched *Jeopardy* together, sharing a super-sized bag of barbeque chips.

"I would turn into a rabbit overnight if it would bring her back," Jeremy had moaned.

But his habits had proved hard to shake. He stayed away at meal times every second or third day now, binge-eating chicken wings, or filling up on scallops and prawns at the wharf.

She wasn't cross with him. The diet had done wonders for her. Doctor Weasley had been impressed by Gina's improved health and weight loss.

She knew Jeremy was glad about it too. They had always been close. Now they lived together again, like they did growing up, when they watched over their dad, scrutinizing the house for hidden Jim Beam and retrieving his unopened mail to make sure the most urgent bills got paid. She wished she could reward Jeremy for his kindness to her with chicken casserole and meatloaf, but those were pleasures of the past.

Gina shoved the grocery store container in the cupboard under the sink, where it would wait until the delivery driver took it away on his next visit.

She cut open the plastic bag of pine nuts, poured its contents in a stoneware bowl and covered them with water from the filter jug. They would make a delicious creamy dressing.

The peaches looked tempting. Smooth and untouched, like forbidden fruit. Although she wouldn't be able to tell, she had never had any.

Gina washed them gently in the sink and did the same with the grapes. She arranged both on a simple white china platter and placed it on the dining table. She would deal with the other groceries later.

Gina squinted. The kitchen was getting so bright. Sunrays entered through the patio windows, drenching the table and the wet fruits on it in radiance. She decided to hide herself in the guest room and drill sea glass until Abbie came back from the shore.

# *Four*

## ABALONE
FRIDAY AFTERNOON

*I* dance on broken glass. It does not injure me because the surf has smoothed it. Every step the little mermaid took on solid ground, though, felt like knives piercing her soles. I don't think my feet will hurt in the deep. It's easy to avoid touching the ocean floor, and the coldness of the water should soothe any pain.

But if not, I will gladly bear it.

How will it feel to dance with them, to sing with them? I miss singing. Sometimes I hum on the way to the beach; it is not speaking. My mind plays music when I dance to the rhythm of the waves breaking at the shore, and I try to imagine the tunes and chants of the merpeople.

The story says they have beautiful voices, nicer than any human's could ever be.

Uncuru told me that sound travels four times faster underwater than on land and that a diver can hear much higher frequencies. "In the ocean you hear with the bone behind your ear, little seal," he said and tapped his finger against the side of my head to show me where it is located.

So maybe their voices are high-pitched like ultrasound, or completely different, like the singing of whales. I sometimes hear their moaning and purring when they swim by at a distance and wonder what it would be like to travel with them from Alaska to the sunny strands of the south.

I do love the way water magnifies sounds: the clicking of the shrimps, the crackles and pops, fish swooshing and zinging around me like hummingbirds, the soft gurgling my body creates when I glide through the water.

What I detest is the rumbling of engines, the coughing of the trawlers, the growling of the giant fans propelling merchant ships. All this Prop-made noise thundering through the peaceful blue. The merpeople will take me to places where we will not be disturbed by any reminder of its existence. They will hold my hands. I will breathe water and be transformed. I will marvel at the underwater gardens. See the living flowers on the palace walls. Hear their beautiful singing with the bone behind my ear. Dance their dances. Learn the way they speak. Maybe I will even be rewarded with a tail.

Yet what I am most anxious to find out is: Will I meet Mommy there?

# *Five*

## DAN
### FRIDAY AFTERNOON

Dan lifted his binoculars and grinned: his shift for the Mendocino Abalone Watch was over, but he still watched Abalone. The girl capered about at the waterline, tall and slender, but developed. Almost a carbon copy of her mother.

After she came to land in her small boat, she had sat on one of the boulders. Long legs slightly bent, monofin flat on the stone. Her gray-brown wetsuit glistened like seal skin in the afternoon sun. Her dripping hair reached almost down to her waist. Waves licked all around the dark rock. Quite picturesque. Now she pirouetted in the glimmering surf while seaweed wiggled between her feet.

A surreal scene. To think this stretch of the shoreline had been a garbage heap for nearly sixty years in the last century. The Dumps. They finally got cleaned up by the end of the Nineties. The skeletons of old cars and appliances were long gone, everything else washed away — except for the colorful pebble-sized pieces of glass. These days the beach was a destination, coveted by the visitors, who thought its sparkly covering a commodity. A handful of people dotted the area between the rocky cliffs right now, their searching and shoveling activities suspended as they gazed in awe at the twirling girl. It would make a great closing scene for a tourism commercial. Filmed as an angled view from the cliff or maybe an aerial shot coming in off the ocean: Glass Beach, where mermaids dance.

Dan lowered the binoculars again and wished he had brought the camcorder instead. He could use it as filler material for the documentary his boss was planning. But of course, even if he got footage of this alluring beach performance, Dan doubted they would ever receive permission to air it, for, sadly, the girl was mental, refusing to speak, living in her own world, obsessed with the sea. You could see it in her absent bi-colored stare.

Now she picked up one of the thick brown kelp strings and made it dance with her. She looked just as smashing in a wetsuit as her mother, who had been a major attraction when she went out with Fuertes for his freediving events, on a boat full of stock brokers and computer nerds.

Once, Dan had shot a short promo video for the website of Abalone Adventures. Ruben Fuertes had been pleasant to deal with and paid well, a nice guy, not arrogant at all.

Some dudes at the harbor, though, guessed he had been in the poaching business, using his diving outfit as a disguise. A few even believed he was involved in the drug trade, connected to the grow ops sprouting like malignant lesions in the forests of the backcountry.

The liberal fashion in which he handled his money, the yacht used for his excursions, and the wealthy clientele he attracted had rubbed some people the wrong way.

All hearsay, though. People talked too much and cared too little.

The girl stopped twirling and dragged her boat out of the water, along the small sandy path that led up from the beach. In the cliff face, just above the high tide level, was a small opening. She shoved the dinghy into it.

The people on the glass still watched as she tossed her weight-belt to the ground and shed the neoprene skin, revealing a one-piece bathing suit. She pulled a bundle out of the boat: a long brownish gown, almost medieval in style, and a pair of black rubber boots.

After dressing and carefully braiding kelp strings around her waist, she went up the last part of the path, carrying her pelt over one arm. She stopped at the edge of the bluff to behold the sea, solemn, rapt — hair, dress, and the leaves around her waist moving in the gentle wind — looking as if she had just stepped out of a fantasy novel. A princess disguised as a peasant girl.

Dan sighed; the camera would love her. What a waste. The sea glass collectors on the beach finally returned their attention to the ground as the girl walked toward her backyard out of their sight.

She threw the wetsuit over the weathered wooden pickets that marked the end of the property, before she grabbed the pink children's bicycle leaning against the fence, mounted it and vanished down Glass Beach Trail.

# Six

## GINA
### FRIDAY AFTERNOON

"*Buenos dias*, Señor Limón."

Gina opened the cage door.

"*Buenos dias.*" The large green bird leaped onto her thigh and fluffed up its head feathers in anticipation of the daily crown massage. "*Que pasa?*"

Gina roamed her fingertips gently through Señor Limón's silken plumage. She tried to keep him company as often as she could. He missed his former life as a social butterfly, spending his days perched next to the cash register in the dive shop, where he interacted with store patrons, welcoming every new customer with a buoyant *Ha del barco!*

All attempts to teach him the equivalent *Ahoy there!* had failed; however, Señor Limón learned to imitate the doorbell instead, so that he could summon Gina or Ru out of the backrooms with a salvo of rings whenever he felt in need of attention. He still did it at least twice a day, at unpredictable times, giving Gina a jolt as she washed romaine lettuce in the kitchen sink or pulled sheets out of the dryer in the bathroom.

The delicious split-second of joy before memory kicked in. The brief delusion that she could still rush to the front of the store. She would find Señor Limón peeking at her with a smirk in his black pearl eyes, and would see Ru come out of his office to scold him — before he embraced her while their parrot hopped up and down on the horizontal bars in his cage, demanding *un beso, un beso*.

More than once, this had led to them hanging the *Closed* sign on the door for half an hour.

Gina gave the bird a last tender pat. Knowing their routine, he spread his wings and took off, flashing sap-green brightness. Gina loved his stunning color, fresh as the first leaves of spring, all beauty and promise. She had persuaded Ru, who originally fancied a macaw, to purchase him, and Señor Limón rewarded them with a happy temper and astounding cleverness.

He landed on top of the wardrobe next to the cardboard storage box with the copied investigation reports and pecked at the frazzled end of the tape sealing the carton while he waited for his cue.

Gina grabbed the safety mask out of the shelf and rolled her chair over to the workstation.

The drill's old diamond bit had to be replaced. Some water needed to be added into the little plastic bowl, over the slice of cedar that protected the bottom from being pierced.

Señor Limón flung himself in the air and landed next to her on the desk; his talons tapped the wood amidst the sea glass she intended to get ready for Abbie. He liked to play with it, sorting colors, moving pieces back and forth from one pile to the other with his scarlet-red beak as if counting them according to a special system only known to ring-necked parakeets.

Gina chose a chunk of frosted lavender and pressed it down in the bowl so that the water covered it.

She switched on the drill. The vibration echoed through her body; she could feel it even in the dead parts. Señor Limón eyed the diamond bit coming down on the glass and cleared his throat. He had a special talent for sound mimicry. Soon they buzzed together like two busy dentists fighting decay.

Gina sighed. If only there was a way to bore the nagging questions out of her brain, the disappointment out of her heart, the loneliness out of her life.

She stopped and turned the glass piece around to reduce the danger of fracturing it.

Señor Limón waited for her to continue. She glanced at him with a wistful smile and handed her mind over again to the soothing monotony of the drill.

Abbie's grandmother Melody had purchased the high-speed Dremel as a present years ago after seeing the pieces of art Abbie produced in her studio.

She also regularly sent her granddaughter small parcels

containing freshwater pearls, pink tourmaline, lapis lazuli and other tiny gemstone beads.

Abbie loved to use them in her designs but disliked the sound of the diamond bit gnawing through the glass. Gina never worked the drill when Abbie was in the house. Every morning the fruit of her noisy work got inspected, and the chosen items disappeared from the table Jeremy had constructed around a vintage printer's tray.

Gina stopped the drill and placed the finished piece in the section for the light purples and pinks: a beautiful and rare color, produced by the chemical reaction of sunlight with the manganese in colorless glassware from the early nineteen-hundreds.

She looked over her shoulder and checked the time on the antique wooden ship's wheel that her brother had fashioned into a wall clock — a leftover from The Abyss. Half past four.

Abbie being out alone in the *Baby Clam* still made her uneasy. She would have understood if her niece had never ever boarded a boat again, but Abbie loved the dinghy and attempts to separate them had not gone over well.

Señor Limón strutted back and forth across the desk, shoveling the glass with his scaly gray feet, while muttering unintelligible words. After picking at a couple of cornflower blues, he tilted his head and selected a teal-colored oval, which he carefully lifted with his hook-shaped upper bill and carried to the plastic bowl where he dropped it into the water.

"*Muchas gracias*, Señor Limón."

"*Un beso, un beso,*" the parrot replied, but Gina scratched him under the beak instead, knowing how much he enjoyed it. His green head bobbed against her palm until the bird shifted away from her hand and started nipping at the bowl, the sign that he wished to continue their duet. Gina fixed the sea glass in place with two fingers and lowered the drill again.

Things had settled down over the last three years, into a joyless but industrious routine. Jeremy sawed and planed in his workshop, and Abbie created jewelry in her studio at the back fence.

Gina spent most of the day by herself, wheeling her way through the housework, keeping the books for Macklintock Carpentry and Abalone's Own, managing the shop on Etsy and preparing incoming online orders for a FedEx pick up.

It kept her hands and tires busy but couldn't stop her thoughts from wandering.

Who would have guessed a silly old tale could have such an impact? It had comforted Abbie. She never cried one tear when Gina read it with her. They cuddled together in Abbie's bed, under the mural, the large book on their knees. A special edition of Hans Christian Anderson's *The Little Mermaid*, featuring the mesmerizing illustrations of Fern Macklintock. The colorful double-spread drawings created by her mother enabled Abbie to escape into the world of the young fishtailed princess — and Gina accompanied her willingly, although she had to swallow her tears much more than once.

Every evening, they entered a secret realm, deep down at the bottom of the sea, where the earth was the finest sand, not white but the color of burning sulphur.

They dreamed themselves into the mer-king's palace, where living anemones adorned the walls and fish flitted in and out of amber windows. There, they petted sea stars and squid, and the blue tinge to everything suited their mood.

She had hoped the story would help Abbie get over whatever she had seen; instead, it fueled an obsession. It came on gradually, though, while all of them suffered from the aftermath.

Gina stopped the drill. She took the wet teal piece out of the bowl and held it in her palm. It looked perfect, clear and gemlike. No chips marred its smooth surface. And in a small while, it would dry in her hand, transform itself, take on an opaque coating like armor or a disguise.

She stroked her fingertips over the already matt surface. As fascinating as its changing appearance were its journey and its resurrection. Weathered by sand and surf and salt, a discarded shard was reborn as a treasure.

"*Que pasa?*" Señor Limón cawed and kicked his left foot against a lump of seafoam green.

"Patience, grasshopper," Gina said and gently nudged the parrot with her knuckles. She added the teal piece to its equals in the collector's table and picked up Señor Limón's suggestion.

The Dremel sang again, drilling through the whitish glass with the pretty blue-green hue, probably the remains of an old Coca Cola bottle. The glass dust swirled through the water in the bowl. Sea foam.

She had not been alarmed the first time she found Abbie lying in the tub. In her favorite costume with the tulle fish tail and the belt made out of tiny white moon shells.

Head underwater. Eyes open. Staring at the bathroom ceiling as if it had a hole allowing a view of the night sky. Gina waited behind the half open door until she heard Abbie coming to the surface to gulp air. Everybody had to find their own ways to cope.

But when it happened again two days later, she ran straight to the workshop to fetch Jeremy.

He came, knelt down close to the tub and lowered his hand gently as not to startle Abbie. Gina had not been prepared for what happened next. Jeremy dunked both arms under Abbie and ripped her out of her bath, liquid splashing everywhere while she screamed, "Leave me. Leave me!"

"Quickly, Gina! Open the plug and turn the hot water on!" Jeremy pressed Abbie against himself, rubbing her back with his hands while her dripping-wet hair and mermaid gown soaked his T-shirt and jeans. "Tell me when it's getting warm!"

The water in the tub had been ice-cold.

The same evening, Jeremy changed the doorknob to one that couldn't lock from the inside and forbade Abbie from taking unsupervised baths.

But she found other ways to keep them on their toes. Three weeks later, seeing her waddling into the kitchen, the legs of her pants weirdly attached to each other, Gina and Jeremy had actually laughed — a welcome distraction from the depressing atmosphere in the house, but short-lived.

"Please, Abbie, go and change. It's a quarter to eight," Jeremy said still smiling, "I'll drop you off at school with the Sprinter before I finish the Millers' kitchen."

Abbie stood by the fridge and shook her head.

"You won't be able to play b-ball at recess with your legs shackled. Go and put on your Spurs shorts."

Abbie stared at him with her bright dissimilar eyes as if he spoke a language she had never heard before in her life. It felt like the room temperature had dropped below thirty-two.

Gina jumped up from the table and took her niece's hand. "Come, honey, let's go and find you a pretty skirt. Maybe the green one with the sweet peas," she said and gently pulled her away, out of the kitchen. Not daring to look back: she had seen a shadow of fear on her brother's face.

Abbie did not go to school that morning, and the Millers waited in vain for Jeremy to install their kitchen cupboards.

It took Gina and Jeremy two hours to unpick the seams Abbie had used to connect the legs of all her pants, done in tiny meticulous backstitches joined so tightly as if they had to last forever. Abbie had also inserted a cord into the hem of every single skirt she owned, so she could wrap and fasten the fabric around her legs. She must have worked on this for many days. Amazing handiwork for an eight-year-old.

The phone rang. "*Ha del barco!*" Señor Limón screamed and chimed in to the ringing with his doorbell impersonation.

Gina switched off the drill. She reached over her shoulder and grabbed the handset out of the back pocket on her wheelchair.

"Georgina Fuertes." She removed her mask.

"Hi, Georgie," said a familiar voice.

She frowned. "Elon."

# Seven

## JEREMY
### FRIDAY AFTERNOON

Jeremy sat behind the table and checked his finished display, sucking on sweets the organizers gave out in their exhibitor's package every year. Hard candy with a light coating of icing sugar, fashioned to look like sea glass. The tin was half empty already. His craving for treats seemed to increase every day. He was fortunate his profession demanded manual labor.

The goods on his two tables looked awesome, outstanding. Even if he lacked the joys of a regular dad, he relished the pride of being the father of a promising young artist. His daughter's pieces could just as well be for sale at Tiffany.

He picked a wisp of lint from one of the small velvet

cushions on which he had arranged the gold and silver wire bracelets made of lovers' knots. On the connecting jump rings hung sea glass charms — and iridescent abalone beads. Rainbow pearls. Alien gems. Gleaming like an oil spill. The only part of Abbie's creations he disliked. But people gushed about them as if they were crown jewels.

To his left, Mr. and Ms. Harstrom covered their tables with white sheets, and he watched them with a mixture of awe and envy. Whenever they opened another folded cloth, their hands touched. They often bumped into each other during the day, but not because of deteriorating eyesight; they still appreciated being together after forty-seven years. He knew they would spend the evening in their rental kayaks paddling the Estuary, enjoying great blue herons and snowy egrets in the sunset. Every year, the Harstroms flew over from Fairview, Pennsylvania, to showcase their pendants made from beautifully frosted Lake Erie marbles, wrapped with silver wire to look like Japanese fishing floats.

The couple waved goodbye to him before they turned to leave. Their hands joined for good as they strolled to the exit. On the ceiling over the double door, Jeremy spotted a helium balloon leaning against the cedar beams, as if out of breath.

*Just Married!* was still legible on the crumpled scarlet foil.

He glanced across the hall. Some of the other exhibitors were already gone, but Tessa sat by her small display, hunched over her mobile with busy fingers, pretending to be in demand but probably playing Angry Birds.

Jeremy pulled his phone out of his jacket. He checked in with Gina at least twice a day. She was completely self-sufficient at home by now, but since her car accident five and a half years ago, he felt an urge to stay in control, the need to protect what was left of his world. The phone icon had a small red dot attached to it. He tapped: three calls from Gina!

How did he miss them? Oh, yes, when he was out walking on the pier, twenty minutes ago, gobbling down two pulled pork burgers.

"To review your messages, press one," said the phone-bot, who knew nothing of urgency. He cut her off with a tap on the required number.

"Jeremy!" He rose from his chair as if somebody had set it on fire. "They have arrested Abbie. She's at the police station. Please come back as fast as you can. Elon is on his way from Ukiah. He has given instructions to wait for him —"

"Saralyn," Jeremy hollered to the girl who stood five tables down the aisle, handing out promo T-shirts for the Battered Fish Shack, one of the festival sponsors.

She turned her head. "Mr. Macklintock?"

"Have you ever worked in sales?" he asked while Gina still talked into his ear.

Saralyn was at his stand in no time. "I've helped at the church bazaar and sold tickets for our high school musical. We did *The Beauty and the Beast*."

"Good enough. I'll pay you two hundred bucks and the seahorse of your choice if you manage my stand this weekend."

Saralyn almost dropped her shirts. "You're kidding? You're not kidding. Oh my gosh." She looked like she had found the Shard of the Year.

"Of course I'll do it! I'll tell Grandma and get Kane to take over my duties. Back in a flash!"

Jeremy touched nine to save the message and gazed at the teenage girl bouncing down the hall. Happiness, normality — places he was barred from. Getting braces adjusted, joining the basketball team, arguing over curfews and boyfriends, making plans for college.

Being arrested for assault.

The ground crumbled under his feet. He steadied himself on the shaking fragments pulling further and further apart. Why would his gentle, silent daughter attack somebody?

With a weapon?

Seven years of practice had given him the prowess to cope with emotional blows while keeping at least an outward calm.

He took his jacket from the chair and slipped the phone into the side pocket.

"Jeremy, are you okay?" Tessa asked. He hadn't seen her coming.

"A domestic emergency. Saralyn is replacing me."

"Nothing serious I hope." Tessa touched his arm.

"I don't know yet. Could you arrange stuff with Saralyn and her grandma? She's getting two hundred and a horse. I'll phone you about it." He grabbed his car keys. "I have to go now."

"Sure, honey," Tessa said and squeezed his elbow. "Leave it to me. Drive carefully."

He walked out of the hall into the low standing sun. Good thing he had decided to set up the tables before checking into the hotel.

He opened the door of his Dodge Caravan and crawled behind the steering wheel.

Child Welfare Services would surely be all over this, chomping at the bit to declare him unfit as a guardian, accusing him of negligence — again. Veterans of an ongoing, almost seven yearlong homeschooling battle.

He remembered Mrs. Hotchkins's scathing soprano. "How are we going to evaluate her skills and competencies, Mr. Macklintock? Collect sea glass with her?"

Ignorant cow.

He had asked her to show him other preteens who had taught themselves the art of jewelry-making from a stack of library books.

But his opponent had been unflinching.

"We have determined development issues. I have reviewed Dr. Baker's new assessment. How will we ensure that Abalone maintains healthy relationships in the future if you are so uncooperative? And the problem with her nutritional choices."

Blah blah blah . . .

He put the key in the ignition, cursing the four hundred miles lying before him.

# *Eight*

## LEIF
FRIDAY AFTERNOON

*N*urse da Silva stuffed a cotton plug into his nostril. "You're lucky," she said.

Mugged by Abalone Macklintock. The resident artist slash village idiot. The sea witch with the mismatched eyes. This didn't fit Leif's definition of lucky. The nurse had meant his nose, of course. Dr. Cooper had seen immediately that it wasn't broken.

Leif hoped the story would at least not make it into the local newspaper. Gordon, his best friend (although right now Leif felt like subjecting this status to a serious review), had already shared the news on Twitter with a shot of him protecting his head with both arms.

At least school was out for the summer, so he wouldn't have to face his smirking peers on Monday. Leif generally preferred to keep a low profile. His top marks might have boxed him in with the nerds were it not for the saving grace of his attachment to Gordon, who intellectually was a bottom feeder, but greatly revered for his three-point percentage and the cool parties on his father's diving school day boat.

Leif exhaled loudly through his mouth as his nose was now plugged with cotton wool.

Only one more year before he would be free to pursue his real interests.

Now, this afternoon's weird event had dragged him out into the open. Although, so far the comments and reactions pouring in during the last twenty minutes had been mostly good-natured. He would have to develop a much thicker skin for standing in the limelight. This was an exercise in learning to cope with people's reaction to his performance. He wished, though, Gordon could have done the right thing and helped him instead of turning into a paparazzo. Thanks, bud.

Leif and Gordon had been in a hushed conversation about their Saturday harvesting trip and didn't notice the girl going into the coffee shop or coming out. She appeared like a ghost, sucking on the straw in her vegetable smoothie, long redwood mane flowing in the afternoon breeze, braided kelp wrapped around her waist. The sun illuminated her ivory face and the long sea glass strings around her neck sparkled in the colors of her eyes — deep aqua and seaweed green, peering right at him.

Leif winced: Nurse da Silva disinfected the scrapes on his forehead left by the zipper's metal teeth.

When the girl had dropped her drink and barged toward him, her swamp-colored goth dress billowing, pieces of kelp slipping to the ground, and ripped the racquet out of Gordon's kitbag, Leif was too stunned to do anything other than bear her onslaught. It had felt like being in the twilight zone. Instead of taking pictures, Gordon, the moron, could have wrestled the racquet out of her hand. After all, he was six foot five inches.

It had been strangely fascinating though. She was pretty, even in her fury, her stare mesmerizing.

He smiled, which made his nose hurt.

"I'll get you some painkillers," Nurse da Silva said and walked over to a metal cabinet.

Leif rubbed his bruised arms. At least the cover had still been on the racquet. She was pretty strong for such a slim person. Probably from all the swimming.

He had believed, though, that she was mute. According to town reports, she had lost her voice after the incident with her mother. He and his friends had only been ten when it happened. A long time ago, and he did not remember any details.

Anyway, this afternoon, when Mr. Ogilvy came running out of the coffee shop and grabbed her by the waist, she had started screaming like a banshee, dropped the racquet, clawed her hands into Leif's arm and wouldn't let got. She tried to wiggle her fingers into his bracelet, which made it easier for Deputy Flynn to handcuff her when he arrived with screeching brakes only moments later.

Leif was sure this juicy tale would dwarf the glass beach dispute for at least a couple of weeks.

He touched the bracelet. Underneath, his skin was streaked with red. Had she wanted to rip it of his wrist? It made him feel funny. He had heard she was a good diver. Had she seen him?

Maybe he should have tried to find the owner by putting an ad in the local paper's lost and found section. But who knew how long it had been lying there. He had easily convinced himself that one of the rich jerks from Silicon Valley had lost it. They only came for a day or two and had the means to replace it. Finders, keepers.

It was a charm bracelet, but manly, with a nice weight to it. Pirate-themed. Leif fingered the shiny pendants hanging from the broad rose-gold curb link chain: a fish skeleton, a musket, a wooden leg, a doubloon with the number ten on it, a parrot, a grinning skull. Original, and fun.

Why would she want it? It wasn't girl's stuff.

And she made jewelry herself. His mother had bought a necklace and earrings in one of the local gift stores. "It's so sad," she had said, "such a tragedy."

He should have left it there. Leif untied the toggle clasp and stuffed the bracelet into the front pocket of his jeans.

The nurse came back with a couple of single dose Advil sachets on her palm.

"Here," she said and handed them to Leif. "You should go home now and rest your head for a while. And put some ice packs on your arms."

# Nine

## GINA
### FRIDAY AFTERNOON

"Pardon, what did you say?" Gina shifted in her seat. She had forgotten her shades on the hall table, and the sun reflected into her eyes from the windshields speeding across the intersection. Not to mention the air conditioning that blasted through Pam Fowley's SUV like a November storm.

"Have you heard about the petition?" her friend asked. They waited at the corner of Elm and Main for the light to turn. Pam peered into the rear-view mirror and rearranged the faux diamonds dangling from her statement necklace. The silver bangles on her wrist slipped over her crimson silk cuff.

As usual, she was dressed up as if she ran a Fortune 500 corporation, when in fact she managed her little chain of dog spas mostly from her home office since she had developed an allergy to animal hair.

"Which one?" Gina asked.

"The one to replenish Glass Beach, of course."

"Yes, I've read about it in the *Advocate-News* and had your flier in my mailbox."

"I have the board of the business owners' association unanimously standing behind me supporting the idea," Pam said and accelerated. "And you know how impossible that is."

Why had she asked Pam to give her a ride? Obviously not because of her empathy skills. She lived down the road and had a van. Abbie sat alone and terrified at the police station, and Pam could only think politics. Although, there had been a time when Gina cared about it too. Her two-year stint as vice chairman of the business association had been fun, and her success in dealing with controversial matters had led her to consider running for city council. Pam regularly asked her to pick up where she had left off.

"The mayor is proving a hard nut to crack, though," Pam mumbled, this remark being among the nicer things she had to say about her ex-husband.

Gina sighed. The plan was to toss tumbled shards into the ocean to replace the decreasing stock.

The replenishment advocates seemed hell-bent on remodeling the town into Glass Disney Land. What could authenticity avail against greed?

But what other ways were there to attract more people

to this charming corner of the world, with its interesting past, the little museums and quaint stores in the historic downtown area, the natural beauty of the coastal scenery, and the added wackiness of the leftover flower children kicking around?

The sawmill had closed many years ago, and still the empty site lay like an open wound between town and ocean. This sleepy city needed a boost — surviving on salmon fishing and tourism alone was difficult, and even harder with the additional burden of a stagnant economy and the never-ending drought. A Stage One Water Emergency had been declared only days ago, the city manager urging everybody to conserve and be prepared for smell and discoloration issues when they turned on their taps. There were bigger issues to be considered than throwing glass into the sea.

Gina adjusted her legs.

However, why should she be concerned with plans for the future of other people when she had none to look forward to? Another twenty yards and they would drive past *The Abyss*.

She found it painful to even glance at the mural on the storefront.

Loved by everybody, it still was an eye-catcher; although the faded underwater scenery badly needed some touch-ups. One of the divers' silhouettes even had a chink in its chest. Fern had taken care of the maintenance in the past. Maybe somebody should just whitewash the wall, and then Gina could pretend it had never been there.

Every day, she had waited for good news, or bad news, until any news would have been welcome.

Eventually, she canceled all freediving events and operated the shop with some hired help. But she couldn't stand to be alone in the store, and sometimes when she explained something to a customer, for example the advantages of a low volume spearfishing mask with two lenses, a sinkhole opened under her feet and she dropped through the planet into space and drifted forever in its infinite darkness.

Her home wasn't much better. Shadows lurked in every room, eager to grab her ankles and make her sit down at the bay window or in the easy chair or on any step of the staircase or just the kitchen floor for hours on end. After a while, Gina threw white sheets over the furniture, locked the doors and moved in with her brother and niece. About a year after Ru disappeared, she sold to Trevor Abornut, who revived Abalone Adventures and almost returned it to its former popularity.

"If we don't act now, Glass Beach will be a name-only attraction very soon," Pam said and honked at a truck in front of them. "Our magical site is a magnet for sea glass lovers from all around the world. But we have to give our visitors an experience. They want to take souvenirs home."

"Tell me about it," Gina mumbled.

Daily, she saw the scavengers along the path by the backyard fence with their buckets and zip-lock bags. They could count themselves lucky that she wasn't able to drive across the bumpy lawn. Who on earth needed that much? Ruining the experience for everybody in the long run, not for a second considering there wasn't an endless supply. Poacher mentality.

These creeps deserved to be fed counterfeits. The new trails would open soon, making the other two spots accessible. Why not add free parking on the beach? And complimentary tools so they could shovel the glass right into their trunks?

Gina had read once that the police in Greece arrested everyone who dared to pick up even a speck of marble from their ancient temple sites. Of course she wouldn't go that far. But report cards or check points might curb the appetite of the people stuffing their pockets at the silica smorgasbord — or a pricey license. And fines for anybody who took uncooked pieces.

Abbie only collected small amounts and never came home with anything less than perfectly rounded, smooth and immaculate. She hunted for these gems in the caves that were inaccessible from the beach, untouched treasure chests, guarded by the tricky waters around them.

Gina used to go out with her in the *Baby Clam*, before what had become known as *the accident*, making sure Abbie took precautions and had a buoy with her always. Her niece had been so small then, ignorant of the dangers of the raging surf, the sneaker waves. Abbie's lack of fear still scared her.

"Gina?" Pam touched her arm.

"Sorry, what did you say?"

"Will Elon be there?" she asked and took the corner onto Cypress Street.

"Yes." Good grief, Pam had the gift of cluelessness.

Elon Wagner, Gina's prom night date, an excellent dancer with great timing. Not like his clumsy peers, stumbling over their partners' feet. He knew how to lead then; now he commanded the county police force.

"He's still in love with you," Pam had said a couple of years ago when they had sat on her deck watching the sun set.

"How would you know?" Gina took a toothpick and tried to stab a black olive.

"My mother plays bingo with his mother."

"You think he fancies an old woman in a wheelchair?"

The olive jumped onto the table, rolled off the edge and disappeared through a crack between the deck's cedar boards.

"He has never married, Gina," Pam said. "It broke his heart when you came back from San Francisco with a Latin lover instead of an accounting degree. And you're forty-one, not eighty!"

"I can't believe he still feels the same after all these years — and events," Gina muttered into her ginger ale, feeling like she had been smacked across the face.

"Why don't you try to find out?" Pam asked and stuffed another shrimp dim sum in her mouth.

"Because I am already married," Gina had replied in a tone that caused Pam to chew her dumpling twice as long as necessary and change the subject afterward.

Elon was a friend, maybe not even that. It had been frustrating to deal with him regarding her efforts to reopen the case.

"My hands are tied, Georgie," he had told her. "Without new evidence, it's impossible to get another investigation, no matter how much I want it."

He had given her copies of all the files, though, bending the rules, maybe to let her know that he was not to blame for the dissatisfying outcome.

She had studied them endlessly, unable to detect an oversight or form a theory with the sparse facts. An empty boat, a dead woman, and a missing man.

A child found in a dinghy fifty miles down the coast.

Whatever had happened on the *True Limpet* on the twenty-third of August almost seven years ago remained unknown.

"Here we are," Pam said.

# *Jen*

## ABALONE
FRIDAY AFTERNOON

*I* have acted unwisely. Sometimes my understanding is slow, like the tide building up on a day when nothing disturbs the glossy stillness of the sea.

Today I lost control. Sounds escaped my mouth. I wish I could retreat to the serenity of the kelp to calm my thoughts. What if this iniquity has blighted my fortune?

The place I'm confined to is ugly and without peace. Props are passing by through the corridor; I can see them from the table I'm sitting at through a glass divider. They talk with harsh voices. Their heels attack the floor.

A female Prop in a plus-size oatmeal-colored pant suit is preventing my escape. She crouches by the exit on a plastic chair and skims through a binder containing many papers. Whenever she peeks over at me, I pretend to study the patterns in the slanted ceiling tiles.

I am well acquainted with her face, with the long creases on both sides of her mouth that make her resemble a ventriloquist's doll, though she never has anything funny to say. Her forehead gets red as fireweed when the parent Prop yells at her, which usually happens not long after she arrives to check on me.

The door opens and one of the uniformed Props comes in. He bears the name Steve Flynn. He visits the house often to pick up the parent Prop. They go to kill lingcod together.

"Abbie, your aunt Gina will be here shortly. And your father has just called. He will be home tonight. Do you want a glass of water? Or shall we get you a spinach smoothie?"

I shake my head.

"Mrs. Hotchkins," he addresses my guard, "Mrs. Fuertes is on the way. Would you like something to drink?"

"Thank you, Officer, a cup of tea would be nice. With milk." Her salt-and-pepper locks shiver when she speaks.

The uniformed Prop leaves the room. I remember how he stopped his vehicle as soon as it had taken the next street corner and was out of view of the coffee shop.

He asked me to lift my hands. "I don't think we need these," he said and removed the metal from my wrists. "And don't worry, whatever he has done to you, we will get him."

I wasn't paying attention, though, because I had to think about the little mermaid. She could not stab the prince because she loved him too much. And she never went back to her people.

Commotion in the corridor. "Where's Abbie?" I hear Auntie Gina's voice before her chair rolls into the room.

# Eleven

## GINA
FRIDAY EVENING

Gina took another sip of mint tea while her email account opened. An order notification from Etsy.

A store in Monterey requested a quote for a custom-made collector's chest. Reach-in closets at Hare Creek for Jeremy to refurbish. A message from Pam asking if all had gone well after she left Gina at the police station. Attached was the Glass Beach Replenishment petition and an invitation to join the business association for their bi-weekly lunch meeting. Gina typed a few short replies and closed the email program.

Far down on the left of the desktop sat the icon of the folder with her private photos.

Somehow the cursor felt like shimmying over there and opened it.

Seven years had passed without one new image being uploaded. Why had she even copied them from her old computer when she bought the new laptop? She didn't have to look at the billowing sails and the smiling faces; it was all fresh in her memory.

On the twenty-second of August, they had celebrated their anniversary with a splash.

At Gina's request, the wedding in San Francisco had been an intimate ceremony with only his parents, her brother and a few close friends. Ru laughed when she told him she'd never bought into the idea that this was supposed to be the happiest day in a woman's life, as she intended to have a truckload of at least equally happy days with him in the future. She wasn't the girl for six-tier-cakes and horse-drawn carriages and all the pomp and circumstance people liked to stress themselves out with.

It was only half of the truth, though. Planning a big wedding didn't seem like an overwhelming challenge to her organizing talent, but she would have never felt comfortable to spend a fortune on a single day, even if Ru was willing and able to afford it.

She couldn't so easily shed the stinginess she had acquired growing up. Especially during the time she took her distance-learning course and worked in one of the harborside restaurants frying fish and potatoes while her brother finished grade twelve — after their father had left them a ramshackle bungalow and three hundred dollars in bottle refunds.

Over the years though, Ru's generosity had rubbed off on her, and both agreed to make their first double-digit anniversary a special one. They decided on a Pirates of the Caribbean party and rented a beautiful schooner that came all the way from Sausalito the evening before.

"Hella narrow harbor passage you have," the captain had said as they greeted him at the dock. "Awesome to be here."

Early the next day, over two hundred guests boarded the tall ship, gazed at by locals and welcomed by Ru and Señor Limón, who perched on Ru's shoulder wearing a little red harness with a leash, voicing his delight to be in the middle of the bustling affair with frequent calls of his trademark *Ha del barco!*

The decks filled with family members and friends, business contacts and customers, all in theme costumes; even crew and caterers were dressed up as buccaneers.

Gina wore her cream-white wedding dress again, the elegant long-sleeved silk gown being perfect for the part of the kidnapped beauty. For added fun, she accessorized it with a striped neckerchief and two wooden flintlock pistols from Ru's collection, while he had one of his original eighteenth century cutlasses in a leather scabbard hanging from his belt. The white Renaissance cotton shirt and simple brown knee breeches suited him like he had never worn anything else.

He was closing in on fifty, but his looks still made her heart beat faster. He had the gait of a much younger man. No gray streaked the wavy black peeking out under the red bandana. The golden ring in his ear gave him an air of dauntlessness.

He stood on the outside deck saluting their guests, as if he had just climbed down the rigging from the crow's nest to shake their hands.

The morning was warm and sunny with enough wind to fill the sails and gently fluff up your hair. The Jolly Roger capered on the top mast. Not a few people slowed down their cars on the 101 highway bridge to watch the boatload of swashbucklers leave port for a day of fun and fabulous food.

Ten years since Ruben and Gina tied the knot. Nine since they opened up the diving school. A time of celebration, and the crowning of a wonderful week. Jeremy had won the bid for the renovation of the Sea Star Inn, a project that would give him creative freedom in designing the interior of nine luxury cottages. Abbie had turned eight two days before, and Fern's first illustrated book had been released.

Mother and daughter wore similar mermaid costumes and were asked frequently to pose for pictures. Waving tulle tails and tossing shiny tousles of hair over bare shoulders, they basked in the sun and the general attention.

The schooner sailed up the coastline. MacKerricher State Park flew by; the harbor seals grunted greetings from their rocks at Laguna Point; the dunes of Inglenook Fen gleamed in the morning light; in the distance dwelled the blue mountains of the Coast Range.

What a blessing to live here, Gina thought. She looked over at Ru, who handed out eye patches to some of their younger guests. And to be loved.

At the height of Ten Mile River, the captain aimed for the open ocean.

People were encouraged to assist the crew in raising the sails and handling the lines, or to have a try at driving the ship with the helmsman standing by. The first mate explained how to calculate water depth and boat speed using traditional techniques. As afternoon entertainment, the crew was scheduled to sing sea shanties and teach everybody how to dance like a scallywag.

Before the opening of the lunch buffet, ten shots were fired out of a traditional ship's cannon. Never would Gina have believed as she stood next to Ru on the bridge, receiving the toasts of their friends, feeling she couldn't possibly be any happier, that at the end of a day spent in such high spirits she would be downcast like never before in her life. It was only a foretaste though; twenty-four hours later, the world as she knew it would be hit and destroyed.

Gina closed the folder.

Seven years had gone by since that fateful day, the time required in California before a missing person could be declared dead. The Presumption of Death Law. Gina had no intention to apply it. The insurance would never pay a cent of the 1.5 million dollar benefit without physical evidence. The representative had made this clear to her. Ru had an accidental death policy; after all he was in a high-risk profession. He had wanted his family to be taken care of. Nobody could have foreseen the circumstances of his disappearance.

Gina wasn't pressed for money. She knew how to get by on little if need be. She had access to all accounts and investments. Ru had put them in both their names after they were married.

But the fortune had dwindled during the years she spent in and out of various hospitals. And she insisted on sending her father-in-law the monthly check she knew his son would have wanted him to receive.

She knew Ru was dead.

Of course, she had no proof, just as she had no proof he hadn't done what some people suspected him of and run for cover afterward.

In her heart, though, Gina was certain these people were wrong. Ru wouldn't hide in a hole like a rat for the rest of his life; he would stand by his actions and take responsibility. He would make sure the people he loved did not have to live in the shadow of rumors and uncertainty.

However, she still preferred to be his wife rather than his widow.

# Twelve

## JEREMY
FRIDAY EVENING

Jeremy gunned up the last stretch of US-101, imagining he was driving along the twisty coastal road instead. Barely thirty miles west, the sun was setting over its breathtaking scenery and the many spots with special meaning to his family.

The gallery in Gualala, where Fern exhibited the large canvases of her *Trees of Mystery* project and got a small mention in Art in America.

Schooner Gulch, where a tourist found Abbie sleeping in her dinghy, stuck between the surreal sandstone formations at the shore that look like it had rained over-sized bowling balls.

Point Arena, where he and Fern made love in the back of his truck, above them the stars and the circling beam of the lighthouse, beneath them a blanket with wood splinters — after she had admitted that she was pregnant and he improvised a proposal using a clamp collar as a ring.

The cliffs at Manchester, where Abbie saw her first gray whales: a pod of three spouting giants on their migration route from the icy waters of the north to subtropical lagoons.

"In their lifetime they swim the distance to the moon and back," Fern had said.

"And they are so big that their tongue weighs more than ten Abbies," Jeremy added and threw his daughter into the air so that she would know how it felt to be a breaching whale.

She laughed and clapped her hands and soon after cried because she wasn't allowed to ride on them to Mexico.

The curve at the exit of Elk, the sweet little coastal town forever tainted by Gina's car swerving off the road and crashing down the bluff side, when she came back from burying Ru's mother in San Jose.

Little River, where he was introduced to Fern's parents, during a gourmet lunch between two rounds of golf; her mother having too much Chardonnay, relieved they were going to do the right thing; her father jovially recounting his own humble beginnings. Both unsuccessful in their efforts to hide their disappointment about Fern's inferior catch.

The meticulous lawn of the boutique hotel in Mendocino, where their marriage began.

Noyo Harbor's swaying jetties, where it ended.

Jeremy grabbed the plastic bottle from the cup holder and poured the foaming liquid down his throat. "I can't drink this stuff anymore," Gina had said a while ago, the girl who had thrived on diet cola for the last twenty years. "It tastes like battery acid now."

He had phoned the police from the gas station.

"Abalone is fine," Steve had said. "And the boy has only minor injuries. Couple of bruises. His nose might be broken. That will add some character to his face."

Gina had called Jeremy twice.

As he drove through Salinas, she told him to take his time and not to worry, because she was already back home with Abbie, who seemed unaffected by the afternoon's unsettling event. Three hours later, shortly before he reached Petaluma, she phoned just to make sure he would be home soon. Only because he knew her better than anybody else had he been able to detect the tremor in her voice.

As Jeremy descended from Ridgewood Summit, the highest elevation on U.S. Route 101 between the Mexican and Canadian border, he thought of his daughter again.

Was this event the climax of Abbie's story or the turning point? Would there be a chance for her to come down to normal or would she go off the deep end now? Six or seven psychologists had tried with her over the years, but what do you do with a child that does not talk? Art therapy had been useless; although Abbie could have drawn the most expressive pictures, she refused to even touch a pen. Nor did she consent to build any little scenes in a sandtray, the play approach Mrs. Hotchkins had so highly recommended.

The outskirts of Willits appeared.

The Redwood Highway became Main Street. Papa Murphy flashed his lights at him and Jeremy's mouth watered.

He should go in and order a large five-meat stuffed pizza, take it home and bake it in his own oven in his own house.

Jeremy groaned. Everything had slipped beyond his control. He had to get on top of things again. Although, had he really ever been?

He passed the shopping center, switched the radio on and tuned into the familiar station of The Coast. He turned westward, and the slim moon lit his way until the Dodge entered the darkness of Jackson State Forest: fifty-thousand acres of Douglas firs, mystical sequoias and joyful memories.

They had come here every year on Abbie's birthday since she was three.

She loved riding the Skunk Train through the towering redwoods. They had hiked on the old logging trails and picnicked in secret groves.

On their last birthday together, Abbie and Fern had climbed up onto one of the old-growth stumps. Jeremy took pictures of them with Fern's first generation iPhone that her father had gotten for her from friends in San Francisco before its official release.

His girls had twirled around on the platform with locked arms, singing 'A Sailor went to Sea'.

Jeremy could hear their voices now, bouncing back and forth through the black tree trunks. *And all that he could see, see, see was the bottom of the deep blue sea, sea, sea.* Strange song to be sung in the woods.

He glanced at the mileage counter. About twenty-six miles left. Twenty-six. Fern's age when she finally fell in love with him.

He took one last gulp of Pepsi and threw the bottle on the mat in front of the passenger seat.

Fern Westfield, gorgeous and talented, a year older than him, daughter of Captain Chester Westfield and Jeremy's one and only high school crush.

He had joined the theater group just to watch her paint stage settings, volunteered for the production team of *The Current* to photocopy her cover illustrations and caricatures depicting the teaching staff.

As a teenager, she had designed logos for local businesses; Jeremy still flinched whenever the signets of Gray Fin Tours or Martha's Dry Cleaning caught him unaware.

Her lavish cinnamon-red hair and heart-shaped face made her stand out, as well as her habit of cladding herself most of the time in jeans and her father's old dress shirts with ever-changing patterns of acrylic paint smudges. As a less unconventional notion, she had dated Bryant Cranmore (Tyrant Cranmore to his enemies, and heir apparent of Cranmore Constructions), delighting two sets of parents.

After her graduation, she vanished; Jeremy heard she had gone to New York to pursue a career in the arts. Her abandoned boyfriend comforted himself with the homecoming queen and got married soon after, while Jeremy spent the last year of high school mourning Fern's absence, and went on to let his love for woodworking fill the gap — an unsuccessful venture, like the string of short and shallow relationships with girls he found wanting.

The radio played Bryan Adams now. *This is torture. This is pain.* Jeremy turned it off and massaged his temples. *Baby, when you're gone.*

And then one day, without a warning, Fern had reappeared. Gina and her husband Ruben, recently retired from competitive apnea diving, had moved into town three months earlier and were working on their dream to open a diving school offering under-sea adventures with spear-fishing and abalone harvesting for stressed business managers from San Francisco.

Jeremy had been hired by his brother-in-law to refurbish the seminar room and adjacent shop in a manner that would make people gape. Inspired by pictures of old Spanish galleons, he fashioned the store to look like the interior of a sunken ship, using redwood planks and oak paneling coated with glaze finish in pale greens and blues; sailcloth dividers between the sections; and old barrels, trunks and treasure chests to store small merchandise.

Jeremy was smoothing the side of a drawer for the cabinets behind the counter when he heard heels clack on the wooden floor boards; Ru must have left the front door open.

"Excuse me," said a voice he recognized in a heartbeat. "Are you Ruben?"

He stopped sanding and turned around.

"Hi." The slender young woman in a flowing peacock-blue summer dress extended her hand.

"Ahem," he said, unable to arrange his thoughts. The heart-shaped face. The luminous red hair, trimmed into a shoulder-length feathery bob.

"My name is Fern Westfield."

Her hand still stuck out into the air between them. "Ruben Fuertes asked me to design a brochure for Abalone Adventures."

And he forgot to mention it to me, Jeremy thought and muttered another, "Ahem." Not only did she not recognize him, she would now think him an imbecile. He straightened his shoulders, dumped the sanding block on the counter and took her hand.

"I'm Jeremy Macklintock," he said. Her skin was soft and cool. The first time he ever touched her. "Ru is my brother-in-law. He just went to get us some coffee. Would you like to wait in his office?"

"I remember you." Her aqua eyes sparkled at him. "From the theater group. You were so funny as Bottom."

"One of my greatest accomplishments," he said, thrilled by the ease of their conversation.

"You have changed a lot, though," Fern remarked with a frank smile. Was she alluding to the fact that the woodworking had put muscles on his lanky frame? That she liked it?

She glanced around in the store.

"Is this here your design?"

Jeremy nodded. He felt her fingers warming up against his dusty palm.

"Love it. Looks almost real." She realized that their bodies were still connected. "Oh, I'm sorry." She let go of his hand. But not hastily, as if she was embarrassed; she released it like one sets free a young bird, with care, aware of its frailty.

"Nothing to be sorry about," Jeremy said, his eyes fastened onto hers, encouraged by the firmness in his voice and the bold questions forming in his mind.

What did you do for the last eight years?

Would you like to go for a glass of something?

Are you back for good?

"Hello, you must be Fern," Ru said and put the coffee traveler and the pastry tray he was carrying on the counter. "I'm Ruben Fuertes."

"Pleased to meet you," Fern said. They shook hands. "Your store looks great."

"Jeremy is a true artist," Ru said and distributed paper cups. "My wife Gina will be here in ten minutes. Let's have some java while we wait."

After they ran out of coffee, Ru invited everybody for lunch, and the idea was born for Fern to paint the front of the store and some of the inside walls with underwater scenes in exchange for diving lessons, which caused her to be in and around the shop for the following days, while Jeremy put the finishing touches on the cabinetry in a state of blissful disbelief.

At the end of the week, after his sister and brother-in-law had showed up for half an hour with two bottles of sparkling wine from the Anderson Valley to celebrate their work, Fern and Jeremy found themselves lying on the planks behind the counter in a close embrace, applying traces of paint and sawdust to each other.

Soon after taking up diving, Fern became crazy about abalones, and her enthusiasm was contagious. Jeremy started using the mother of pearl as inlays in the furniture he produced, and throughout the summer they ate them as often as the legal limit allowed it.

By the start of the next harvesting season, they were husband and wife, and Fern was five months into her pregnancy. When the ultrasound revealed that they were expecting a girl, she had no difficulty persuading him to name their daughter Abalone.

Jeremy reached into the bag of beef jerky on the dashboard. His fingers raked the leftovers into a pile and threw them in his mouth. There was another bag for later. To be devoured after Gina had informed him about the day's strange occurrence.

The meat scraps released their flavor on his tongue. Through all the years with Fern, he had been content. Living with her fulfilled him. She needed her space, but he understood. She loved him. She was content. They shared ideas. They admired each other's work. And together they raised their beautiful daughter, who was an inspiration.

As a present for Abbie's sixth birthday, Fern created a picture book of *The Little Mermaid* and had it printed. For the double-page illustrations, she used black ink combined with iridescent shell patterns in a blend of Art Nouveau style drawings and the psychedelic images of the Seventies. Beardsley on LSD, she had called it.

It was mind-blowing. Jeremy had urged her to make more copies and send them out to agents.

Not surprisingly a New York agency took Fern on and soon after offered her a contract for an exclusive collection of illustrated fairy tales with a renowned publisher of high-end gift books.

At this time, Jeremy had considered abalones the lucky charms of his existence.

He had only begun hating them on the day his life turned into a bad trip, when the Mendocino County Coast Guard Auxiliary fished Fern out of Noyo Bay with fragments of iridescent shell stuck in her forehead.

Jeremy slowed and pulled into the driveway in front of the workshop. The light of the kitchen lamp fell through the side window. Right outside stood the basketball net they had given Abbie for her seventh birthday, its large black silhouette looming like the Ghost of Christmas Yet to Come.

He could see his sister at the table, her head resting in her hands. As he cut the engine, she waved to him.

# Thirteen

## ABALONE
FRIDAY EVENING

I have finished my work. The light is off. On the corduroy couch pushed against the large window, I lie like in a nest, cradled by the back and the high armrests, and the cold glass pane I often touch to be connected with the outside. I view the sky and feel the cool of the sea.

I am calmer now; though thoughts still swirl through my head like the surf around the rocks at the shore. Why do I have to deal with long forgotten desolation at a time that sees the day of my departure approaching fast? The waning moon's sickle hangs above me, looking sharp as a razor blade. It was not my choice to stay on land with the Props for all this extra time.

I would have visited the sea witch right away had I known where she lived. Trying to cut off my tongue by myself proved more difficult than I had imagined. The pain made me faint and I hit my head on the washbasin. Auntie Gina discovered me on the fleece of the white bathmat, blood trickling out of the corner of my mouth, leaving a stain that looked like a sea flower, like one of the bright-red blossoms in the little mermaid's garden.

The cut healed, and in the days when I learned to keep my tongue fixed against my lower teeth so it wouldn't hurt, I understood that if I didn't use it the result would be the same. For a sacrifice is needed. I also tried not to employ my two lower extremities when I was younger, but it didn't work out. I had to move around somehow. So I began to cover their unsightliness with skirts and dresses and longed for the hours I could put on my fin and swim. Uncuru had taught me the dolphin kick. I also learned from him how to hold my breath underwater. I am almost at six minutes now. He could go for close to eight and said a man from a small country called Austria can even do it for over nine.

When we didn't exercise, Uncuru told me stories of the wonderful Ama, Japanese women who dive for pearls and seaweed like their ancestors did for two thousand years.

"Imagine," Uncuru said as we sat on the deck of his boat and peeled out of our wetsuits. "For eight to ten hours a day, they search the chilly coastal waters for treasures. And they wear nothing but a loincloth."

I also loved to hear about the Moken, whom he had visited himself. They live on small wooden boats called *kabang* between the islands of the Andaman Sea, where the ocean is like a sparkling sapphire and the temperature of the surface water never sinks under eighty degrees.

"On a single breath, they dive down to depths of over sixty feet, without any additional weight," Uncuru said. "They take walks across the sandy seabed or stay motionless over their prey when hunting for groupers or threadfin with a simple bamboo rod. Or they drift with the current along the coastline of an island and gather lobster, oysters or sea urchins. And imagine — they never wear diving masks. Their eyes are adapted to the liquid environment," Uncuru explained to me. "Their underwater vision is better than any other human's."

I wish I had asked him how their voices sound.

Whenever the ocean allows it, I improve my diving skills. Sometimes though, I just float along the shore pretending to be a tropical nomad harvesting food. I collect the tender blades of bullwhip kelp, off the floating bubbles bobbing on the waves like little heads.

"Never take the stuff that has washed up on the beach," Uncuru had warned me one day when we were out together. He stood, half of his body in the water half in the mid-day sun, but I was still small and had to paddle. "Pluck them directly from a rock or the sand, or from the top of a stem. Then you know they're edible." He vanished under the shiny surface for a couple of minutes. "Look what I found," he said, appearing again, waving a feathery miniature tree. Drops of ocean flew all around. "A sea palm. Rare and tasty."

His fingers pulled off the fronds' light-green tips. "Open up." He put some on my tongue and some on his. "Chew," he said and smiled.

They were fresh and salty and melted in my mouth. I still have to figure out how to eat them underwater though.

The kelp forest is one of my favorite places. The high and slender stalks with long leaves, always in motion, hang down like frilly party garlands from a bright-blue ceiling. When I submerge along one of the flowing strings, its color changes with the depth of the water, from ochre and orange, where the sun rays touch it at the surface, to olive and turquoise, and emerald at the bottom of the sea.

I love to dive by Seal Rock and meet its occupants; they always enjoy themselves when they rollick in the kelp. I swim among the gray-brown bodies and try to imitate the way they fly through the water — their elegant moves, dashing here, dashing there, twisting and turning, swift and effortless, while rays of light frolic over their speckled skin. Whenever the seal pups peek at me, some timid, some curious, I'm reminded that I started diving when I was their size. They have such sweet faces, long white whiskers spreading out wide, fore-flippers waving happily, the line in their snouts curving up on both sides into a welcoming smile.

When they see my tail fin, do they wonder if I'm a mermaid? For once in a while, one of them swims close and looks at me with big melancholy eyes as if it wants to tell me something important and doesn't know how.

When I get exhausted, I crawl onto a rock close to the beach and sit there in my rubbery skin that is not like fish scales but not like the pale human covering either. Without it the water feels icy and I cannot stay for very long; although I have tried my best to get used to the low temperature.

The seals are lucky to possess a thick layer of blubber to keep them warm. How are the Ama able to take it for so many hours?

But at least I don't have to put a mask on. Uncuru taught me the trick that Moken children learn when they are very young.

"Seawater is close to tear water. Your vision can adapt to the liquid environment," he explained. "When you open your eyes underwater, the pupils automatically widen as far as they can. Everything gets blurry. The secret is to narrow them, then you can see twice as good."

Then we dove under, Uncuru and Mommy looking at me through their diving goggles while I practiced adjusting my pupils.

"I knew it. You are a little Moken," Uncuru said to me when we all were back on board of the *True Limpet*.

"You're wrong," Mommy said, laughing, and shook the water out of her beautiful hair. "Can't you see that my daughter has mermaid's eyes?"

When I rest on a rock, I squeeze my props together so they look like a tail and spread my fin on the wet stone.

Should merpeople be nearby, they must see that I am worthy of being one of them.

In the meantime, I busy myself preparing gifts for them to show my appreciation. I use precious metal thread, shell beads and gemstones, and the colorful treasures I find on the bottom of the caves close to the shoreline.

Only my best work is good enough for them. All other pieces I hand over to the parent Prop in exchange for food and clothing and the use of the small wooden house that still smells faintly of linseed oil and turpentine used there before it became my temporary shelter, where I lie now, gazing at the sickle moon.

I reach out and press my palm flat against the glass in front of me.

Coolness seeps into my flesh. My hand moves over the pane to repeat the comforting sensation in another spot.

I will not miss this little place; yet I have liked living here. And I will hold on forever to the memories it contains. On the worktable, Mommy showed me how to draw with charcoal and pastel chalk. I had my own small easel and a flat wooden box that contained silvery tubes with oily paints. Their mysterious names still ring in my ears: Cerulean blue, alizarin crimson, viridian. These days, I only use colored pencils to sketch my ideas.

But I follow everything she taught me about composition and proportion, perspective and how to create the illusion of depth with light and shadow. We drew the ocean view together, or a vase with lupines from the garden, or each other's face. "Forget that it's a nose, Abbie," she said, reached over and touched mine with the wooden end of her No. 5 brush, "there are only shapes and lines. You must see the negative spaces."

I still remember the time when we decorated the back wall with the glimmering glass we loved to collect together at the beach.

The Props have many polished names for it: sea glass, surf gems, mermaids' tears, beach jewels.

But originally, it was trash. Hurled over the cliff top into the unsuspecting waters.

They violated the ocean — but the ocean did not retaliate by sending furious waves, dispersing their settlements and drowning their infants. No. It chose to make them a present. Turning offense into beauty, in an act of undeserved forgiveness.

Leaving Auntie Gina behind will be my only regret. She, too, has detached herself from the Props, refusing to walk. But it is impossible to take her with me.

I am counting the days.

# Fourteen

## LEIF
### SATURDAY MORNING

"What do you mean you don't want to press charges? We can't let the girl get away with assault and battery."

"I don't want to cause more trouble for her, Dad," Leif answered and reached out for the local section of the newspaper.

His hoodie sleeve creeped up, revealing the streaks on his wrist. The crimson had paled to light pink overnight. The suspicions about the bracelet, however, had increased while he tossed and turned, trying to come up with an explanation for the bizarre event in the coffee shop. Maybe Abalone Macklintock was stark raving mad. Or, more probable, the bracelet had a mystery attached to it.

Bad decision to keep it and wear it, even though only sporadically when with his friend. Leif wished he could tell his father, admit where he found it. But that would lead to questions. Questions he wasn't prepared to answer. For now, it would have to remain a secret; another one in the cocoon of lies and omissions he had already spun around himself.

"After all that has happened to her family," he added and opened the newspaper.

His father rubbed his freshly-shaven chin. He was in dress shirt and tie, his suit jacket ready for action over the back of the chair next to him.

"I know," he said. "But it's not in your hands. I wish you could exercise your legal mind more. The sheriff will decide if he wants to forward the case to prosecution. What if she is developing violent tendencies and becomes a threat to society?" His father possessed the odd habit of crafting most of his sentences as if he had to impress a judge with it.

"She's only confused, Dad," Leif mumbled, wondering if he had a legal mind, or even wanted to.

The stupid bling. Why hadn't he just left it buried in the sand? He had to find out why it had outraged her so much.

He threw the paper on the empty chair next to him. At least he wasn't featured in the weekend issue.

"I think she needs another shrink," his father said and took a hearty bite off his greasy breakfast sausage.

Leif winced.

"Sorry, sonny, that was really less than charitable." His dad wiped the fat off his mouth. "It's nice of you to think this way. Don't worry, she won't go to prison for it. I'm sure

Family Services will have a talk with her father and decide what's best for her." He took the Heinz bottle and squished some more ketchup onto his plate. "Anyway, how's your nose?"

"A little tender."

"Do you want to go over what you will say?"

"Why?"

"Just in case."

"In case of what? She beat *me* up, Dad!" Leif grabbed his half-eaten bowl of Froot Loops and carried it over to the sink. "I'm taking Gutsy for a walk along the ocean." A wheeze came out from under the table as their pug acknowledged the mention of her name.

"Okay, son. Be back at a quarter to eleven."

"I will," Leif said and snatched one of the leftover sausages from the pan. He pulled up the table cloth and showed Gutsy the bait.

"Come on, girl, let's go." As she crawled out of her hiding place, an annoyed look on her little black face, Leif attached the leash to her collar. He could tell she wasn't keen on exchanging her comfy spot in the beguilingly smelling kitchen with the great outdoors. The treat appeased her, though, and she let herself be dragged into the hallway.

He wasn't worried about the interview. Although Gordon had been upset they had to cancel their Saturday night trip, Leif knew his friend would lie for him. If only to cover his own butt. Every Friday, from one to three, they played racquetball together.

He would protect their mutual dream: to buy Harleys and drive down to Los Angeles.

Leif grabbed his car key from the hall table and wondered how he had managed to entangle himself in so many falsehoods in seventeen short years.

Hey, Gordon, let me tell you what my real dream is: to sing at the Met! As soon as Gordon figured out what that actually meant, he would become the first ever recorded case of lethal laughing.

Leif went down the front steps and waved goodbye to his mother, who knelt in the flowerbed by the side fence and weeded between the hollyhocks. His car was parked at the curb. He unlocked it and lifted Gutsy onto the beige leather of the passenger seat. Although she couldn't see much more than traffic lights and sky through the windows, she loved sitting next to him when he drove. Again he marveled at the adorable mix of cute and ugly in her little face.

When they went to the shelter four years ago, after his sheepdog, Hobo, had died of cancer, Leif had expected to come home with a Collie or a Retriever, but inexplicably his whole family fell for a wingless bat with weight issues.

He took his phone and connected it to the stereo receiver. For the next ten minutes, Cecilia Bartoli sang, all the way to Glass Beach Trail, accompanied by Gutsy's wheezing, while Leif listened intently to the soprano's pronunciation.

He stopped the T-bird at the end of Elm Street. It was still early and only one other car sat in the parking lot.

Nobody but Gutsy witnessed him putting on sunglasses and his black Giants cap. If at all possible, he planned to encounter the girl in disguise.

What would he say? He hadn't really given it much thought so far. But he would talk from a distance and not present her with the opportunity to attack again, in case she was insane. Which he dearly hoped she wasn't.

Leif opened the passenger door. His pug hopped out and lolloped toward the sign the city had erected at the entrance of Glass Beach Trail to warn careless beachcombers of the perils of the sea. 'Even on calm days, large waves can form without warning', it said. 'As you enjoy the beach, please remain aware of the surf.'

Gutsy sniffed around the base of the pole for additional messages. Leif picked up the leash end and pulled her away, and they set out toward the ocean.

As far as he had found out on Google maps, the Macklintock property bordered on a small part of the trail. He could linger there for a while; maybe she would go for a walk to the beach by herself, where he could approach her.

Gutsy plodded at his side as he turned to the left around the wire fence. *Stop Poaching* said the small sign hung up by the enemy, the self-appointed snail protectors. Leif was at a loss to understand their infatuation. Apart from the pretty name and tasty meat, abalones offered little charm. These creatures were not pandas. And what did they do? Just sit on a rock stuffing themselves. Taking a dozen a week, maybe two, three at the most — where was the harm? The waters of the Mendocino coast supplied an abundance. And he only picked the large ones, not juveniles, nothing under seven inches. Giant mollusks fattened by dead kelp.

Max Nguyen had urged them to go out more often; his contacts in San Francisco were screaming for wild red abalone, but it was already difficult to conceal their activity from peers and parents, the cunningly camouflaged wardens and from the nosy members of the MAW, patrolling the coast from Navarro River up to Glass Beach. At least, they were easy to spot in their yellow caps and jackets.

Leif looked around: none of them on duty this morning on the windswept cliffs.

Yes, it was poaching. Yes, it was illegal. The limit per person in the season from April to November was eighteen, total, never more than three at once at any given time. You were required to tag every abalone immediately and record it in your stamp card, not to mention that it was outlawed to use scuba diving gear or go at night, and whatever you harvested you were not allowed to sell, period.

Gordon and he would be in a load of trouble if the fish and game wardens ever got wind of their lucrative little business. But then, Jack London had made some money being an oyster pirate in the Bay of San Francisco to support his family. Wouldn't you let a starving man get away with stealing a loaf of bread? Why could nobody live off the land or the sea anymore? East-coast Canadians were still allowed to club seal babies over the head. And what about dolphins and other mammals dying in fishing dragnets? Why this overprotection for a slab of meat with a gaudy shell?

Gutsy pulled on the leash and disappeared behind a small shrub. Good girl, she had the happy knack of pooping in hidden places.

She came back, grunted at a hole in the ground and started munching on Leif's shoelace. He bent down, took it out of her mouth, and they continued their walk along the trail.

Of course, Leif had to admit he was not starving. He was properly fed and wore clothes that allowed him to blend in and did not attract ridicule from the popular crowd. The car he drove, a mint-blue 1962 Thunderbird Hardtop inherited from his grandfather, was even regarded as cool.

His parents had money earmarked for his university education, so he could learn to twist the truth, preferably at Stanford or Berkeley, but at least at Loyola Law School like his father, who earned a living by facilitating the collapse of other people's love stories.

Leif sighed. For twisting the truth he would of course not need further tuition and if he wanted to steer off the designated path, he had to fend for himself. His share of the booty got deposited in the account at the Citibank in Richmond District, opened when Max had invited Gordon and Leif to come and see the Giants last October.

He had a long way to go still, considering the unimaginable thirty-eight thousand per academic year at his favorite pick, the Juilliard School in New York, without even having paid for any accommodations or a morsel to live off.

So his best choice would be to try out for the San Francisco Conservatory of Music, which still charged a whopping twenty thousand dollars, and apply for financial assistance like a California State Grant.

Ms. Panetta said he had the talent.

They were working right now on the repertoire for the required audio recording, which requested an Italian aria from the eighteenth century, an English art song and one piece of his choice.

If he passed the pre-screening process, there would be a live audition in San Francisco.

But doubts had come up lately. In May, a poacher had been sent to state prison for three years and fined fifteen thousand dollars on top for taking a fraction of what Gordon and Leif hauled away in a month.

A career built on ill-gotten gain, was that really what he wanted? Putting his life in danger to make his dream come true? Up to a dozen divers got killed every year hunting the prized snails.

Leif reached the edge of the cliff. The sea was calm, the tide out. The patches of beach holding sparkling treasures still slept in the shadow cast by the bluff. He loved the rough coastline, the fissured rocks and boulders, waves tossing and swirling around them, the ever-changing colors of the water. It reminded him of opera: the turmoil of emotions, drama and beauty that capture the senses.

He felt like singing, but close to him, two middle-aged women climbed up from the beach, each carrying a small bulging plastic bag.

Lately, the Parks Department tried to discourage people from taking glass home, although there was no legal ground for it, as his mother had informed him. She co-owned Sea Star Cottages, an upscale Bed and Breakfast Inn by Pudding Creek, and supported the idea of throwing shards into the sea to let the surf recycle them. The tourists would be happy, she said, and the minerals from the glass would seep into the water and benefit the marine biology.

Maybe it would be also good for the abalones. The cove at Glass Beach was a favorite spot for the locals, with plenty of abalone and targets for spear-fishing. You could always get your limits there. The bottom sloped gently to a depth of twenty-five feet, before it dropped away past the last wash rock. He knew the area so well, strange that he had never come across the girl before, but she probably never left the shallow waters as she was only freediving.

The two glass collectors had made it safely up the cliff. Gutsy greeted them with a snort, and they smiled as they passed by.

Their catch was not even worth anything, Leif thought, contrary to his. Max charged one hundred forty per snail and paid Gordon and him forty bucks each, which was a fair deal. His first couple of payments had bought a second-hand Yamaha CP50 stage piano, worth about four hundred fifty dollars as he had told his parents instead of the thousand three hundred he had really paid for it.

He practiced every evening with earphones for at least one hour when they thought him wrapped up in homework or World of Warcraft. Music as a career — his father would not even entertain the thought. He had never come once to hear Leif in all the years he sang on Sunday in the choir of Emmanuel Baptist. Luckily, Gordon hadn't either; his friend thought he was taking piano lessons to become the next Ray Manzarek.

Leif examined the beach and the cliffs: no sign of the girl. Gutsy had started digging in the sandy ground and Leif pulled her away, returning to the path. He slowly approached the Macklintocks' backyard. Five or maybe six meters away from the low wooden fence stood a cabin, its glass front facing the ocean.

A person moved by the sidewall.

Leif ducked behind a bush. He glanced down at Gutsy, afraid she might snarl, but she didn't show any interest. He peeked through the twigs and exhaled. It was only a wetsuit, dangling from a hook.

A thin rope extended from one end of the cabin to the other between the protruding beams of the roof construction. On it hung long and narrow leaves, fastened with clothes pegs. Bull kelp blades drying in the morning air, wafting like dark-green bunting.

Under them slept the girl.

## JEREMY
### SATURDAY MORNING

Jeremy spooned black powder into the Melitta filter. The house was quiet except for the sound of water gurgling out of the bathtub at the end of the hallway and the hissing kettle on the stove. He glanced through the open patio doors into the backyard, marveling at the beautiful and rare sight: an August morning without fog. Ocean air flowed into the kitchen, perfumed with lavender and thyme from the giant planters Gina kept on the deck.

The rays of the rising sun reflected in the cobalt-blue sea glass of the small oval window of Abbie's studio, gleamed in the wave and spiral mosaics grouted onto its east-facing wall.

He took the kettle off the stove and slowly decanted the hot water into the pour-over brewer. The rich flavor steamed up, together with a glorious vision of scrambled eggs and half a dozen rashers of sizzling bacon. The lavish breakfast feasts this kitchen had seen, sumptuous Sunday brunches with no shortage of meat or dairy products and happy people chatting at the reclaimed redwood table, Fern in the center of the action baking buttery scones and blueberry pancakes laden with whipped cream.

These days he would have been content with two pieces of plain white toast. He bent down and placed the kettle back on the burner. After the complete make-over he had given it three and a half years ago, the place looked like it was home to the seven dwarfs, but it allowed Gina an independence that had lifted her spirits.

Jeremy opened the refrigerator to review his breakfast options. Soaked oats and nuts. Dehydrated mushrooms. Meh. A handful of blueberries maybe? But he was not going to slurp a liquefied head of lettuce. Or eat pickled kelp stipe. What did he expect? Sausages and hash browns? Maybe there would be time to dash down to Boatyard Drive for two Egg McMuffins before he met Elon.

The rubber seal of the fridge smacked like lips as Jeremy closed it. Abbie laughed at him from a photo, the one where she dunked the basketball, taken almost eight years ago.

She was a miniature Fern in everything: hair, bone-structure, the cream color of her skin, even the seven-year-old nose already elegant and proud, the curve of her earlobes — except for her smiling green eye. That was his contribution.

He loved the photos of them together. On the train, cuddling. Playing b-ball. He taught her how to dribble and stop, make crisp passes, fake out a defender. Her arms were strong because of the swimming; throwing the ball was easy for her.

The other pictures he just glanced over. He had left them on the fridge as a reminder for Abbie. Maybe that had been a bad idea.

The phone on the kitchen table buzzed like a furious wasp. Jeremy flinched. He gave the brewer a longing look. At least two unpleasant calls lay in wait for him this morning; he would have to take the first one on an empty stomach. No sense in trying to avoid the unavoidable.

He braced himself.

"Macklintock."

"Jerry!"

"Good morning, Chester."

"Jerry, what's going on with Abalone?" Anger, badly disguised by his father-in-law's Rotary Club chairman voice. "Melody had a melt-down before breakfast when she checked her phone. Please explain to me why Abalone beat up Kent Saunders's son in the Bean and Bagel!"

"I wish I knew, Chester." The 'Dad' days were long gone. "I came home at eleven last night; I haven't even seen her yet."

"The photos are all over Facebook. Striking the boy with a tennis racket. And that stuff hanging from her waist. She looks like a lunatic. Has he done something to her?"

The thought had crossed Jeremy's mind more than once in the early hours of the morning as he lay in bed checking the ceiling for irregularities.

"We don't know yet, Chester," Jeremy said and slumped down on a chair at the kitchen table. "Elon and I are going to visit him at eleven this morning."

"So he's not in the hospital?"

"No."

"Good. She will need a lawyer. I golf with Ross Thompson from Bergman Thompson Shaw. They're experts in damage suits."

"Chester, I'm sure this will not be necessary. We have to talk to the boy. And before I go I want to hear Abbie's side first."

A snort. "And how are you going to do that?"

The king of sarcasm. No wonder Melody had resorted to Prozac.

Her husband wasn't much comfort in a crisis. They had moved permanently to their penthouse in Sacramento two months after Fern's funeral. Officially to be closer to headquarters, but Jeremy knew that his mother-in-law had found it impossible to bear the ocean vista any longer. Who could blame her.

"Give me two days to sort things out."

"Jerry, are you handling this the right way?" Performance review voice now.

"Two days, Chester." Jeremy could feel another offer approaching.

"Why don't you come over and stay with us for a while? Professor Velasquez has made contact with a trauma specialist in Seattle. Dr. Van Mellen is willing to come down to see Abalone. Don't worry about the financial side of it."

"I'm not forcing Abbie through this again! Being landlocked in Sacramento is not going to improve her condition."

"I'm sure you know what to do with a chunk of wood, Jerry. But these people are experts in child psychology!"

"And I'm an expert in Abbie!"

"Okay, Jerry, you have two days. Good talking to you." His father-in-law hung up.

Jeremy ended the call on his side.

Photos on Facebook! He had counted on the town gossips to speedily deliver the news to his parents-in-law, but the existence of visual material caught him off guard.

The brewer dripped on the counter as Jeremy carried it over to the sink. He ripped open two sachets of sugar. He always took extras when he got himself lunch at the coffee shop. Why sugar was on the list of undesirable food items remained a mystery to him, like the whole raw regime that had been established in his house.

But he had given up hoping things would bounce back to normal and went along with whatever made Abbie and Gina happy.

At least he was allowed a cup of coffee at home in the morning. Stirring the sweet crystals into the hot liquid, he congratulated himself that he was not somebody who fancied cream in his joe.

Jeremy sat down at the table and stared at the icons on the green display until he had emptied half of the mug and was prepared to log into his Facebook account. Although it was almost a year since he last did so, he had no problem remembering his password: Abalone.

After the initial excitement of connecting with a couple of old friends, he had found the daily flood of claptrap tiring.

And for the last seven years, he only went there once in a while, feeling his status updates were better left unwritten: 'Hey, today it's three years since my daughter has last spoken to me.' 'Driving my sis to the hospital for her next operation.' 'By the way, has anybody seen my brother-in-law lately?'

He flinched: *Married to Fern Macklintock* it said on the left; he never had the heart to change it or to delete her account. His profile picture still showed his wife and daughter dancing on the remains of a giant redwood.

Tessa's friend request sat sulking in the top bar, ignored since it came in four years ago.

Jeremy didn't have to scroll down far in his news feed. At least five posts and shares showed his daughter brandishing a racquet, her lovely countenance contorted into absurd grimaces. In a supporting role, Leif Saunders turtled in his plastic chair, while a couple of coffee shop extras beheld the crime with shocked faces.

Abbie's expressions almost made him happy; her mouth was open in several pictures. Had she shouted at the boy?

But what struck Jeremy, harder than any racquet could, was how grown-up Abbie looked: the spitting image of his wife when he had first laid eyes on her, at lunch break on a Wednesday in early September.

"The new girl. Just moved over from Sacramento a couple of days ago. Her dad's loaded," his friend Steve had said, pointing at Fern. "Isn't she a knockout?"

She had sat by herself in the grass, leaning against the trunk of a plane tree, listening to music fed to her ears by a Walkman in the lap of her acid-washed jeans. Glossy dark-red hair cascaded over her shoulders.

Her soft sweater had slipped off one of them and exposed her skin. She smiled, looking up into the green canopy. The leaves filtered the noon sun and showered her with golden specks of light. He could not remember having ever seen anything so beautiful.

Jeremy's brain had just suggested the idea of going over and introducing himself — after all she was new at school and alone and to say welcome seemed a perfectly normal thing to do — when Tracy McFadden and her blonde ponytail appeared, boyfriend Bryant Cranmore and some of her cheerleader entourage in tow. Soon all of them were chatting and laughing under the sunny tree as if they were old friends.

"Of course she will be one of them," Steve snorted. "C'mon, Jay. Nothing here for us to see." But Jeremy stayed and watched them, until the bell rang and he noticed he hadn't even taken one bite of his baloney sandwich.

Fern had risen and for a second peeked over at him, before she hooked arms with Tracy and Bryant and strolled toward the school entrance.

Jeremy shook off the memory and focused again on the photos in his feed.

Here was his daughter, his little girl, on the brink of womanhood. What would the future hold for her?

In his head the Hotchkins tape repeated itself: how will Abalone maintain healthy relationships?

How would she maintain any relationships?

She had no relationships at all. His protection had allowed her to slip away from reality, had stunted her. He should have done something to rip her out of her agony, especially after he had it in black and white that she was his, but that would have meant to leave his own weird state of hibernation. Instead, he had floated through the last seven years, acting like there was all the time in the world to make amends. Only for her to turn violent in the end.

Jeremy switched off his phone and slid it into his pocket. He crossed the hallway and entered Abbie's room. After they found Fern, and then Abbie the next morning, time had started stretching like a never-ending sleepless night. He had fought through every hour as one cutting his way across a hostile jungle. Yet now, it seemed that he had helped Fern with the mural only yesterday.

He gazed at the painting spreading over three walls — no wonder Abbie lived in a dream world. They all had contributed to this madness. Escorted by smiling dolphins, a little girl rode through the ocean spray in a shell-shaped carriage drawn by six seahorses. The other two walls showed a choir of starfish holding song sheets, accompanied by a harp-playing octopus, and a palace at the bottom of the ocean surrounded by waving kelp trees.

Jeremy had broken abalone shells into pieces and Fern decorated the carriage with the delicate mother of pearl. Around her neck and in her hair the girl wore real sea glass. Of course she had Abbie's sweet features, and the same red locks, painted as a swell around her head like in one of the Alphonse Mucha illustrations Fern adored.

Her most favorite artist, though, was the Victorian John William Waterhouse (not the least reason being that Fern resembled all the glorious women in his works in one way or the other). A couple of years before she died, Jeremy had given Fern a newly-released monograph for her birthday, and as embarrassing as it was, once in a while, he still locked himself in his bedroom with the book, to search for his wife's face among Waterhouse's seductive sirens and nymphs.

"The worst thing is I still like the picture." His sister stood in the doorway, wrapped in her powder-blue morning robe, a towel around her head, balancing herself on two under-arm crutches. She was almost as skinny as before the accident now, but her carefree pixie smile had vanished for good.

"Yes, Gina," Jeremy said, "strangely, I do too."

"Was that Chester on the phone?" Gina slowly approached him.

He liked seeing her upright, even though the high-tech constructions on her legs made her look as if she had been partly assimilated by the Borg. She limited the stick crawl, as she called it, to bathroom visits and her daily exercises.

"It sure was." Jeremy pulled a face.

"So the news has already reached him." Gina sighed. "It was to be expected."

"He wants Abbie to see another specialist."

"I'm sure she had a good reason," Gina said.

"No doubt. But we can't let her go on like this forever."

Gina gave a short, hard laugh. "Yes, maybe we all need our heads examined."

"I never felt good about allowing her to stay in the studio overnight," Jeremy mumbled. "And I shouldn't be away for a whole weekend with you not able to reach her there."

Gina shook her head. "She was perfectly fine when she went to the beach after lunch yesterday. And you saw her in the morning before you left for Cayucos."

Part of her towel had come loose and flapped down in front of Gina's left eye. She shifted around on the underarm crutches.

Jeremy stepped toward her. He knew she wasn't able to get her hand up standing like this.

"Steve said as far as he knows the boy had been at racquetball practice with his friend since one o'clock before he encountered Abbie in the coffee shop," she said.

"You told me so last night."

Jeremy gently tucked the peach-colored terry cloth back into Gina's turban.

"But what caused her to freak out like this then? She was furious. Wild. Have we missed a sign? Some change in her?"

"No, Jeremy. There has been nothing out of the ordinary." She exhaled. "Or out of what we have come to accept as the ordinary."

They glanced at each other with despondent smiles.

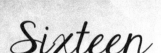

## Sixteen

### GINA
#### SATURDAY MORNING

*G*ina lowered the crutches and let herself drop onto the bed. She grabbed the pillow and pressed her face into it. He was still hurting so much. Was it wrong that she had never told him? Did it even matter anymore? And how could she bring up the truth about Fern now after all those years? Her silence had allowed Jeremy an untarnished memory, and given the amount of her own injuries, enduring one more made no difference; although it had been the worst, the one that never even started healing. No scar tissue was able to cover this wound. She felt the black tide rising, but these days she managed well standing against its surge.

She hurled the pillow across the room and punched the mattress until her knuckles reddened. How she wished she could kick something too. Gina looked down at her legs and feet. The engine block had smashed into her lower half, bones splintered like china on stone tiles. Yet, they were tolerably mended now, reconstructed into their human shape. A notable surgical success it had been, avoiding the near certain amputation.

The option of another string of expensive operations was still open to her, holding the possibility of walking again with just a cane. But why should she make the effort and endure the pain? For whom?

A drop of water ran out of the turban along the back of her neck into the bath robe and down her spine. Gina untied the towel and gave her hair another rub.

The road had been wet, the low standing sun blinding, her mind occupied, causing a fatal moment of distraction.

Can you die of a broken heart? Ru's mother had. She had just faded away, Ru's father said. Gina had spent three weeks with him after the funeral and helped him to empty out his three-bedroom ranch home in Edenvale. He was already over eighty then, suffering from diabetes, and with his wife gone and his son nowhere to be found, his days of independence had come to an end.

Gina had asked him to relocate and live with her, but he wouldn't hear anything of it.

"You're still a young woman, *querida*," he had said when he kissed her goodbye. "Don't give up on life yet."

Waving to the old man in the parking lot of Sunny Meadows, situated at a major highway with no discernible meadows in sight, she had wondered how long he would last there.

But time had proven Gina wrong. Now close to ninety, he phoned every two or three weeks to encourage her, and to report on his budding friendship with Mrs. Delgado, who shared his fondness for playing backgammon and didn't mind when he smoked a cigar right under her nose.

Gina dug into the pile of stuff that coiled up behind her on the bed. She didn't make a fuss about her wardrobe anymore. The pants and blouses from the days when she had been thirty pounds heavier still served their purpose; although they made her look like a child dressing in her mom's clothes. The old skirts and dresses had retired to the bottom of the closet. Knee-skimming was for other girls now. And nobody was left who cared what she wore or how she looked anyway.

She turned her head to check the time on her alarm clock. In front of it gleamed a small heap of gold and green. Abbie must have sneaked in during her bath. She leaned over and picked up the chain — gold wire twisted into lovers' knots with seven green sea glass charms, shiny as emeralds and every one of them heart-shaped.

Gina swallowed. What a sweet gift. She knew how relieved her niece had been to see her yesterday. When Gina had rolled into the room, Abbie jumped up, took her hand and didn't let go of it until they were in the parking lot of the police station.

Upon Gina's entrance, Mrs. Hotchkins had also risen, her face glowing with self-righteousness, as if Abbie's arrest confirmed all her suspicions, justified her frequently voiced warnings, and constituted the culmination of and the deserved rebuke for the criminal laissez-faire-attitude displayed by Abalone's father and aunt. Thankfully, before she had been able to put these thoughts into words, the sheriff-coroner walked into the room and rescued them.

At home, Gina and Abbie had eaten a quiet bowl of gazpacho together. Gina had not been able to detect any further emotional unbalances in her supper companion, before Abbie had retreated to her studio with a plate of cashews and a glass of orange juice.

Gina wrapped the bracelet around her wrist and fastened the clasp. She moved her arm and let it slip up and down. The rose-gold matched her wedding ring, the only piece of jewelry she wore these days.

# Seventeen

## ABALONE
### SATURDAY MORNING

*M*emories are coming to me now, for the first time in years, of a day I thought forgotten. Pictures flood my mind with the force of a spring tide. When I get up later, I will put them on paper, showing how Mommy floated on her back like a sea otter, her face next to the boat; how she stared into the sky.

I knew she wouldn't turn into foam on the crest of the waves. I held her arm, my elbow locked into her elbow, but the ocean roared and crying made me tired and then she was gone.

I was afraid she had sunken into the deep waters where the polypi seized her, strangled her with their numerous little arms and consumed her flesh until only her white bones were left to cling to.

Later, people tried to make me believe that she lay in a wooden chest with lilies in her hair, and does now rest forever at the end of East Spruce Street, a meadow covering her body.

I stayed in the dinghy, hoping in vain I would see her again, her pale cheek bobbing out of the blue and the long hair whirling and curling with the motion of the swell.

The wind picked up and the sky became pearl gray and the waves the color of ashes.

I took the knife out of the supply box and cut the rope connection to the big boat so that my small boat could float away to where she had gone.

After a while, it started raining and I crawled under the tarp and hugged my knees.

When I woke up, moonlight bounced on the choppy water, and wispy clouds drifted across the black sky as if they wanted to be somewhere else fast. Then it dawned on me that I would never play hide and seek again with her in the kelp. I bent over the gunwale and screamed for the merpeople to come and salvage me while the chilly sea frothed up into my face, as salty as my tears.

I got thirsty, and after I had watched the stars and the hurrying clouds for a while, sprawled out on the bottom of the boat where the spume drenched my shorts and blouse, I got hungry as well. Uncuru used to put trail mix and orange pop in the supply box when I went out with them, because I loved to sit in the dinghy by myself and pretend it was a carriage drawn by seahorses with shimmering harnesses.

But he hadn't known I would be there, and the box was empty. I drank a little rainwater from a crease in the tarp and coiled up under its plastic skin, shivering from cold and loss.

I awakened again when somebody spoke to me: a wrinkled woman with tiny blue-gray locks who wore sneakers and a purple cardigan. Although she had no toads or water snakes with her, only a small off-white poodle that jumped into the boat and tried to lick my face, I believed a kind fate had guided me to her. For in the sand all around us, up and down the shoreline as far as I could see in the light of the morning sun, lay giant orbs of light-brown stone, and my dinghy was stuck among them. Naturally, I thought the beach to be one of the sorceress's playgrounds, like the road of foaming whirlpools or the turfmoor.

So, I told her I needed a tail because I wanted to live in the deep. That I was willing to offer my hair and even my voice for her powerful draught. However, she did not listen but continued to yell into her phone while she cowered next to me on the seating board with her arm around my shoulders.

Soon, others appeared on the shore.

I was carried up a steep path by a broad-shouldered man whose breath smelled of smoke and Tic Tacs. Two men in police uniforms dragged my boat behind us because I had refused to leave the beach without it. When we reached the top of the cliff, I got put on a stretcher in the back of a large white van.

The mint man wrapped me in a blanket that looked like golden tin foil, and the old woman, who was not the sea witch, fed me lukewarm tea and crackers with sesame seeds on top.

I hold my breath and listen: someone is wheezing.

I sit up. A shadow crouches behind the conifer at the fence.

Knocking on my door. "Abbie, please open up," the parent Prop pleads. "I have to speak to you."

# Eighteen

## LEIF
SATURDAY MORNING

His mother had prepared a thermos jug and a plate with ginger snaps and short bread before she left for her Pilates class.

His father had offered coffee and treats when their visitors came in, and now three adult males were sitting with Leif at the harvest table in the dining room, sipping coffee out of mugs illustrated with Dr. Seuss characters. Surely his mom must have been in a hurry, as she was not known for bouts of zany humor.

Mr. Wagner, the sheriff–coroner, easily identifiable in his short-sleeved sand-colored shirt with a shiny star on his chest, and Mr. Macklintock, who wore jeans and a navy-blue wind-breaker, had taken the two chairs in front of the china hutch. Leif sat with his back to the window beside his father, now dressed in his full suit and a facial expression of readiness-to-object.

Their visitors had somehow ended up with the Thing One and Thing Two mugs, which provided a slightly similar effect for Leif as the old trick of imagining an intimidating opponent naked.

Mr. Wagner had asked him to recount the unfortunate event for them in detail, and he had done so, omitting only the bracelet and his suspicions about it.

"Then she clung to my wrist until Deputy Flynn handcuffed her," he concluded his account, glad nobody had interrupted to ask any questions.

The sheriff–coroner looked at him over his blue mug and took another swig of coffee.

"I've seen the pictures," said Abalone's father, who had seemed eager to talk since he had entered the dining room. "Her mouth was open. Did she say anything?"

"She screamed at me."

"Could you understand any words?" Mr. Macklintock persisted despite a couple of coughs from the sheriff–coroner, clearly intended to re-establish his authority as the main investigator.

"It sounded like '*you, you*' or something close to that."

"And what do you think she meant?"

"How should I know?"

"Thank you, Jeremy," the sheriff–coroner said loudly, and placed Thing One on the table. "Leif, could you tell me why you didn't try to stop her?"

"I was surprised. It happened so fast, and I guess I was waiting for Gordon to disarm her. I didn't want to hit a girl."

"When Abalone came out of the coffee shop, were you or your friend doing anything to attract her attention?"

"No. Gordon and I were just sitting there, talking and waiting for our salmon paninis. As I told you I didn't see her until she was standing next to me."

Leif looked down at the smirking feline with the striped hat on his coffee mug. He couldn't blame anybody else but himself for the chaos in his life. It was all his doing, and things were not funny anymore.

"So you said nothing to her? No little joke or remark she could have misunderstood?"

"Not a word!"

"And did you have any prior contact with her?"

"Yes," Mr. Macklintock interjected, and his arm came down hard on the table, almost tipping over Thing Two. "Did you ever meet her at the beach?" He bent forward, his face flushed. "Or come close to her studio?"

Leif squirmed in his seat. Never, except for this morning. Once more, he had the impression telling the truth would only complicate matters.

He had cowered behind the low fence and a strategically well-positioned stubby pine tree and watched the girl, who lay on a sofa shoved against the window panes that made up the west wall of her tiny house, like a fairy tale beauty in a glass coffin. The rays of the rising sun had fallen into the dark room through a small round opening in the wall behind her, filling the room with a blue glow — as if she slept underwater.

Her white face had shone out of the masses of hair curling all over the fabric of the couch and the soft sheet outlining her body's contours. She had rested on her side, one hand cupping her chin while the other touched the glass in front of her.

Leif had felt the urge to leave his hiding place, to press his palm against hers, to kneel by the sofa until she opened her eyes.

He had flinched out of his trance when she suddenly sat up, and flinched again as he heard somebody talk at the side of the cottage only a moment later, seeing the girl jump over the backrest of the sofa wearing merely a bathing suit. Almost crawling, he had sneaked off, pulling Gutsy behind him, hoping nobody had noticed his presence.

"Talk, boy!" said the voice he had heard at the girl's cottage. "Did you ever come near her?"

Leif glanced at his dad. "What are you implying?" he heard him asking, and the outrage in his voice felt like a hug.

"Nothing," Mr. Wagner said, his arm lifted to curb his companion's fervor. "But we need to establish if there is a history between the two."

"Until yesterday afternoon, I have only ever seen her from a distance," Leif exclaimed. "Never talked to her in my whole life!"

His father got up and put a hand on Leif's shoulder.

"Excuse me, Sheriff–Coroner," he said, "as far as I understand you are here to interview my son as a witness and the victim of a crime. There is no doubt about what has happened. We have abundant visual proof of the attack.

I suggest if you want to find out the reason you should interrogate the assaulter. I have agreed to her father being present, assuming him to be apologetic and not trying to fabricate an allegation against my son."

"Please, Kent," Mr. Wagner said with a brief side glance meant to silence Abalone's father, "nobody suspects Leif of any wrongdoing. You have to understand that Jeremy's daughter displayed extremely atypical behavior yesterday. She is usually very withdrawn, and this explosion of anger must have been triggered by something."

Now was the moment to open his mouth, Leif thought. To tell them all about the bracelet. To clear himself of all suspicions regarding Abalone, and at the same time, incriminate himself of stealing her gastropod namesakes. Not exactly a win-win situation — and there was also the appealingly romantic thought of sharing a secret with the mysterious girl and her beautiful bi-color eyes.

"Well, whatever it was, you will have to go elsewhere for an explanation," his father said to the men, who now also got up from the table. "Leif has given a detailed account of the incident. There is nothing more we can add from our side."

Both men gave Leif a final inquisitive glance before they followed his father to the hallway.

Leif collected the coffee mugs. As The Cat in the Hat joined Thing One and Thing Two and little Sally Walden on the tray, Leif wished for somebody to come and straighten out the mess in his affairs. But the probability of outward help was slim. Leif sighed; all his decisions had seemed so reasonable at the time.

He felt a glimmer of hope, though. Given the way his dad had stood by him, maybe it was possible to at least tell him about the intended change concerning his career plans. Though, maybe his father was only trying to protect his own dream: Saunders & Saunders Law Firm.

Leif carried the tray into the kitchen. Gutsy jumped up on his leg, and he shared a piece of short bread with her before he poured the left-over coffee into the sink.

He heard footsteps on the floor tiles.

Rinsing the last mug, Leif felt his father's hand on his shoulder for the second time this morning. He turned around.

"Son, is there anything you haven't told me?"

# Nineteen

## JEREMY
SATURDAY, LATE MORNING

Jeremy pushed through the crowd, following Elon to the back. The Bean and Bagel resembled an anthill. He had never seen it this busy. Lots of young people, obviously acquainted, as they shouted to each other over the already cringe-worthy level of chatter. Here and there, somebody hit a friend over the head with a stir stick. Great.

Matt Ogilvy waved to them with a paring knife.

"What a frenzy. It seems to be some sort of flash mob. But I don't mind as long as they consume something," he said when they finally reached him. "Hello, Sheriff. Hi, Jeremy," he greeted and continued slicing an avocado. "How can I help you?"

Once, Jeremy remembered, they had seen each other often. Abbie and Thomas, Matt's son, fond of each other in kindergarten, had liked to meet at the Wiggly Giggly playground. A couple of years later, the four of them had started playing basketball together on Sunday afternoons.

Jeremy looked over at the till where Thomas took the orders. He was an upcoming star on his high school team now. A promising point guard.

"As I told you on the phone," Matt said, responding to Elon's request to give his view of the event, "I had just handed her the Veggie Deluxe and said goodbye. When I turned around to rinse the blender, I heard the screaming. I saw Leif ducking in the chair and Abbie thrashing him with the racquet. I galloped outside and tried to drag her away from him."

He artfully placed the avocado wedges around a portion of whitish mush on the plate in front of him, and put the finished creation on the pick-up counter.

"Tabule Andino," he shouted and hit the little silver bell next to it with his palm.

As if this were a signal, a teenager, standing by the gents' door, got smacked on the head with a rolled up newspaper, followed by hoots and laughs from the group surrounding him.

At least some people were getting enjoyment out of this sorry mess, Jeremy thought. It seemed Abbie had supplied the weekend entertainment for the city's bored adolescents.

"She dropped the racquet and gripped his wrist."

Jeremy returned his attention to Matt, who grabbed the last multigrain bagel out of a woven bread basket.

"Leif got up and tried to loosen her fingers, but she wouldn't let go. When Steve appeared and handcuffed her, she collapsed in my arms." Matt stared at the baked loop in his hand as if it held the explanation for this peculiar experience. "Then she followed him to the car like a puppy."

A loud grunt came from one of the corner tables where the newspaper skit was repeated by a trio of pimpled boys, sparking more laughter and snorts.

"Did you overhear anybody saying anything before it happened?" Elon asked and stepped aside for a girl in a hoodie and pajama pants who picked up the quinoa salad and disappeared into the crowd.

"No, Sheriff, I didn't hear Leif or Gordon say anything, only Abbie shouting." Matt cut the bagel in half. "Although it was more like a howling. *Uhhhh, uhhhh*, or so."

He opened a tub of Philadelphia. "Oh, Jeremy, before I forget, I have stored her bicycle by the back door, and don't worry about the smoothie bill for this month." He gestured towards the multitude in his cafe with his cream cheese knife. "As sad as it is, she got me some extra business."

They left Matt to feed his silly customers and jostled their way outside.

"I better get going," Elon said, standing by his car. "Although, I hate to leave it like this. We're none the wiser, are we?"

"True." Jeremy shrugged. "But what can we do? Anyway, thanks for your help." They shook hands. Elon got into his car and left.

Jeremy retrieved Abbie's bicycle from the rear of the cafe and packed it into the loading space of his van.

He closed the hatch and frowned. It wasn't the enlightening morning he had hoped for. He opened the driver's door and slumped behind the steering wheel.

Interrogating Abbie had turned out to be as fruitless as his father-in-law predicted. Every question he asked she had answered with a shake of her head. Do you know the boy? Did you meet him before? Was he mean to you? Has he ever touched you?

Why did you beat him with the racket?

No reaction at all, except a blunt stare. Just as Gina had said, there was no change in her usual composure, her extreme guardedness.

Jeremy pulled a bag of jelly beans out of the glove compartment. He liked to please his taste buds while his brain had to chew on unpalatable matters.

The interview with Kent Saunders and his son had been equally unsatisfying. Leif was a nice kid, lean and athletic, without attitude. Handsome too. He had inherited his mother's looks, the dark mop of hair, the glacier-blue eyes. And Steve was wrong; Leif's face didn't lack character. Jeremy was happy his nose wasn't broken. Leif didn't appear to be a coward or the type who had difficulty getting a girlfriend.

His behavior had been gentlemanly, to sit there and get beaten without striking back. And he had seemed shocked by their suspicions of him having provoked this attack by some improper dealings with Abbie. Jeremy was almost certain Leif had never met his daughter before. However, he had the impression that something was wrong with the boy.

Jeremy glanced at the clock: a quarter to twelve. Lunchtime.

He started the van and directed it toward the wharf. At least he would have a nice, satisfying meal before he returned home. There was little more that could be done, with Abbie unable or unwilling to give a hint about her motivation. It had been kind of Elon to get involved. In the cases concerning Jeremy's family, he had really gone the extra mile. Jeremy reloaded his mouth with sugary beans. Of course, his fancy for Gina was an open secret to anyone who had ever seen him around her.

If his sister could come out of her shell, there might be a chance of happiness for her. She didn't deserve to be a shut-in at forty-three.

Jeremy sighed.

Maybe if he had told her the truth about Ruben, she would have been able to get over her grief; he often thought about it lately.

Jeremy parked in the small parking lot of the Nautilus. Three spots over from where they had arrived in Steve's police cruiser on that devastating afternoon.

Steve had appeared in the workshop like a ghost. He stood by the bookcase that was ready to be delivered the next morning, his left hand holding on to its solid oak, rubbing the back of his neck with the other, and waited for Jeremy to switch off the miter saw.

"Bad news," he said and swallowed. "There was . . . Cal Ashby saw something in the water, and . . ." The tip of his shiny black boot drew circles in the wood chips. "You have to come with me to the wharf. They have found Fern . . ."

It was beginning to drizzle when they got there, after picking up Gina at the dive shop. Jeremy saw a hearse parked at the side of the road, the trunk door open like a maw — ready to swallow his wife.

Small groups of tourists and locals dotted the scenery, some hiding under umbrellas, quiet and motionless. Only once in a while, an arm slowly lifted to point.

Jeremy and Gina followed Steve to the jetties. Inside the restaurant, the patrons stopped eating and stared at them, with the pale faces of waxen dolls, stared at them through the windows and the thin gray threads falling from the sky.

The wooden walkway quivered as Jeremy passed the docked boats, Gina by his side. He had experienced minor quakes — slight rattles occurred now and then in many places on the West Coast — and always wondered how a big shock would feel, the ground under your feet coming to life. The one in 1906 had shaken the core of their little town badly. Many buildings got damaged, some collapsed. Then came the fire. One and a half blocks burnt down.

Screeching on his left. On the cabin roof of a rusty trawler, two seagulls fought over the orange leg of a Dungeness crab. Didn't they know it was forbidden to catch them outside of the season from November to April? Maybe nobody had told them.

His forehead was wet from sweat and rain; he wiped it with his arm. The sawdust on his shirt sleeve itched his skin.

People whom Jeremy knew but couldn't remember surrounded a stretcher. Gina grabbed his hand. Some mumbled words as they came closer. He couldn't understand them.

He only heard the tiny raindrops hitting the dark plastic that covered the body lying on the stretcher.

Tap, tap, tap.

Jeremy realized his fingers were clenched around the steering wheel.

He got out of the van and entered the restaurant. His favorite table by the window was free. Charlotte came by, wearing her checkered pinafore and the smile reserved for regular customers.

"Hi, Charlotte."

"Hi, Jeremy. You look like you could use a seafood platter." She put a glass and a bottle of local ale on the table.

He nodded. No need to communicate to her that he wanted a double portion of Chipotle coleslaw and garlic bread instead of fries; she knew his preferences by heart.

"You got it," she said and vanished through the swinging kitchen door.

He had never possessed a great talent for small talk. It suited him to spend his days alone, working away, his mind focused, but at the same time free to wander, thinking about the next project, an idea for a chair or a chest, or, even worse in the years since Fern had died, locking onto the same questions again and again.

Jeremy sighed. Given the level of noise behind him, both side rooms of the Nautilus were stuffed with large crowds engaged in animated conversation.

He peered out of the window into the peaceful, sunny harbor. Ian Macy's charter boat drove by, full of amateur fisherman eager to catch King Salmon.

Jackson Howard refilled his trawler at the fuel dock.

Louisa Pendergast and her father hoisted the main sail on their catamaran. On the jetty by the fish cleaning station, a giant sea lion lolled in the sun.

Jeremy heard Trevor Arbornut's booming voice bring on a toast. Glasses clinked. The freediving events were still popular. It was so sad his brother-in-law wasn't around to enjoy the success of the business he created. Ru had also come up with the idea of having a partnership with the Nautilus: a harvesting session in the morning followed by a lunch. The divers supplied the abalones, and the restaurant crew turned them into a banquet complimented by local wines and artisan beers.

"Jeremy!"

He turned his head. Pam Fowley steered toward him.

"Hi, Pam. Thanks for your help yesterday."

"No big deal, Jeremy," she said and sat down opposite to him. "You know I'm happy to be there for you guys." She reached over and patted his hand. Although she was only a few years older, she had a motherly way of interacting with him. They had known each other since the days when he and Gina had been frequent sleepover guests at her family's home because of their own father's business trips, which was the agreed-upon euphemism for a long weekend's absence after a dry spell had come to an end.

Pam always made sure her mother cooked something nice for Georgina's little brother.

"I hope all is well with Abbie," Pam said. "And Jeremy," she leaned forward, "we need to drag Gina out of her hole. She won't hear anything about coming back to the association." Pam gestured toward the side room.

"I'm over there with the board. We're preparing for the special council meeting and planning our media event at Glass Beach on Thursday."

As usual, Jeremy tried not to watch her mouth when she spoke. Pam was blonde and overall not unattractive, but she possessed the irritating habit of matching the loud reds of her lipsticks and silk blouses. It looked like she had cut two wave-shaped pieces of fabric out of her top and glued them under her nose.

"Do you really think replenishing is a good idea?" he asked the table cloth. Personally, he thought it harebrained; equal to dumping the garbage over the cliff in the first place. When the genuine things were gone, they were gone. And what would prevent other coastal towns from turning their beaches into bogus attractions once it was done here?

"It's not harmful to the environment," Pam said. "I don't know why everybody has their knickers in a knot. We're not talking nuclear waste." She grabbed the salt shaker and waved it in front of him. "Glass is silicon dioxide. It's made of sand."

"But aren't the collectors after vintage shards?" Jeremy dared to suggest. "Is it the same for them if the pieces they take have been wine bottles just six months ago?"

Pam swiped away his doubts with another wave of the shaker, showering the small arrangement of asters in the middle of the table with white crystals.

"It's glass on the beach. That's what counts. It's our unique selling feature. Tourism is key for the region. We have to capitalize on our assets. There is demand and we can meet it."

She put the shaker down and leaned toward him again. "And don't you think we should try to offer our children some other job options than managing grow ops?"

"Touché, Pam," Jeremy said, picking up his napkin as he saw Charlotte approaching with a tray.

Pam's crimson lips smiled and she got up. "I should go back to my board; they're getting fidgety. Enjoy your shrimps, Hollow Legs." She patted his hand again and nodded to Charlotte, who placed a large platter on the table.

"Thanks, Charlotte. It looks great, as always," Jeremy said after Pam had rejoined her board in the side room, and the waitress had arranged his order in front of him.

"Bon Appetit, Hollow Legs," she said, smiling, and left with her empty tray.

Jeremy poured beer into his glass and took a bite of the battered cod. Only it wasn't fish he tasted, but the unique flavor of red abalone, somewhere between calamari and sweet oyster. Charlotte must have sneaked a slice from Arbornut's harvest on his plate, thinking she was doing him a favor. Jeremy hadn't eaten the odious mollusks for what seemed ages. The texture was good, soft and succulent. He cut off another piece, dipped it into the cocktail sauce and put it in his mouth. The cook knew how to treat the meat right. Jeremy's tongue delved through the delicious mush.

He watched the sea lion slip into the water and remembered how he and Fern had prepared their first abalones. How they had struggled to get the shell off and cut the tough body, then beat the pieces too short and fried them too long so that they ended up as rubbery as car mats.

But they quickly became experts.

Sharp knives were purchased, and a fisherman at the wharf showed them how to shuck the shell, skin the snail, and trim knob and foot. Jeremy always joked that the result looked like an old-fashioned planer.

They learned to slice them into half-inch steaks, pound a tenderizer onto them until they almost fell apart, to bread them using lightly seasoned sourdough crumbs mixed with parsley and Parmesan, and sauté them in hot vegetable oil just about thirty seconds on each side so that they remained soft.

Every time, it was a feast. And Fern never forgot to squeeze the gut with her fingers to check if a treasure had developed inside; over the years she collected a small but stunning amount of iridescent, oddly-shaped pearls.

After a while, Gina and Fern came up with new recipes, turning the delicious meat into stir-fries and chowders, sushi and wontons.

The year before Fern died, they formed a team, called themselves Neptune's Maids and competed in the Abalone Cookoff in Noyo Harbor, the annual festival where people from all over the West Coast presented their elaborate creations. On the afternoon prior to the event, both couples and Abbie went diving together — luckily the sea was calm with great visibility underwater — and everybody got three abs; although Jeremy and Gina only splashed around on the surface while Fern, Ru and Abbie dove down to collect the allocated number of snails.

To everybody's surprise, on the following day, they won the popular vote grand prize for their abalone cakes with lemon-caper sauce.

A beaming Abbie lifted the trophy; she had suggested using the recipe because it was her favorite.

"Have you heard what Macklintock's little freak did yesterday?" A guy somewhere behind Jeremy's back chuckled.

"Yeah, I saw the picture on Twitter. I almost laughed my ass off. What a retard," a different voice said, snorting.

Jeremy's hands tensed into fists around his fork and knife. He could get up and stuff his cutlery into the creeps' gullets easily, but the prospect of two members of his family getting booked for assault on one single weekend kept him on his chair.

"Shut your ugly faces," Charlotte hissed at the men who sat on the other side of the wooden bar, "or you can finish your grub outside."

# Twenty

## GINA
### SATURDAY, NOON

Nine down, one to go. Gina moaned; her legs were getting zonked. Just one more round from the chair to the kitchen door at the other end of the house, then back to the chair before she would freshen herself up a bit and prepare a quick lunch: stuffed mushrooms with a simple green salad. Abbie liked that.

One more step. And another. The long hallway with the skylights cutting through the whole length of the house made for an excellent training ground. Its gray stone tiles gave the rubber tips of her crutches a good grip yet let her soles glide forward easily. Left stick, right stick, left stick, right stick, left stick, right stick.

For every yard she had to move each crutch three times. The distance from the painting with blurry redwoods to the grainy black-and-white portrait of Abbie and her mother smiling at each other, their noses touching.

Gina looked up at the band of panes in the ceiling. Daylight fell through it, bright and cheerful, filling the hallway like peals of laughter.

Jeremy had designed and constructed the house himself, on the lot his in-laws had bought as a wedding gift. A minimalistic over-sized cabin, all glass and wood, its roof ascending towards the west as if a cheeky ocean breeze tried to lift it off its massive timber beams. Floor to ceiling patio windows ready to slide open to the large deck and the panorama of the backyard, the cliff top and the merging blues of sea and sky. The view made Gina feel less restrained, and the seamless connection between the inside and outside floors allowed her to enjoy the elements as often as she wanted.

Nevertheless, it wasn't her kind of architecture and the relics of Fern irked her, but overall the house had her brother's spirit, and Gina was thankful it had welcomed her when she needed a sanctuary.

Still, she longed for the yellow Victorian on Brandon Way with its ornaments and decorations, the mantelpieces and crown moldings, and the stained-glass windows casting rainbows onto the living room floor.

The steep front steps and narrow staircase connecting the levels had snuffed any hope of ever living there again after she unexpectedly woke up from steering her Corolla into the setting sun at Elk.

The house was now rented to a nice young couple whose children played hide and seek in the nooks of the attic and climbed in the old cork oak that stretched its branches high up against the roof and tapped at the little eyebrow window watching over the back lawn.

Children. She had wished for two, Ru had wanted four, but none had come into being. A miscarriage in the first year of their marriage and another one in the third crushed their hopes, but they promised each other to happily take on whatever life hurled at them as long as they were together, and aimed their love at their niece, who responded like she knew of their grief. Abbie doted on her Auntie Gina and adored Uncle Ru, who introduced the eager four-year-old to the wonders of the underwater world and pet-named her his *pequeña foca* because she was as natural at diving as a baby seal.

Gina had reached the entry area when the doorbell sputtered its ringing toward her.

"*Dichosos los ojos!*" came the caw from the guest room at the other end of the hallway. Gina wrinkled her nose. The prospect of visitors always excited Señor Limón, but she wasn't happy to see anybody right now.

In less than five minutes she would have been back in her chair, ready to speed down the corridor to the entrance, to take deliveries and sign for parcels. On crutches she felt vulnerable, reluctant to open the door to strangers; few of her acquaintances knew she stick-walked, even Pam had not seen her more than twice.

Gina leaned to the right and peeked through the narrow glass panel in the entrance door: Elon!

She steadied herself. Shouldn't he be interviewing Abbie's victim?

He had been kind yesterday though: made sure she could take her niece home right away, wrapped up the formalities in record time, fought off Hotch the Dragon (Jeremy's apt nick name for Mrs. Hotchkins), and then gave them a lift in his car.

After all the anxiety of the afternoon, she had squeezed Elon's hand when they said goodbye and told him how much she appreciated his help. It took her by surprise when he bent down and hugged her.

And now he stood at her door again, barely a day later. Gina sneaked another look. He wasn't aware of her presence; his head bent, working his phone with concentration. His thick ash-blond brush cut had darkened a bit over the years, and the side-burns ended in tufts of gray. But he still had the wide mouth that seemed to smile even when the rest of the man looked stern.

Overall the sheriff–coroner appeared much bulkier than the tall youngster who had picked her up on her graduation night in one of the smart suits he used for helping out at his parents' dance school.

Gina remembered him telling her about the fights at home after he had revealed his intention to join the police force. On the late summer evenings when they sat together, talking and smoking, in their favorite spot overlooking seal rock, she encouraged him to follow his heart. He became a police officer — and he never married.

Gina glanced into the large mirror next to the door. He had already seen her yesterday in her baggy black sweatpants and she didn't care one straw what he thought about her outfit. They were comfy, easy to pull over her stubborn legs in the morning, and disguised most of the awful knee and ankle braces she had to wear for exercising. She wished she could cover her upper part as well. The clingy white tank top wasn't something she felt comfortable in to receive an ex-lover. Ex-lover. This expression made her even more uncomfortable. What then? A former boyfriend? The man she once thought to be her destiny?

Gina stared at her naked shoulders. Powering the wheelchair had given them and her arms a nice toning.

You had to know the scars to trace their pale, meandering lines.

The top didn't show too much cleavage, and her boobs still fared fine without support; however, she found it inappropriate. Furthermore, the blender had spilled some of her mashed breakfast, and she looked as if an alien baby had vomited all over her midriff. But it couldn't be helped, the cotton blouse hung on the back of the chair at the end of the hallway.

Her brown curls were still a bit damp, sticking out in all four cardinal directions. But the light tan suited her well, and it smoothed the contrast between the skin of her cheeks and the shadows below her eyes.

Abbie's elegant gift dangled on her wrist. The kelly-green glass matched the color of her eyes and the splotches on her top. Gina hadn't been in the mood to wear decorations in a long time.

The realization that she might still be considered pretty caused a vague smile to appear on her face.

The bell rang again, setting off its feathered counterpart in the guest room.

What was she doing standing around assessing herself like this? She couldn't even remember the last time she had been concerned about the way she looked. So why now? She pressed the crutches into her armpits and stretched out her hand toward the door knob.

Elon stood in front of her like someone struck by summer lightning. "Heavens, Georgie" he muttered. "You walk?"

"Hello, Elon." Gina wished she had crawled away and left the door closed. "I wouldn't exactly call it walking. It feels as if I'm a badly drawn matchstick man."

"You never said a word." He brushed his left hand back and forth over the bristles on his head.

"I don't like to entertain people with my sick stories."

"Am I *people* to you?" Judging by his facial expression, his question had surprised him as much as her. Gina felt a weakening of her legs that was more than the usual strain from exercising.

"Did you miss Jeremy?" she asked. "I thought you wanted to meet Leif Saunders together." The metal of the door knob was heating up under her squeeze. "Anyway, he's still out. On Saturdays, he likes to frequent either the Nautilus or King Tide Burgers. In case it's urgent."

Elon straightened himself, visibly taking hold of his emotions as if grabbing an unruly dog by the collar.

"Not quite," he said. "We have talked to the boy and his father. But since then, a piece of evidence has surfaced that I would like you and your brother to review and tell me if you have any knowledge about it."

He fumbled around in the breast pocket of his well-ironed uniform shirt. "I have to drive back to Ukiah, and if you don't mind I could leave it with you for the weekend and you can show it to Jeremy and give me a call later."

He opened his hand in front of her.

"Leif Saunders thinks Abalone attacked him because he had this on his wrist."

Gina gazed at the rose-gold bracelet lying in Elon's palm.

"He said he found it by a rock close to glass beach when he was snorkeling." His voice came to her from afar through a wall of fog.

This must be a joke, Gina thought, before the crutches slid away and Elon lunged toward her.

# Twenty-One

## DAN
### SUNDAY MORNING

The wet glass stirred under the soles of his gumboots with short crunching sounds, as if disgruntled to be awoken by his steps. Dan zipped up his yellow windbreaker. Even though it was mid-August, the early hours could be quite chilly close to the ocean, and the mellow morning sun did not supply any warmth.

Fog whirled over the undulating water like puffs from a giant doobie. He sat down on a weathered log and gazed westward, where the string of rocky islands rising tall out of the ebbing sea formed a dark border covering the horizon, like a fortification to protect the hoard piling up on the beach.

Their effort was in vain, of course, as the pilferers usually attacked from the other direction. However, right now, he had the pleasure of enjoying the scenery by himself, except for the ground squirrel whose twitching nose poked out of a burrow entrance by the bluff, a few seagulls bickering over their clam breakfast in the tide pools, and the lone guy in neoprene who had just walked down the cliff path and waded into the compliant surf, gauge in hand.

Dan glanced at his wristwatch: 7:58 a.m. — two minutes to the legal time window for taking red abalone. He opened his waist pouch and pulled out his yellow baseball cap with the MAW logo. Showing presence was important, to make sure the pickers never forgot they were being watched.

"Don't you dare touch one before it turns eight," Dan whispered, placing the cap on his head while eyeing the small figure closing in on the wet base of a giant boulder, green with algae and rockweed.

Of course, this scenario could not be compared with the onslaught in April when each of the seventeen minus tides attracted a multitude dressed in black wetsuits, roaming around between the exposed rocks like a murder of crows looking for treats in a parking lot.

Picked over by up to three hundred people seventeen times, with all of them getting their limit, meant a monthly 'harvest' of 11,700 abalone here at Glass Beach alone. The Department of Fisheries estimated the total legally taken amount of snails in Mendocino and Sonoma Counties at 200,000 to 250,000 each year. Without the official regulations, this situation would develop into a free-for-all in no time.

He had little mercy for guys who messed with oceanic wildlife. A mere slap on the wrist was not going to cut it for them. There were still too many poachers around, undeterred by the penalties the county judges doled out these days. What difference did losing the fishing license make to a poacher? At least they usually got fined a whack of cash, every penny well deserved. If he had his way, they would all rot in prison until they came to their senses, instead of doing some puny community service.

The rock picker had found his first prey; luckily for him, it was now 8:05 a.m.

Dan turned his head to the left, as the high-pitched sounds of animated chatter drifted toward his ears, rivaling the gulls' clamorous palaver. Three ladies descended the dirt path and, upon reaching the bottom, immediately stooped down, uttering shrill declarations of delight, thereby causing the frightened squirrel, who had ventured out to take a morning stroll, to scurry back into its hole in the ground.

He had noticed before that for middle-aged women sea glass seemed to possess a particular pull.

After a few additional shrieks of amazement, the trio sat down and started raking their hands through the objects of their admiration.

Whatever one personally felt about the allure of Glass Beach, nobody could deny that its popularity with out-of-town visitors was increasing. Dan scooped up a handful of shiny bits: mostly white pieces, fair-sized and rounded; some bright greens, resembling drops of lime Jell-O; and browns in various shades.

After whisking through them with his index finger, he discovered one tiny speck of pale blue.

Not all that exciting.

Maybe the Glass Beach Cassandras were actually right. On Thursday, he would be here again for the filming of a PR event held by the local business association, campaigning for the conservation of the place, or better put: its maintenance.

For him, protecting the fragile balance of the marine ecosystem was a no-brainer, but the glass wasn't a natural resource, and it wouldn't grow back even if carefully managed.

So, should they throw new trash on the old dump site to keep it attractive? It was quite a unique problem.

Dan tossed the glass to the ground and glanced up. The beach was still empty except for the rock picker, who had returned to land with three big snails and was attaching his tags to them, and the ladies, who continued to examine the beach's treasures in a state of blissful hypnosis. But in the water, about twenty yards in front of Dan, stood Abalone Macklintock with her back to him, clad in an emerald wetsuit, her red locks illuminated by the rising sun — beautiful and serene, unchanged from when he had seen her last Friday frolicking through the surf before she had proceeded to establish her reputation as the town's madwoman.

Although everybody was dying of curiosity, Dan knew his boss had already decided not to follow up on the story, with both persons involved under age; though the boy's father being one of his drinking buddies surely had factored in as well, and no doubt, Captain Westfield had used his connections to guarantee his granddaughter didn't get any further media exposure.

Now, nothing resembled the raging girl he had seen on Twitter, swinging the racquet as if she intended to chop wood. Maybe she was even crazier than initially thought, and taking a wide berth around her advisable. At this very moment, though, she quietly walked into the surf, carrying a monofin, while the fog floated near as if trying to shroud her.

As soon as the water reached her thighs, she crouched down. The last thing Dan saw of the girl was the curved blade of her black fin vanishing between the gentle blue waves.

## Twenty-Two

### LEIF
SUNDAY AFTERNOON

He loved diving at high tide when the water was the clearest. The noon sun pierced the calm surface for perfect visibility. Leif looked up to the *Wave Runner* maybe ten feet above him. Gordon's shadow hung over the gunwale, distorted by the slight ripples Leif's descent had created.

His friend always stayed on board now. He never had developed a liking for the underwater world, much to the dismay of his father.

But in all the years that Mr. Abornut took them out, teaching them the basics, and later employing them during the season, he never held it against Leif that he surpassed his son in every aspect of the sport.

Before Leif had switched to the scuba set twelve months ago, the two of them had been freediving together for the abs, but Gordon sucked at it; he could never relax. Equalization was a constant problem. His ears didn't clear properly. But worst of all, the thought of shallow water blackout terrified him.

Often, the ocean was rough. Whirled-up particles made it seem as if fog had sunk into the water. Kelp strings wafted like cobwebs and fish materialized out of nowhere. The perfect setting for a spooky movie. You would not have been surprised to spot a woman in a nightgown, wandering through the haze with flowing hair and holding a candlestick. Or see seal specters flying towards you, shouting *boo*.

In such conditions his friend had been a liability rather than a help. They had settled the matter, and it was a fair split of responsibilities. Gordon supplied the equipment and the boat, a 1995 Duckworth Jet in excellent shape, and spent the time fishing, thus disguising the operation. Leif only had to do the collecting, unencumbered by the worry his diving partner might entangle himself in the kelp.

Leif kicked his legs and turned towards the sea floor. Orange bat stars littered the crusted ground, palm-sized and pretty, glowing like reflectors in the muted blues and browns.

Leif loved the big purple ones best, though, with their five pudgy rays. Last year in fall, he had found a cluster of at least thirty youngsters; their small spines made them look furry, like plush toys. Sometimes he came across a sunflower star with twenty arms, giants among their kind, almost as big as a bicycle tire, and also the fastest: almost forty inches per minute, on their little tube feet.

The wildlife down here never ceased to amaze him. All the different fish, the crabs, shrimps, slugs and snails, spiky sea urchins, and the colorful anemones with their long waving polyps.

He had encountered a mola mola once, an immense disc of a fish, basking at the surface above Leif's head, and been freaked out, at night, when the beam of his diving light hit the monstrous face of a wolf eel, staring at him open-mouthed, fangs exposed.

Every dive was an adventure, in a world of constant flux. Among the maze of the bullwhip kelp, surrounded by swaying seaweed, he imagined being an ant scuttling around between the green blades of a meadow while the current blew through it like a summer gale.

Some people thought these waters to be the best diving ground in Northern California. This strange, wild realm. A submerged jungle. Complete with predators — for out there, behind the kelp, lurked the great whites, craving a gentle pinniped.

Leif had never encountered one when he ventured out into the deeper areas. He was worried, but not enough to be scared off, nor were all the other divers, locals and tourists, and the guys who surfed at Virgin Creek. The statistics were on their side. One hundred and fourteen unprovoked shark attacks authenticated off California since 1926. Total number of deadly encounters: ten.

It was also ten years since the only ever confirmed fatality in Mendocino County.

It had happened right here, only fifteen miles up the coast, on an ordinary August day. Kibesillah Rock, a site Leif had no intention to dive at, ever.

According to marine biologists, the number of great whites was on the rise. A couple of years ago, a friend of Gordon's father had told them to avoid diving in the early morning, when the sunlight hits the sea at an angle that might make it difficult for sharks to see.

He said they were very cautious, investigating what they had in front of them, and attacks on divers at the coast were mostly cases of mistaken identity. Leif found him a credible source of information, given the fact that he operated a shark diving business at Isla Guadalupe.

"Just watch the sea lions," he had said and smirked. "If they're all on the rocks, somebody might be looking for dinner."

In any case, Leif always submerged with a dive knife in a sheath fastened to his leg. It would also come in handy in the unlikely event he should get entangled in the bull kelp or a fishing line. Even without shark involvement, diving was a dangerous sport. People died every year in these waters. The unpredictable sea, its chilly temperature, the sudden surge that could suck you into a hole or crevice, or just exhaustion leading to heart attacks, there were plenty of causes that kept the search and rescue helicopters busy.

The gauge in his hand gleamed as Leif slowly checked one ab after another. He didn't like to hurry; he had air for about an hour.

His arm reached out again with the measuring tool attached to its end like a silver claw.

The shiny metal reminded him of how he had discovered the bracelet, lying on the ground by a large opening in the rocks, between two abs, partly covered by a nudibranch.

Telling the half-truth had cleared him of all suspicions, Leif hoped. He wished though, he could have come up with this story when Mr. Wagner and Mr. Macklintock sat with him in the dining room. His father had swallowed the tale and phoned the sheriff–coroner right away.

"I discovered it at Glass Beach," Leif told him when he showed up only twenty minutes later, "and thought I could keep it. Maybe she lost it there."

He had found it. That was the main point. No shenanigans involved. Where he found it? None of their beeswax. Mr. Wagner had seemed happy about this new development.

Leif checked the gauge. Nine inches. He never took anything under eight, to make sure Max could get a higher price. It was said the bigger the abalone, the tougher the meat. But Leif couldn't tell; he only ate them once in a blue moon. He owned a fishing license and a report card. Sometimes he brought a snail home as a treat for his mother, who loved seafood of any kind but seldom got it because his father was a meat-and-potato man.

According to Max, the abs Leif harvested got shipped to Hong Kong, where the rare shellfish was the must-have dish for festivals and wedding banquets. Well-off families would pay up to two thousand dollars for a whole dried snail.

He grabbed his ab iron. If only he could sell directly to those people. The loot from a couple of months would pay for four years at Julliard.

Leif inserted his blunt instrument under the shell and pried the ugly mollusk loose. It was all about surprising them.

He heard humming and froze: an engine.

After a short time, a boat went by and the sound ceased. Leif put the snail in his bag.

To be out at this time was a risk, a Sunday in August at high noon. Glass Beach teemed with tourists. Other divers were in the water. But after the cancellation yesterday, Max urged them to go out as soon as possible.

Although Leif's sore nose had improved, the diving mask's pressure felt unpleasant. The last thing he needed now was a patrol boat containing zealous wardens. Leif had practiced dropping his buoyancy compensator and tank in an instant, if Gordon gave the come-up signal. He would get to the surface with a perfectly innocent expression on his face. Diving for abalones? No, not today. If Gordon signaled 'stay down', the plan was to hide by the cliffs and later swim to Glass Beach. Gordon would come back in his truck and pick him up. But luckily, they hadn't ever been checked. The *Wave Runner* was known to everyone. Nobody suspected Arbornut's son to be an abalone poacher. Trevor played by the rules. His customers left money in town, stayed at local inns, ate in local restaurants. The boys were out there to find a site for the next event, or enjoying themselves spearfishing. Leif made sure to always get a lingcod or a couple of kelp greenlings when he was done collecting abs. His mother turned the fish into a nice supper on evenings when his father had his guys' night out at the taproom of the Tide Pool Brewery.

Leif looked up. How limpid the water was today. He could still see the bottom of the boat and the silhouette of Gordon's upper body leaning over the gunwale. A dark arm moved back and forth. Smoking weed, no doubt.

Leif inhaled more clean air through his mouthpiece. He couldn't stand the smell of pot. It hit him right in the stomach. He had never taken up smoking anything because he feared for his voice. Even being around the musty odor nauseated him. Gordon was toying with the idea of growing some as an additional source of income. Just last Tuesday he'd bugged Leif about it again.

They had embarked from Noyo Harbor for one of their night dives, and motored south to Caspar Cove, from where Leif usually sneaked into the Point Cabrillo Reserve, an area with strict prohibition of taking any form of marine flora or fauna. They were already breaking so many rules that it didn't matter anymore. Leif detested how the narrow-mindedness of land life encroached on the underwater freedoms. Don't do this — don't do that. Don't take abalone in the winter. Don't take Dungeness crabs in the summer. Don't retrieve stuff from the wreck of the *Frolic*.

The sleek clipper had rested in thirty-five feet of water, by the cliff just north of the lighthouse, since the evening of July 25, 1850. It had carried Chinese luxury items and household goods to be sold in San Francisco, but originally ran drugs from India to China in the days when opium was all the rage.

Many artifacts were now on show in the lighthouse and in the museum in Willits, but Leif knew that not a few families in the area still had a shard of china or some other little treasure in their possession. The cove close to the wreck had been nicknamed Pottery Beach because of the porcelain pieces that washed ashore.

Leif remembered what he had been told about the surviving sailors who finally made it to San Francisco, how their tales of the enormous native trees they had seen sparked the timber boom. Amazing what impact one little event could have on the life of so many people. To think this cove once was a busy port and home of a flourishing lumber mill. The business that shaped Leif's home county. Now, a new commodity was taking over, and Gordon seemed determined to have his cut.

"Do you need more lube?" Gordon had asked, sitting on the deck at the stern of the *Wave Runner*, where Leif prepared for his dive. The upward shadows on his grinning face, caused by the halogen lamp in his lap, made him look like a ghoul.

The waves murmured against the hull of their boat; Leif could barely see them. The cliffs stood like a black fortress, and the sky only offered glimpses of the stars and the sickle moon.

But the flash of the lighthouse's third-order Fresnel lens sliced through the dark as if it was part of a search party looking for nightly poachers.

"Shut up, Gord." Leif wrestled into his tight-fitting Farmer John wetsuit. Its open-cell lining provided more warmth in the fifty-two-degree water than a loose scuba suit, but the thing had no zippers and getting into it was a pain in the butt.

Leif applied liquid to the inside of his top and swished it around to make sure it got into the arms and the hood. He always prepared his own thermos with lube now: scent-free hair conditioner mixed with hot water. Much better than Gordon's coconut and apple blossom shampoos from the Dollar Tree.

"Come on, bro, it's easy money. The zip-tie permits are voluntary now," said Gordon and took the thermos Leif held toward him. "We don't even have to spend a buck on registration. We could start with twenty-five plants, all legal."

Leif slid his arms into the sleeves, refusing to give this nonsense any acknowledgment.

"But we need a plot," Gordon added and dropped the lube in Leif's gear bag. "What about your grandpa's place at Hare Creek?"

"Forget it!" Leif pulled the hood over his head. "Mom is turning it into a vacation rental."

"Maybe we could clear a space somewhere up river."

Sometimes Leif felt like Pinky and the Brain with Gordon. "Don't count me in, Gord," he had said and fastened the beavertail clips to the front of his jacket. "I'd rather work on a skunk farm. Those plants smell worse than shit."

No way was he going into drug dealing. He still saw his career in singing, not in organized crime. However, Gordon continued to talk about it as frequently as he smoked the stuff.

Leif didn't understand the attraction in the first place. He appreciated a beer or two, but he would never want to be sloshed out of his mind, or fogged up like somebody had soaked his brain in fabric softener, and smell as if he shoveled horse manure for a living.

Here, underwater, his senses sharpened. If he wanted to lose himself, he just had to listen to a couple of Bach cantatas, and singing did the trick whenever he required an emotional boost. His life didn't lack excitement, and he needed his mind alert to conceal his activities and keep all his stories straight. Often, he worried that, when drunk or stoned, Gordon might accidentally let the cat out of the bag by bragging about their escapades. Or in a weak moment with one of his chicks.

Leif popped another ab close to nine inches, and two slightly smaller ones. His refined technique let the snails come off with ease. The trick was not to disturb them, to give them no chance to clamp down on the rock with their muscular feet, which would make it impossible to remove them. Leif added the three abs to the others in his collection bag. His hands worked deftly while his thoughts wandered again.

Gordon wasn't picky when it came to girls. And he liked to talk about it. And tease Leif about his refusal to do the same. But at least not in a mean way. Leif was too valuable to him. Gordon would never want to piss him off on purpose. He had profusely apologized for the photos and the postings of Friday's event.

It was not that Leif didn't enjoy being with girls. He did. He had kissed Marisa Potts and Eleanor Longdale, and made out twice with Kelly Petersen in the T-bird. Gordon knew that. But Gordon didn't know that Leif loved his music more than he was attracted to any of these girls.

That he didn't fancy a relationship as a mere means of satisfying his own desires. For a true emotional involvement, Leif believed, he would have to open up about his secret life. Which, at the present, meant more dangers than benefits.

"Taylor Swift is so awesome," Eleanor had said when he walked her home after harvesting baby spinach together in the Learning Garden on the school campus. Leif had mumbled some general consent, tempted to ask her if she had ever heard Diana Damrau sing 'La Traviata'.

It wasn't these girls' fault that he was a misfit, and to spare everybody embarrassment, he stayed single, and planned to fall in love with a sexy coloratura soprano in his first semester.

Leif's hands worked away without much input from his brain. Measure and pop, measure and pop. Ab after ab went into his mesh bag.

How could he tell anybody? He stopped performing in the choir at fourteen. The half year of struggling with his voice led him to believe that his singing days were over. To find out his soprano was still there had surprised him and Mrs. Panetta, who agreed to teach him secretly because she understood his predicament.

At a time when most of his peers already shaved daily, he discovered that he could still warble like a girl. Countertenor: the voice of a castrato. He found that hard to cope with at first. But the urge to sing and the enjoyment it gave him were overwhelming.

Mrs. Panetta had encouraged him. "Your voice is a gift from God," she said. "Don't neglect something so special. Be thankful."

So he performed in hiding, in the church basement where Mrs. Panetta had her grand piano, because it didn't fit in the pastor's apartment; at home after school when his parents were still at work, his half-sister already being away at college; later, in the T-bird, driving up and down the coast, and on deserted beaches and lonely rocks.

Once he had discovered a cavern in the cliffs. The acoustics there had been like in a cathedral.

Too bad he couldn't sing underwater. It would be the ideal place to practice; without his noisy breathing apparatus of course. Now, he only heard the bubbles gurgling and fizzing as they ascended to the surface, and his regular inhaling that almost sounded like Gutsy's.

A school of shimmering sea bass flitted by in front of him. If only he had his speargun handy and wasn't burdened with tank, tools and mesh bags. He had to spend some fun time down here again, unencumbered by work.

Out of the kelp dashed a seal. Its skin looked pale blue and speckled like a robin's egg. Leif plucked another ab, watched by a pair of inquisitive black eyes. Reproachful eyes. What are you doing here, human, in scuba gear, with a sack full of abalones?

The seal shot toward him, swerved, and showed off its swimming skills by floating past Leif, back down. He felt like petting the round white belly, but the seal spun again and zipped away, its two flat hind flippers waving goodbye.

Leif imagined Abalone appearing out of the kelp, swimming in her long, billowing dress. Her hair flowing like red algae, and her eyes fixed on him, ocean blue and seaweed green.

He longed to see her again. Which probably meant she had caused him some serious brain damage.

His lips managed to smile despite the mouthpiece.

He turned right towards a large crevice, checking out the hidden spots always proved fruitful. Tilting his head, he peeked into the crack, hoping it wasn't inhabited by another creepy eel.

What he saw, though, gave him a shiver of elation. There, right in front of him, sat a monster ab; he guessed it was far over twelve inches. His gauge confirmed it: 13.05. Gosh! He almost forgot to breathe.

The biggest one ever recorded was 12.34 inches, discovered by John Pepper somewhere in Humboldt County, four years before Leif was born. And in 2007, somebody had found the heaviest one at the coastline off Gualala. After cleaning and trimming it provided seven and a half pounds of meat and fed fifteen people, a Christmas turkey of an ab.

Leif knew there was a bunch of guys competing with each other to find the ultimate trophy 'hog', the thirteen-inch monster abalone; with this snail, he could outdo them all.

He looked at the ugly oval shell encrusted with barnacles and other critters, mimicking the ground it sat on. A hideous rock wart. A whopper among its kinsfolk that grew everywhere, spreading like tumors. An alien disease mushrooming all over the sea floor.

Leif stopped, his ab iron suspended over the giant snail. When had he started to vilify these creatures? They would die because of him.

Why did he have to malign them on top of it?

The answer came easily: to feel less guilty.

They didn't harm anyone. They sat here peacefully on the rocks, in nobody's way. Gentle herbivores, keeping the algae growth in check. Kelp cows.

How old was this giant? Abs needed at least ten years to grow to the legal size of seven inches. Somebody had told Leif that they could live thirty to fifty years. This one here had managed to hide from divers, cabezon, and hungry star fish.

Shreds of the future flashed through his mind: a newspaper article showing a photo of him holding the monster snail; MENDO Live knocking at his door; seasoned freedivers, old enough to be his grandpa, patting his shoulders; the fraudulent record haunting him for the rest of his life.

Leif put the iron back on his belt. He didn't want to be the one who killed this big guy. It had to end.

Leif reached into his bag and pulled out an ab. He turned it around; the foot showed no injuries. His iron wasn't sharp and he knew how to handle it. An abalone would bleed to death if the sensitive skin got damaged. Carefully, he placed the snail on an empty spot not far from the thirteen inch one.

Gordon would be miffed. With the moody weather conditions here at the coast they needed to take advantage of calm and clear days.

He had promised Max two nets: at least sixty abs. The contact man was prepared to come after dark and pick up the large collection bags.

As always, Gordon would text him the location to the secret number. Leif only had to attach a couple of yellow glow sticks to the bags' metal handles. Invisible by day, but easy to spot at night, they would illuminate the booty for the next twelve hours.

Gently, he placed another ab on the rock in front of him.

He would stay down for the whole hour and pretend the job was done — and then insist that the glow sticks malfunctioned. Hey, what could you expect for sixty-five cents apiece? Maybe somebody else had found the bags by coincidence. At least once his talent for lying would be used for good.

Leif and Gordon had delivered duly for over two years; Max might not clue in too soon. Leif would feign illness for a while, say his parents were limiting his free time, forcing him to take on a job. School would start again with an increased workload.

But what would happen to his money? The profits of two years of crime and deception. Would Max give him access to the account?

As Leif returned the last abalone to the rocky ground, it came to life.

Instead of hunkering down, it budged. He had seen abalone move before, once escaping a predatory starfish. They were astonishingly fast on their one big foot. He gave the wandering shell a nudge. No need to run from me anymore, buddy, he thought. I've made a decision.

Leif dropped the two empty nets, stuffed them into a small crevice and put a couple of stones on top. The air bubbled cheerfully behind him.

The seal emerged from a patch of eelgrass.

Leif looked at his watch: thirty-two minutes left. Enough time for a stroll in the kelp.

# Twenty-Three

## JEREMY
TUESDAY MORNING

"Why don't you move in yourself?" Jeremy asked while he maneuvered around an assortment of Home Depot boxes hogging the space between the sofas. The leftovers of someone's existence in the process of being packed up and scrapped. The living room air smelled of cardboard and dust.

He stopped at the double door to the deck. Ten yards down, Hare Creek Beach lounged in the midday sun; its sandy half-moon set between curving bluffs. It was empty except for a young woman walking her dog, and a lone guy sitting next to his surf board waiting for the waves to make a better effort.

With the abundance of pretty coves up and down the coastline, it never got crowded. You could always find a stretch of beach for yourself.

"It's an awesome view," Jeremy said. His hands played with the folding ruler he had brought to take the measurements for three new wall closets.

Deidre's chiffon skirt rustled as she stepped up beside him. "I'd love to live here," she said and shrugged. "But Kent, you know . . ." She opened the sliding door, allowing a breeze to enter and play in her hair.

Yes, Jeremy knew, or at least was able to make an educated guess. Easy-going Deidre Ratcliffe — how on earth did she end up with Kent Saunders, so much older and boring with a capital B. At least he was good at his job. He had been Pam's divorce lawyer, and she couldn't praise him enough.

Was Deidre happy with her choice? Absentmindedly, Jeremy fanned out the ruler and closed it again. If only he could have looked at her without the she's-not-Fern glasses. Their eleven months together, he twenty-one and she only nineteen, he had spoiled them by his hesitance and refusal to commit. Such a sweet and caring girl. Good wife material. If he hadn't been so dumb.

"Kent thinks it will be a real moneymaker. He's right. When you have to put two kids through university."

Deidre exhaled.

"And I have procrastinated long enough; Dad's been gone for over a year now."

She turned her face toward him. Her blue eyes seemed to be a tad duller than when he used to look into them close up. Jeremy knew how much she had loved her father.

"He was a good guy," he said and glanced back at the beach. The surfer talked to the girl while patting her Labrador.

Deidre's dad, Don Ratcliffe, had been senior saw filer at the lumber mill. A couple of times, Jeremy visited him in the filing room, intrigued by the silvery band saws, giant metal loops as long and wide as tank tracks. Don showed him how they repaired the blades, explained the gumming, the fitting and benching; from him Jeremy learned how to keep his own tools sharp. He knew Don approved of him. A child of the mill. Son of a former dry kiln foreman. Raised to the singing of the saws. Able to tell the time by the toot of the shift-change whistles.

And a talented woodworker, already at his young age. Deidre had exalted him to her parents for the improvements he did to his home. And she adored the little Shaker-style box he made for her. A skill acquired from his dad, who had a workshop in the garden shack where he crafted oval containers of different sizes, put together for sale in nested sets of three.

As a preschooler, Jeremy had watched his father steaming the wood, cutting the swallowtails, smoothing the hot bands around the forms, fixing them with copper tacks, creating bottoms and tight-fitting lids.

As Jeremy grew older, he was trusted to hand-sand the finished boxes and to paint some in sage green or carmine, and a paler shade of cornflower blue similar to his mother's eyes.

Jeremy sighed. He hadn't made one in a long time. When Fern found an old set in his apartment, she had urged him to produce some for her.

Abbie had just been born and Fern wanted a simple activity to fit in with her new motherly duties.

For a while, they were a team. He made the oval boxes, applied several coats of oil finish and buffed them until the cherry wood glowed, then Fern took over and decorated the lids with animal vignettes: snowy plovers in their sandy nests, suckling black bear cubs, sea lions fighting for rocky islands, pelicans in flight. They sold well in two local gift stores until Abbie got weaned and Fern lost interest in doing crafts.

Had Deidre kept the little red box?

Her father supported Jeremy's plan to work as a carpenter. "I don't think there is much future for lumber in this town," he had said.

Their break-up left everybody sad, but they stayed on good terms.

Once in a while, when Jeremy met Don by chance, they had a beer and discussed the state of the mill and later the reasons for its shutdown. Sometimes, they just sat together saying nothing.

Jeremy glanced over at the quiet woman next to him. Obviously, Don's daughter was able to endure gaps in conversation as well.

Deidre shifted and took off her cardigan, revealing a thin sleeveless blouse. Jeremy felt a bit warm himself. The beams of the high-standing sun falling through the window reached up to his navel. But he didn't have any surplus clothing to shed. The air seeping in through the open door did nothing to refresh him; it only carried Deidre's light magnolia scent into his nostrils.

"Dad would want me to move on." Deidre threw the cardigan over the couch behind her. "Do you remember when we played horseshoes with him?"

Jeremy peered over to the lawn at the side of the house. The sand pits and stakes were still there.

"Yeah. He had a good straight swing."

"He liked you," she said. "You threw a ringer with your first shoe."

"I remember it," Jeremy said. He also recalled how she had guided his hand under her sweater after the game, in the eucalyptus grove, on the way to the beach.

She fell silent again.

Jeremy watched her out of the corner of his eye.

The muscles in her slim arm moved slightly as her fingertips wandered through the ruffles on the front of her blouse.

The smooth fabric was slightly see-through. He didn't want to discern what she wore beneath, so he looked up at her face. Twenty years hadn't spoiled her profile, the high cheekbones, the chin that stuck out a bit more than necessary but not enough to disturb the overall effect.

The tip of her tongue massaged the little fleshy bump in the middle of her upper lip. Was she indulging in the same memory? What a weird moment of intimacy with a woman he had barely seen for two decades.

The last time they met had been when he renovated the Sea Star cottages, a month after Fern died. How had their interactions been? Had she said anything suggestive? Anyhow, in his fogged-up state of mind, he wouldn't have noticed if she had thrown herself naked at his feet.

"Is Leif feeling better?" he asked. "I'm sorry that happened to him. But, at least, now we know the reason why."

"Yes. Kent told me about the bracelet. Did your daughter lose it at the beach? It must be very important to her."

"It isn't hers," Jeremy said, shaking his head. "It belonged to her uncle. To Ruben."

"Her uncle Ruben." The way she whispered these three short words, Deidre managed to condense seven years of town gossip. Jeremy felt he had said enough and just stared out the window at the sandy tongue that divided the calm creek water from the spuming surf.

"Leif is fine," Deidre said, louder now, like somebody had adjusted her volume button. "He acts as if nothing happened. I guess his pride is hurt. First, being beat up by a girl, and then paraded on social media." She was obviously trying to talk away her embarrassment. "It's hard to know what's going on inside of him."

"I'm happy he decided to tell the truth," Jeremy said, turning his face toward hers. The light gleamed in her eyes. The ruler was getting slippery in his sweaty fingers.

"Do you ever have these moments," she said and swallowed, "when you think you don't even know your kid anymore?" She covered her mouth with her hand. "I'm so sorry, I didn't mean —"

"It's okay, Deidre," Jeremy said, looking away to avoid any further display of unbridled emotion. "I should be able to give some expert advice on this. But I never got used to it."

Just like he had never gotten used to women pitying him. Otherwise, telling his woeful tale could have been an unfailing tool to bed them.

"Shall we have a look at the closets now?" he said, and only then, it dawned on him that one of the three would be in Deidre's old room. He hoped the Bon Jovi posters were off the walls, but the thought of the red Hoppity Horse she had employed as a desk chair almost made him smile. And she used to hide her cigarettes from her parents in Barbie's Country Camper under the bed, next to a clutch of troll dolls.

Sometimes they had met here in the early afternoons, her father and older brother being at the mill and her mother nursing at the District Hospital, but mostly spent time at the bungalow, and after they fooled around, Deidre watched Jeremy work, putting new windows in, grinding down and painting the wooden siding, replacing the roof shingles with cedar shakes. Gina had managed to get a small mortgage that enabled them to buy material and new tools. "I'll get this house back into shape," Jeremy had promised her, "and then we get rid of it."

Occasionally, Deidre fixed lunch for the two of them, neatly setting the old oak table, arranging sea hollies from the garden in his mother's Fenton Amberina vase, bright-eyed and eager to please. But in a kitchen where tension had shriveled up the wallpaper and quarrels had been a daily dish, freshly cut flowers and crisp hash browns served with a smile did little to brighten Jeremy's outlook on things.

He feared a replica of his parents' life materializing, marrying quickly and getting weary of each other even faster — which, he was convinced, would not happen if he could find someone like Fern, whose presence he imagined glorious and inspiring.

"Of course," Deidre said. "That's what you're here for." Her high-heeled sandals click-clacked on the wooden floor as she passed the kitchen door. Jeremy followed her tanned calves through the hallway, pretending he didn't know his way around, feeling awkward to revisit this long forgotten bit of his life.

Looking at the might-have-been with the knowledge of his present regrets — he wished he had told Gina to decline the request.

"You know, your floor boards are a bit worn-down," he said, wanting to slap himself immediately.

"Yeah, I thought about freshening them up," Deidre answered. "They still have a lot of life in them."

"They sure do. I could give them a work out, if you want." Jeremy flinched; every word just got a ridiculous extra layer of meaning. "They should be sanded and resealed," he said with an added dose of matter-of-factness in his voice. What was he thinking, turning this into a century project, hovering around his married ex-girlfriend, waiting for their passion to be rekindled?

"But I should check my schedule with Gina first. I'm probably booked up already. Bert Tucker might be your man. I can give you his number."

To his relief, the bedrooms had been completely emptied of furniture and all decorations. They briefly talked about how to remodel the reach-in closets, and then Deidre left him alone to take his measurements. He heard her walking around in the living room, wasting time; she wasn't dressed for packing.

He unfolded his ruler.

She wanted to reduce the return walls and have new oak fronts; six-panel bi-fold closet doors with off-white glaze. Between the two hanging sections, Jeremy was going to fit in a shelf and three drawers at the bottom, and another shelf up to halfway under the left rod. He slid a notepad out of his pocket.

The sound of Deidre's slender heels on the living room floor didn't help him to focus, or to forget the view of her walking in front of him, sheer fabric swishing over the backs of her knees.

Ninety-four inches wide. Door height: seventy-nine inches. He sketched a mini plan onto his notepad and proceeded to the inside. When he was done, he tiptoed across the hallway to the next closet.

Deidre's old room. He looked around. It seemed her parents had never painted the walls after she moved out; virgin-white rectangles marked the spaces where her posters once hung.

The castors of the bed frame had left deep imprints in the carpet.

One of the brakes didn't lock properly, Jeremy remembered, and sometimes the bed started swaying like a boat at sea.

Deidre and he used to joke around with the stuffed toy Cat in the Hat that sat on her night table: she complained that Jeremy was making her messy, and he called her breasts Thing One and Thing Two.

Deidre hadn't been present on Saturday morning when he visited her home with the sheriff. Of course, he had noticed the cups right away.

But so what, everybody loved Dr. Seuss. Was she trying to communicate with him? His daughter had just walloped her son. Who would see this as a signal to resume an ancient relationship? These were just fantasies, born of severe starvation.

However, Deidre was only a few steps away from him, dressed in pleats and frill. The living room still contained two couches. Why didn't he just go over there and make a pass at her?

Jeremy pushed his ruler into the closet. Because he'd never done anything with a married woman and he wasn't going to start now.

He sighed. Prior to last Friday, he would have thought it impossible for things to get worse. Now his daughter had turned into a young offender, Ru's bracelet had been found at Glass Beach of all places, and Gina had bounced back into gloom.

Time for him to come out of his torpor and deal with the past — and the present. He glanced around in the emptied bedroom again. Tidy up his life and start anew. But how? Maybe Deidre could kiss him awake. "Stop it," he hissed at himself.

Anyway, some action needed to be taken.

He heard water gushing into a sink. Deidre must have turned on the tap in the kitchen. Jeremy frowned. He had to get out of here before he did something that he would regret. A strange time of emotional turmoil this was. He still tried to make sense of last Saturday afternoon, when he had arrived home from lunch to find Gina and Elon on the couch in the living room, necking.

Yet instead of celebrating their reunion, things turned awkward. Elon jumped to his feet and mumbled he had to get going, and Gina stared at Jeremy, her already red and swollen eyes welling up. Her fingers lifted the bracelet, before she collapsed sideways and sobbed uncontrollably into the cotton hopsack of the sofa cushions.

After Elon's abrupt departure, she had locked herself in her bedroom and rarely been seen since. Jeremy tried to talk to her twice with little outcome.

Was every member of his family to be provoked to an overboard reaction by the retrieval of a stupid piece of jewelry? Of course, the appearance of the bracelet disturbed him, but he would not give in to this madness.

Jeremy scribbled the last dimensions onto his notepad, and darted toward the last bedroom when his back pocket started chiming. The old-fashioned telephone ringtone echoed through the hallway, making the silent house shudder. Why hadn't he just left it on vibration mode?

This was surely his father-in-law, exactly the cold shower he needed right now. Last Saturday evening, he had sent him a message about the bracelet, and since then wondered why no reply came in. He knew the explanation wouldn't satisfy Chester. In fact, he expected him to pop up in person any moment now. Chester Westfield wasn't a man of empty promises.

Deidre peeked around the bend from the kitchen holding a watering can in her hand. He gave her an apologetic smile and pulled out his phone.

He checked the number; his finger halted over the display: Tessa. He tapped decline.

Jeremy had messaged her in the morning, after the three texts he received from her since Saturday. She would mail him the four small pieces that were left and a check. Saralyn had proved her talent in sales.

He texted: *"Sorry, working at client's."*

Tessa: *"Hi, what to do with display chest?"*

Jeremy got the impression she already had something in mind.

Jeremy: *"Please mail it."*

Tessa: *"Too large!"*

It was barely the size of a microwave.

Tessa: *"Could drop it off, if u want."*

She lived in Santa Barbara. A stone's throw of eight hours.

Jeremy: *"Don't worry."*

His finger hurried over the keyboard. *"Please keep until next year. If u have space. Thanks."*

He knew she did; her former husband had left her the five-bedroom mansion after cheating on her with her best friend.

He put the phone away and glanced at Deidre, who was plucking dead leaves off a neglected begonia in the corner by the TV. The plant shivered under her touch.

Jeremy stepped into the last bedroom to finish the work and get out of the house without delay. The unopened bag of caramels in the glove compartment would be his reward. He could taste them melting in his mouth even now.

## Twenty-Four

### GINA
TUESDAY, NOON

Gina opened her hand. Her fingers were almost too stiff to move. One of the bracelet's pointy charms, either the musket or the wooden leg, had left a deep hole in her palm. The golden skull grinned at her. Who had come up with that one? She couldn't remember.

She still possessed the sketches Fern and Abbie had made during the two months in late spring when they spent long afternoons at the kitchen table, sometimes in her home, sometimes in theirs, and designed the bracelet together. Fern drew out an idea and Abbie copied her drawings and added her own twist. She had already been so accomplished. And so eager, so excited.

A present for her beloved Uncle Ru. Her aunt's gift to him for their ten-year wedding anniversary. Gina had found a jewelry designer who was able to do it. They all drove to Pacific Heights together to deliver the designs.

She closed her hand around the bracelet again.

Fern was so smashing; she won people over in an instant. Beguiled them. The goldsmith fell over himself to accommodate her, when in fact it was Gina who had phoned to make the appointment, was going to commission the jewelry for her husband, and pay for it in the end. Instead, she felt like Lady Fern's handmaid, accidentally invited to a function she had no business at. Of course her sister-in-law did not observe anything amiss. She was used to servility and adoration, and on the way back along the winding shoreline highway, Gina's silence went unnoticed as Fern and Abbie sang together until they were almost hoarse.

Gina lifted her head and turned the pillow around; it was running out of dry spots.

The finished item arrived via mail two weeks before the anniversary. Gina had it sent to her brother's house for secrecy. When she came to pick up the parcel, Abbie opened the door with the bracelet on her wrist.

"Oh, Abbie, you should have waited for me," Gina said, too peeved to control her voice. "That was very disrespectful of you!"

Abbie looked at her. "But Mommy said...," she mumbled, and her beautiful, bright two-colored eyes filled with tears.

Gina understood, and hugged her. And said nothing further about it; she didn't want to let a fight with Fern spoil the day.

They all sat around the kitchen table and agreed that the goldsmith had done wonderful work. It was better than they could have imagined.

As expected, Ru loved the bracelet. Gina gave it to him in bed when they woke up early on the big day. His thank you was passionate. The last time her skin heated up against his. The last time she felt the hands that could be rough and tender, each at the right time.

Gina moaned and squeezed the metal charms; she didn't care if the musket pierced her flesh.

Eleven years.

Eleven good years.

They had met in the City by the Bay. In the second spring Gina spent away from home.

It had been Pam's mother's idea. Her cousin co-owned an accounting firm in San Francisco. Wouldn't Gina want to broaden her horizons? Why stay a bookkeeper for all her life? City College was affordable, and Gina and Jeremy had a little money now that the bungalow had sold.

Gina thought about it and agreed. Why not? A change in scenery might help. Things tasted stale.

She decided to give it a try and enrolled.

Pam's relative gave her a part-time job in her office, and Gina moved into the basement of the home of a nice Filipino couple with two little girls.

She worked a lot. In her sparse leisure time, she explored the city. But she made sure to always spend some time on the weekends with Tala and Marilag, who liked flying kites with her on the windy slopes of Bernal Heights Hill, exhilarated by the panorama of the city, before they all burst into their mother's kitchen to get fed freshly-fried banana lumpia.

After two terms, though, their grandma Rutchel fell ill and the bachelor apartment was needed for her. To everybody's regret, Gina's lease was canceled. Scrambling for affordable accommodation, she rented a shabby bedroom from Lynette and Aidan Blacksmith, in their little boxy house with a fake-stone facade on Samoset Street.

They were both in their late twenties. Lynette jobbed as receptionist at a real estate office, and Aidan worked as line cook in one of the trendy fusion restaurants. Most weekends saw them performing in bars and clubs with their band, Lynette channeling Courtney Love and Aidan plucking the lead guitar.

The smallest bedroom was let to Birch, a bulky girl with spiky hair in varying color combinations, who was a bartender by night, but dreamed of becoming a special effects make-up artist. Frequently, gargoyles and severed hands spilled out of her space into the hallway, and it was not unusual for somebody to eat supper at the kitchen table with a black eye, powdered wig or slashed wrists.

Once, early on in her tenancy, Gina had been to a gig of Aidan and Lynette's band at a small venue called Bottom of the Hill. She still wore the delicate elf ears Birch had attached in the afternoon while Gina read about commercial law. This and the fact that she never touched a drop of beer only partly accounted for her decision that hearing The Blacksmiths once was more than enough for her.

Months went by, her living situation supplying an interesting backdrop to the bean counting she performed at Swindon-Fitzpatrick, where she was swamped every afternoon by records and receipts.

Until one Tuesday morning. Gina stood at the kitchen counter stirring eggs in a bowl when she felt arms slipping around her waist.

"I can't think straight anymore with you around," Aidan whispered and kissed her neck. His voice sounded sleepy. He leaned his body against her backside and breathed into her hair. Out of the corner of her eye, she saw his naked foot next to her lace-up boot on the linoleum.

She had always thought it the ugliest floor ever. Its faded reddish pattern reminded her of marbled steak. On Aidan's big toe sprouted a streak of black hair, and the seam of his pajama pant leg was ripped.

There had never been an indication that he was interested in her in any way. Gina hardly ever saw him without others being around. She had enough insight to know she wouldn't want to be in Lynette's shoes. Most of the time, though, Aidan had been kind and funny. The guy who treated them to California roll or crème brûlée on his day off.

He pulled her closer. She could feel the heat of his body; he wore no T-shirt.

It was neither funny nor a treat. Gina cursed Birch, a bear in hibernation before eleven in the morning. Calling her for help would be futile. Lynette had left at seven for a doctor's appointment to discuss the two positive pregnancy tests, now buried at the bottom of the trash can — unbeknownst to Aidan, who had slept on the couch for the previous ten days because she had caught him by the back door of their last concert venue smooching a fan.

Gina calculated the distance between her hand and a) the knife block and b) the handle of the cast-iron pan heating up on the burner (both out of reach) and decided to have a try at fake submission first.

Aidan's hands rubbed her hips now; the lining of her skirt slithered over her pantyhose. His fingertips dug into her upper thighs. He was muscular.

Quite surprising that slicing carrots and leeks could build up such strength. Apart from guitar lifting, he did not exercise.

Gina tilted her head and smiled at him. His long sandy hair stuck to one side of his head. "I'm not discussing this on an empty stomach," she said, her voice husky, playful. She reached over her shoulder, up to his face, and touched his cheek. "Let me make some breakfast first."

Relieved, she noticed that he moved back a bit.

"You should have some too. And coffee. You look like you're still asleep." Just keep on talking, she urged herself. She stepped over to the stove and poured the eggs into the pan.

"Yes, I'm hungry," he mumbled. His fingers ran up and down her spine, lingering high to squeeze her neck, low to creep into the rift between her buttocks.

"Aidan," she said, willing herself to appear relaxed, although it seemed every fiber in her body had turned into concrete. "I've an appointment with my teacher at nine." She bashed the eggs around with a wooden spatula.

"I can't miss it. He has to review my paper on exit strategies."

Gina reached over to the coffee maker.

"Maybe we can continue this when I'm back, at noon," she suggested while filling one of Lynette's vintage cafe-au-lait bowls.

Aidan took the offered coffee with both hands and settled at the kitchen table. As he took a sip, he peered at her over the pink rim on the porcelain as if wondering how he had gotten there, so far away from her.

Gina turned off the stove, threw the undercooked eggs on a plate, dunked two slices of Wonder Bread into the toaster, prattling on about the importance of the research paper she had just invented.

She excused herself for a moment to go to the washroom — snatched her backpack from the hall floor and ran down the squeaking stairs into the March drizzle, without a coat, and of course too early for the bus to City College. From the coffee shop around the corner, Gina phoned Moira Fitzpatrick. Her employer had been very supportive, and she didn't disappoint in the time of need.

At lunch break, Moira marched into the apartment in her power suit, accompanied by Gina and Dave, senior auditor, armed with Bankers Boxes. Dave, an only slightly shorter Latrell Sprewell lookalike, told a befuddled Aidan he better make himself invisible for the time they gathered Gina's belongings — after he had written a check to reimburse her for the two weeks of rent that were still left in the month.

The packing didn't take much time; Gina had rented the room furnished. Clothes and shoes, books, some small stuff, the Fred Astaire videos.

Three trips to the company van, and soon Gina sat in the passenger seat of Moira's BMW with her bonsai ginkgo on her lap, waving back to Birch, who bade her farewell on the front steps in her Superman bathrobe.

The evening found Gina gazing through the window of a spacious guest room on the top floor of a Painted Lady on Postcard Row, hardly believing her luck when Moira told her she could stay as long as she wanted. Gina knew her daughter had just gone to Boston for her medical internship. Moira, still shaken by the death of her husband two years ago, frequently complained about the vacuum at home.

Gina's offer to pay for room and board was refused and Moira required little other compensation. They went jogging on Saturday mornings and cooked together once or twice a week in Moira's well-equipped but little-used kitchen. Gina saved up her rent money and enjoyed being home early, due to a much shorter bus ride. Once in a while, she left the office together with Moira and got treated to a restaurant meal and inside information of the SF business world.

However, sometimes, when Gina woke up in the morning, among scented Martha Stewart bedding, opening her eyes to walls painted in maroon, a color she would have never chosen for her bedroom; or earlier, seeing the sunlight fall on Lynette's shedding flokati rug through busted Venetian blinds; and even before that, hearing Tala and Marilag giggle in their bedroom upstairs; she felt like a drifter, moving from one alien place to another, longing for a home.

Longing for a home. Gina sighed and pressed her hot face into the pillow. She had come full circle from there. She should get up and make lunch, having missed breakfast already.

Although, she wasn't hungry, and Abbie would get by on a bite of kelp. No need to hurry. Ru would come into her life now.

Shortly before the end of the tax year, her colleague Bess had gone on maternity leave, handing over some of her clients to Gina, among them a rather infamous one.

"Poseidon is coming to see you tomorrow." Katie, the receptionist, stood in the doorway of Gina's small office space, chortling like she had just emptied a bottle of Champagne by herself. "Lucky you!"

"Who's that?" Gina put down the spreadsheet she had been studying.

"Ruben Fuertes. He does this crazy underwater thing." The words bubbled out of Katie. "And he looks like a Greek god."

"Where is he taking you?" Moira asked two weeks later, coming out of the living room when she heard her house guest walk down the stairs.

The expression of care and excitement on Moira's face gave Gina a sting: she realized neither of her parents had ever been there to inspect her before she went on a date, to give her a lecture, or stay up late to make sure she came home at the appointed time.

"I have the address in my purse," Gina said, adjusting the bow on her blouse. "Something French. It starts with a B." Ru had delivered his missing receipts in three installments, personally, instead of mailing them, and by the last time he handed an increasingly smitten Gina a manila envelope, asked her if he could make amends for his flawed organizational skills with a dinner invitation.

"Boulevard?"

Gina nodded.

"Please, don't be offended." Moira touched Gina's rayon jacket sleeve. "You can't go on a date with this man in a pant suit."

Gina glanced down at her best outfit and frowned. Black was always the right choice and she had just bought the cream-colored blouse last month. True, it wasn't glamorous. Her present wardrobe knew only two variations: office look and college gear. The former: four rotating suits, one of them with a pencil skirt; the latter: jeans and sweaters.

She owned pretty clothes too. Their long-time neighbor Mrs. Yelland had given her a large suitcase full of well-cared-for cocktail and party dresses from her heydays in the Fifties and early Sixties, and altered everyone to fit Gina's slimmer waistline. Gina had worn one on her prom night, a mauve organza dream, sleeveless with a full skirt, and found herself praised for being up-to-date with the new vintage trend. But she hadn't bothered to bring any to San Francisco; they were all stored in the spare room of Jeremy's small apartment.

"Boulevard is one of the top restaurants in town," Moira said. "You look like you want to audit it."

She took Gina to her daughter's closet. Lilly Fitzpatrick had left more clothes behind than many other women possessed in their whole life. Some of the carefully stitched-in labels wore designer names people whispered on Oscar nights.

Moira picked a slate-gray slip dress, which fit Gina like it was tailored for her.

The matching pumps were half a size too small, but Gina would have cut her heels off to wear them. A hand-embroidered Kashmir shawl and a small sparkling evening purse from Moira's own collection completed the ensemble.

As Gina stood in the entrance hallway ten minutes later, waiting for the cab, she would not have been surprised to see Moira wave a magic wand and turn one of the terracotta pots on the front steps into a carriage.

On their third date, at another flashy in-place, Gina told Ruben about the Fitzpatricks' wardrobes, the source of her magnificence, wanting to make sure his attentions were sparked by her own plain self and not somebody else's expensive fashion sense. She was the girl sleeping in the ashes by the fireplace, not a pampered princess. Much to her surprise, this revelation led to a Saturday lunch at the wharf in Bodega Bay, where they ate fish and chips without cutlery and occasionally wiped their fingers on each other's jeans.

They stayed until Monday morning in a lodge at the ocean, leaving their suite only once to request a complimentary toothbrush from a smiling receptionist.

For her twenty-fifth birthday, a month later, Ru gave her a Pashmina wrapped around a little red box, containing a diamond ring, and asked her and all her lovely suits to please marry him.

Gina hesitated. She needed to think about it.

The short time they knew each other. The age difference. His knee-melting looks. His dangerous sport. She wanted to finish her studies.

And, of course, there was Elon.

Follow your heart, she had said to him. Wishing him to propose. Expecting him to propose — and take her with him wherever he wanted to go, to study management and communications, to polish his Spanish, to make the perfect moves for his desired career.

But he did not ask. It seemed he took it for granted that she would wait. They had talked about so many things, painful things, even shameful things: her father's drinking; the day her mother left with a man driving a red Chevy truck; his sister dying of leukemia when he was twelve; the time Gina got used to stealing Pop Rocks and Razzles for Jeremy and her, before she was old enough to make some money babysitting and helping Mrs. Yelland with her chores after she broke her hip; the visiting uncle who touched him in a way he wanted to forget. Yet Gina couldn't bring herself to tell Elon she needed to be first in his life. Couldn't bear to hear he was doing it all for her.

She wasn't second fiddle for Ru. He would give up the apnea competitions for her, and develop the idea for Abalone Adventures because she missed her hometown. He had proven himself already, enjoyed his wild days, left his mark.

Now he wanted a family — wanted her.

The frequency of Elon's letters was down to one a month before Ru ever showed up in Gina's office. Their content focused: His prospects; the next big opportunity; a transfer to a new department, even farther away, for an unspecified period of time. They all ended with I love you. But I don't feel it, she should have written back long ago. It had been ten months since they had last seen each other.

"What are you waiting for, Gina?" Moira had asked one Saturday morning as they jogged past the windmills in Golden Gate Park. "You need to have some joy in your life."

Two days after she agreed to marry him, Ru surprised her with a trip to Grand Cayman, where he taught her to snorkel.

One day they boarded a boat with a glass bottom and drove to a sand bar in the middle of nowhere. Gina was mesmerized by the bright-blue beauty that made her feel like being on the inside of a shiny crystal ball — until large dark spots appeared in the shallow sea and congregated around their vessel. Ru hopped overboard and told her to exit the boat too.

"But they have barbs!" she hollered.

"Trust me," he said.

Soon, Gina stood in warm water reaching up to her waist, white softness under her feet, with wild stingrays swirling around Ru and her like a swarm of eagles soaring in a summer breeze, brushing against their calves, nudging their thighs.

Ru beamed at her while he fed the swaying flat fish with little squids from a bucket the skipper of the glass boat supplied.

"I've been here three times before," Ru said when he showed her how to hold a ray. "These guys are puppies."

Soon the creature fell asleep, hanging in Gina's arms, limp like a giant pancake.

There she was under the gleaming Caribbean sky, with her smiling fiancé, hugging a stingray — transported to a parallel universe, a world too good to be true.

During the following couple of months, though, ocean water washed away her doubts, as they continued to travel and snorkel together. Being with Ru was ease and excitement; two things her life had lacked so far. How could you not be in love with a man who knew how to pet stingrays?

I have met somebody, she wrote to Elon, we are going to get married. I hope you will achieve your dreams.

He never answered her letter.

Gina turned her face toward the window and glanced at the bonsai on the ledge. Its roots looked like fingers clawing into the patch of dark soil, contained in a small square pot with cobalt-blue glazing. On top of the short stem sat a bright green triangle, a half-open umbrella made of tiny cleft leaves. *Ginkgo biloba*, symbol of love and hope. Longevity too. It seemed like a heavy burden for such a wee tree.

In any case, her specimen had proved to be a fighter, and survived even the times when she wasn't there to care for it.

# Twenty-Five

## LEIF
### WEDNESDAY MORNING

Leif braked. He jumped off his bike, pushed it onto the sidewalk by the brewery building and sneaked up to the parking lot. Abalone had taken a left turn toward the train depot.

Wisps of fog drifted in from the Pacific, swirled like tumbleweeds over the wasteland of the old mill site, slunk along the tracks, crawled through picket fences.

Overhead, mist wafted around brick chimneys, got caught in the palm tree tops of Stewart Street, veiled the mountains in the north. By lunchtime though, the sun would have eaten it up.

He stuck out his head and peeked around the corner.

We can add another one to the list of my offenses, he thought. Now that he had given up poaching and become a stalker.

Abalone leaned her bicycle against the last in the row of green benches and vanished into the station building.

Leif looked across the rails. The depot bordered on the vast yards between town and ocean, where the lumber used to be stacked. All this wide and barren space, polluted by the ash from the power plant and who knew what else. Georgia Pacific closed the mill in the year Leif went to kindergarten.

His grandpa had told him many stories about the times when it had been the bustling heart of the area. Restricted access was the only thing Leif could remember about it; the city being reduced to the somewhat ludicrous existence of a coastal town without coast. But now a restoration project promised change, the construction of a trail connecting Pudding Creek and Noyo Harbor. For the first time in over a century, people would be able to stroll along their shoreline.

He peered over at the station again. The pink bicycle still leaned against the bench. What was she doing in the building? Hopefully just going to use the washroom. Or did she intend to take the train?

Leif got on his bike and sped through the parking lot toward the entrance. Through the window he saw her standing in a line-up at the ticket counter.

He locked his bicycle to a pole at the side of the building and grabbed his backpack. Did he even have enough cash? Leif fingered his wallet out of the mess inside. He hadn't taken the train since his cousins came down from Oregon five years ago. How much was it now? He would have to pay the adult fare.

And what about his disguise? Giants cap and sunglasses again. He pulled his hood over the cap, just in case, and opened the door.

Abalone waited, next after a group of three elderly couples arguing at the ticket counter. How will I know what she buys? Leif wondered. He ducked behind the display rack and peeked over its advertising brochures for local attractions — Botanical Gardens, Aquatic Center, horseback riding holidays — towards the line-up.

The seniors seemed willing to delay proceedings until they got a larger group discount. To make things worse, Eleanor Longdale sat behind the opening in the old wooden wall, with a rather displeased face as she listened to a woman with short yolk-blonde hair complaining about the prices. He remembered she had told him she was going to work in the gift shop during the summer months.

The door opened and another group of elders shuffled through.

Leif stuffed the flier for the Drive-Through Tree Park back into the rack and hurried over the shiny chessboard floor towards the line-up. Barely making it in time, he hid behind the broad shoulders of the middle-aged tourist who separated him from Abalone. His XXL T-shirt back informed the world of the cities for the History of the Eagles Tour.

Leif peeked past the black cotton. Abalone's beautiful hair was just two arm's lengths away from him now.

Long and lush, it seemed to glow.

"Well, thank you very much, my dear," said the yolk-haired lady. Eleanor had managed to appease the indignant seniors, and they moved on to waste their saved money in the gift shop.

Abalone was next to be served. She stepped forward, pulled a small notepad out of her sling bag and scribbled something down.

"Northspur Station," Eleanor read from the piece of paper held toward her.

Abalone nodded, and Leif sighed in relief.

He turned away as Abalone walked past him. The Eagles fan likewise received his ticket, and then it was Leif's turn to face the girl behind the counter. He moved forward and took off his hood and sunglasses.

"Leif!" Eleanor's hazel eyes widened. They had an expression of slight surprise to begin with, now they looked seriously bewildered. "What do you want?" Her pretty lips tightened into a narrow line, suggesting he wouldn't get anything from her ever again if she had a say in the matter. He should have called her back.

"Hi, Eleanor. A ticket for the Northspur trip, please."

"Sure." She pounded the keyboard in front of her. "Fifty-nine dollars."

Yikes, no wonder the group had wanted a reduction. He took three twenty-dollar bills and held them toward her.

"I'd be careful if I were you," she said, snatching his money with one hand and ripping the ticket out of the printer with the other. "The Macklintock girl will be on the train too."

Eleanor pushed his ticket and change toward him.

"She might whack you again." She sounded as if she contemplated doing it herself.

"Thanks," Leif said and shoved the dollar bill in his pocket. "Enjoy your day."

"Next," Eleanor said.

Leif fled her icy stare but stayed inside the building in a corner by the window.

He saw Abalone sitting down on a bench outside, under the green roof of the passenger shelter. She gazed in the direction of the water tower from where the pride of the California Western Railroad, the restored steam engine No. 45, slowly rolled northward.

The polished bell cheerfully announced its arrival. The smoke stack coughed out black fumes while white puffs emerged from seemingly everywhere around the shiny metal into the already hazy morning.

After a short drive the locomotive stopped and then moved backward on a different track to connect with the four wine-red cars and the open-air platform that waited at the side of the station building — a maneuver overseen by the train's engineer, the fireman, a crew of conductors, and its unlikely but cute mascot: the uniformed skunk.

Leif, as well as every kid in the county, knew how it had come into being. In 1925, self-powered rail cars were introduced for passenger transport, and the incredible stink of their gas fumes earned the whole operation its — now endearing — nickname, Skunk Train, when people started realizing that, "You can smell 'em before you can see 'em!"

Abalone, in her sweeping dress that matched the color of the train, marched toward it while the other passengers kept back and watched as if they had unanimously decided to give her precedence.

Unimpressed by the attention she caused and the steam creeping out between the big metal wheels, Abalone walked past the logo painted on the side of the car she was about to board. The striped animal — blue conductor's hat on its furry head and a little golden watch peeking out of the breast pocket of its red vest — looked sideways, right at her, as if even a skunk on duty could not help but notice the unusual passenger it had the pleasure of serving today.

Leif waited until Abalone had disappeared into the car, then sprinted towards the nearest gate and mingled with the crowd of tourists to enter the train unseen.

With considerable whistling, chiming and chuffing, the Skunk Train left the station for the Redwood Route.

Leif stood next to a barrel in the corner of the open-air platform. They had cleared town a while ago and now lush green welcomed them to the wild. The yolk-haired woman and her crew lined the metal railing on his left, their leader repeatedly pointing into the bushes, exclaiming: "Look at that big tree," although the vegetation so far didn't display any growth unusual enough to justify such excitement.

They still chugged up the Pudding Creek Estuary. The tall redwoods waited for them, Leif remembered from earlier tours, right after the first tunnel, where the train would start zigzagging through the Noyo River Canyon.

Out of the passenger car on the opposite end of the platform walked a guy dressed in an old-fashioned conductor's uniform, guitar in hand, and a harmonica holder in front of his face. The train singer.

"Life is like a mountain railroad," he began and picked the guitar strings. He did a good job. It was a fun idea to have live entertainment on the ride.

The wheels pounded a rattling bass on the old tracks, and the engine huffed and puffed the beat.

Maybe something I could fall back on one day, Leif thought, in case his highfalutin plans didn't work out. Although he wouldn't be able to carry a piano through the train.

"Watch the curves, the fills, the tunnels; never falter, never quail," sang the man, not performing alone any longer, as the yolk-lady and her quintet joined him with vigor but rather unsteady voices.

Leif moved toward the door of the passenger car and peeked through its window again. The girl still sat in the middle on the right and gazed out at the passing landscape.

The interior looked like Leif remembered it: airy and cheerful, painted bright white and flooded with daylight through the band of vertical windows on each side. The shiny curved ceiling with the rows of light fixtures and baggage racks resembling crown moldings gave it an air of elegance. Dispersed on the electric-blue benches on both sides of the middle aisle was a dozen passengers, and to his relief, Leif spotted the meaty back of the Eagles fan, who slouched in one of the turned around seats five rows away from Abalone, not minding to face the wrong direction.

"Keep your hands upon the throttle," yodeled the choir behind Leif, "and your eyes upon the rail."

Initially, he had planned on waiting for tunnel No.1 to sneak into the car in the waning light, but now he pulled his visor deep over his sunglasses, opened the door and dashed inside.

When had he left off being normal? he wondered as he slumped down on the bench. Maybe he never was from the beginning.

The vast black T-shirt shielded him perfectly. He took off his backpack and cowered behind the Eagles fan for a while, before he dared to turn around and cast a furtive look in Abalone's direction.

Everybody else in the car was staring at her overtly.

She, however, didn't seem to notice or ignored the curious eyes and continued to study the outside scenery. Although she sat perfectly still, everything about her seemed to be in motion: the wind coming in the half-open window combed through her hair, tickled the hem of her gown, frolicked in the lavish bell-shaped sleeves.

Today she wore a light fabric of iridescent burgundy, the style similar to the one she had assaulted him in, ankle-length and somehow medieval; instead of algae, a few shells were braided into her flowing mane, and a necklace of white sea glass sparkled on her immaculate skin.

Outside on the platform, the train singer was finishing his song with a vibrant harmonica solo.

Leif felt lightheaded. Was it the trembling car? The music? Or the sight of the quiet girl with the solemn face?

The greenery flew by next to her milky cheek. The blue backrest of the bench set off the bold reds of her hair and dress. The beads around her neck shimmered as if illuminated from the inside. How well she fit in with the look of the old train, this relic from bygone times, Leif thought, an exquisite antique doll herself, an enigmatic artifact, alien among all those folks in shorts and spandex, an envoy from the land of ravishing beauty. The magnificent queen of the people with two-colored eyes.

The lilting glissando of the harmonica got louder. Leif turned around. The door was open and the train singer entered the car with a final tremolo, no doubt trying to escape the enthusiastic amateurs outside. Leif flinched as the guy walked up between the benches and stopped right beside him, the lower part of the guitar only inches away from his face.

Leif ducked deeper behind the Eagles fan's shoulders, to protect his nose from connecting with wood again, and to be concealed in case Abalone looked over at the train's bard, who now strummed a couple of chords, cleared his throat and sang again:

> "Let me be your salty dog,
> or I won't be your little man at all.
> Honey, let me be your salty dog."

The fun old bluegrass classic made Leif aware of the fact that he had followed Abalone around like a lost puppy for the last two days. On Monday afternoon with the T-bird, feeling awkward in his bright-colored car chasing a pink children's bicycle through the city. Exposed and embarrassed, as if everybody he passed easily guessed what he was doing. On top of that, the girl had surprised him with her audacious riding. How did she keep the billowing amber-colored skirt out of the spokes? A couple of times, he almost lost her, when she took a cunning shortcut.

But he didn't think she was aware of him being on her heels, or rather wheels; she just seemed to enjoy the ride, and he managed to trail her to the harbor.

For an hour, she sat by one of the boathouses, after trying the door and finding it looked. On the way back, she stopped at Mr. Abornut's dive shop. Leif parked the T-bird on the other side of the road, and once in a while, he caught a glimpse of her wandering around in the store.

> "Lil' fish, big fish, swimmin' in the water,
> come on here and give me my quarter.
> Honey, let me be your salty dog."

Tuesday morning, he had changed to his old mountain bike and shadowed her to the Wiggly Giggly playground on Laurel Street, where she mounted the little blue seahorse and worked its spring for half an hour before she walked over to the basketball court and started throwing hoops with an imaginary ball.

Later she bought a green drink at the Bean and Bagel while Leif hid in the safety of the outdoor shop across the street and pretended to look at hiking boots. As soon as she had finished the beverage, she hopped on her bike to speed along the old haul road over the Pudding Creek trestle past the SeaStar Inn — Leif praying his mother wouldn't be on one of the decks to wonder what he was doing — toward MacKerricher Park.

Abalone stopped at the visitor center to pet the gray whale skeleton and then rode over the boardwalks in the wildflower meadows.

Leif kept a good distance, but never lost sight of her thanks to her unmistakable hair flying against the bright summer sky.

In the afternoon, she didn't go down to the beach like he had hoped, but stayed at the worktable in her little sun-filled house. Leif cowered behind the bush again and watched her covering sheet after sheet of the sketchpad in front of her with pictures, never looking up once.

"Let me be your salty dog,
or I won't be your little man at all.
Honey, let me be your salty dog."

He wasn't sure what he was trying to achieve by following her. For one thing, he wanted to let her know where he really found the bracelet. The jewelry that had, as his mother told him, belonged to Abalone's uncle who disappeared under strange circumstances. And he longed to tell her that he didn't hold against her what she had done to him. Why chase her instead of just intercept her and get it over with?

Leif glanced at his arms: the bruises were a faded greenish yellow by now. The moment had to be right.

"God made a woman and he made her funny," crooned the train singer, finally moving on down the aisle. "Lips 'round her mouth sweeter than honey. Oh, Honey, let me be your salty dog."

Leif bent forward and looked over his shoulder: Abalone sat unchanged, hands folded in her burgundy lap, gazing out the window with her wonderful spellbinding eyes.

"Honey, let me be your salty dog," Leif whispered.
The whistle tooted as the train approached tunnel No.1.

# Twenty-Six

## ABALONE
### WEDNESDAY MORNING

Coming out of the tunnel, the train crosses a bridge over the river. This is where the tall trees are. I cannot depart without a last look at the emerald giants. Among them I am reminded of being underwater. And I feel it is right to say farewell to the places I have known and enjoyed, as I will never see them again.

The little mermaid sang at her father's party before she took her leave. More sweetly than ever. In the ballroom with its walls of crystal, many hundreds of fires burnt in huge mussels, some with dark red shells, others green as grass, and illuminated the mer-king's palace and the ocean around it with blue radiance.

The fishes passing by listened to the little mermaid; their fins and scales reflected the light and sparkled like silver and gold. She had the prettiest voice of all the creatures on earth or in the sea. And while she sang, she was happy. Mermaids and mermen danced to her tune in the current and applauded her with hands and tails when she was done.

But nothing could make her stay. She crept away from the joyful celebration into her silent garden. I would like to know if she caressed the bright-red flowers, or kissed the marble statue of the handsome prince. It says she sat alone and sorrowful. Alone. My name without the first two letters.

I would never have left. Not for an existence on land among the Props, and the pain and disappointment it brings. Or for a man whose heart is taken by another.

I will venture all for him, she said. He on whom my wishes depend, and in whose hands I want to place the happiness of my life. I have never loved anybody like I love him.

Did she ever think about the happiness of the people she left behind? The father, the sisters, the grandmother? Her decision made all of them suffer.

What if she had told them what she was about to do? Would they have hollered at her? Slapped her across the face so hard that she fell and hurt her head on the coffee table?

The Prop with the guitar is now playing his harmonica. I hope he will sing again soon. It's nice to listen to him. He walks down between the blue benches on his two poles while he makes merry music.

The little mermaid gave up her beautiful voice to get

the ugly props called legs. I imagine her voice as high and vibrating, so sweet it makes your heart skip and so smooth that you think feathers are touching your skin.

I can't remember my own singing, but it was certainly not remarkable. Of course, I was much younger then. It might be nicer now that I am older. Would it still be a worthy sacrifice if I found out that I sound like a squeaky bicycle tire?

Oh, the wonderful greens of the trees have the power to calm my thoughts almost like the kelp. I find myself confused by the questions rising up and the images emerging in my mind since last Friday.

Once more, I have overreacted. The Prop boy had found the bracelet by a rock at the shore, they told me. At my beach, of all places. Can this be true? How did it get there? Of course, I know he has no guilt.

Clapping and hooting all around me. The music Prop has finished with his harmonica and is now strumming the guitar and singing again.

"As I lie awake and listen, I listen for the train.
Wish the railroad didn't run so near,
cause the rattle and the clatter of that old fast freight
keeps a-makin' music in my ear."

Now his song sounds like a train picking up speed.

"Hear the whistle blow. Hear the whistle blow.
Clickety clack, clickety clack.
The wheels are saying to the railroad track."

The passenger car is rocking while he sings, rocking on the tracks like a ship at sea. A powerful engine pulls it, like the big boat pulled my dinghy.

I hear the guitar strings humming, the wheels talking to the rails. I hear the air swishing by the train's windows; they mimic the sound of waves licking the two hulls when we anchored somewhere and I waited for them to be done with cleaning the inside of the boat. Later, we always dove together. But this day was different.

> "Clickety clack, clickety clack.
> The wheels are saying to the railroad track."
> Well, if you go, you can't come back.
> If you go, you can't come back. If you go—
> you can't come back."

When Mommy got up from the living room floor, I clung to her hip, still crying.

"Wait in your room," she said, pressing her palm against her forehead where she had bashed it against the coffee table. "I have to see Ruben first and then I will come and get you."

For a while she rummaged around in the bathroom, and when she came out, a large Band-Aid covered the injury on her head. She didn't have the time to hug me; she just waved at me with the straw hat she held in her hand and told me again to stay in my room. I heard the car roar and decided not to obey her. I ran out of the house and picked up my bicycle from the side fence by the workshop. Inside, the table saw screeched and howled.

In the distance, our big black car stood at the intersection. Then I lost sight of it, but I guessed she was going to meet Uncuru by the boathouse.

My little bicycle flew through the streets to Harbor Drive, cutting through a couple of yards, past the fishmongers, the icehouse, and the little eatery where we often bought battered snapper and fries after our diving tours. A blue delivery truck honked at me as my tires swerved around its red taillights. Soon, I saw the pillars of the bridge and the harbor jetty.

Uncuru stood on the dock by a column of rusty crab pots, talking to Mr. Thurber and another old man whose name I didn't know. I took a wide berth and stopped behind the wooden shack that houses the rowing club, where I pushed my bicycle under a rack with old racing shells. Unseen by the adults, I tiptoed toward the open back door of the boathouse, and sneaked in. In the corner lay a blue tarp, rolled in a ball; I dropped it in the dinghy, climbed in and pulled it over me.

Why did I hide? I don't know. And I didn't have much time to think it over because a car arrived and two familiar voices came closer. They got on board the big boat, and soon, my dinghy started moving.

After a while, I got hot, and the heavy blue canvas weighed upon my body as if the sky had fallen on me. I lay outstretched in the boat, my belly on the floorboards, arms crossed, my forehead resting on the soft bend of my elbow. The planks smelled of fouling fishnets.

The dinghy bobbed on the waves, which I had always enjoyed before when I sat straight on the bench seat, holding a rope end and imagined it to be the reins of my yoke of giant seahorses.

I was the mermaid princess riding in a carriage made of shells and sea glass, one moment flying over the whitecaps in a race with dolphins and porpoises, and in the next galloping down into the blue, toward the bottom of the ocean, to let my horsies feed on the meadows of eelgrass and maiden's hair algae.

But there was no joy in this trip as my mind played again and again the scene I had witnessed, the fist hitting her face, her body flying back and dropping down, the scream of pain — the blood running into her eyebrow. I stayed hidden even as the roaring of the motor stopped and the fierce movement of my dinghy ceased. Only a slight trembling remained, and from time to time, the waves sloshed against the outside of my little wooden hideout.

When I heard loud voices, I crawled forward under the tarp and peeked through one of its silver eyelets.

"If you go, you can't come back. If you go —
you can't come back."

*If you go, you can't come back* is what the wheels are saying to the railroad tracks. But this is also what the sea witch told the little mermaid. "Think again," she said, "for once your shape has become human, you can never return."

Yet in the end, the little mermaid found redemption.

For me, there is none. I have not saved a life like she did, nor have I spared one. I can never be relieved. Never be forgiven.

I have tried to eliminate the visions by putting them on paper. Hopefully they will dissolve soon.

Tomorrow, in the afternoon, I will leave the land to be forever in the sea.

# Twenty-Seven

## LEIF
### WEDNESDAY AFTERNOON

About twenty yards in front of him, Abalone scampered along the wayside of the old logging road. A deserted path, seemingly unused for years. Weeds and saplings had reclaimed its winding slant. Where was she going? And why was he still following her?

They had stopped at Northspur for the forty-five-minute lunch break. She settled at one of the wooden picnic tables, staring into the treetops, and he succumbed to the smell of the barbecue and lined up to get himself a salmon burger while keeping an eye on her.

All fog was gone or had never made it here, and the noon sun pounded down on his black cap.

He had just stowed two bottles of water and a bag of trail mix in his backpack and taken the first bites of fish and bun, when he noticed a flash of burgundy leave the clearing on a small trail behind the concession stand. Trying not to choke on his food or lose sight of Abalone's swaying dress, he ran after her into the redwoods.

Of course he assumed she was just taking a short stroll. Yet when the whistle signal from the station rang out through the forest, calling the passengers back on the train, and the girl in front of him didn't flinch (unlike himself) or slow down her marching tempo, he realized she had never intended to return.

At least she stayed on the path, making it easy to retrace the way to Northspur and catch the afternoon train, or wander along the road that connected it to the highway through Jackson State Forest. They could hitchhike from there, or maybe somebody would still be at the station and give them a ride. Leif emitted a snort: a bit rash to infer that they would go home together.

Maybe twenty more minutes had passed when she stopped at a hedgerow.

He crouched down behind a bush and watched her foraging for what had to be blackberries. Her hands worked busily; fruit after fruit went into her mouth. When she was content, she produced a small canteen out of her sling bag and took a couple of sips.

Leif opened his backpack, pulled out one of his water bottles and had a generous gulp himself. It was scorching. Wishing for a refreshing ocean breeze to sweep into the woods, he packed away the bottle, shouldered his backpack again and looked over toward Abalone — just in time to see her turn left and vanish behind the thorny thicket. He scrambled up and darted forward.

She walked on a narrow trail winding through the dark tree columns, second growth, but still tall enough to cast patches of shadow onto the ferns and bushes living between the bases. The dizzying pattern of light and dark reminded him of being down in the kelp. Fortunately, the colors of Abalone's hair and gown continued to flare up in each sunny spot, helping his eyes to focus. He felt like a Cub Scout practicing stalking. Good grief, she was steering into the bushes now, onto an even narrower, almost indiscernible path. Its soft ground swallowed their steps. The sun stood high over the green canopy, making it hard to guess which direction she would take. In any case, they went deeper and deeper into the wilderness.

Leif's uneasiness was growing. Weird. He carelessly dove in a region frequented by sharks. Why would he be concerned about the dangers in the woods? He had never considered himself a coward, but maybe this was how Gordon felt underwater. Here, no boat was waiting overhead. Furthermore, a healthy black bear population roamed this region, and the painted mountain lion on one of the Skunk Train's passenger cars had many real brothers and sisters. On top of that, he feared stumbling across one of the illegal grow ops. The guys operating these sites preferred to be left alone, and Leif didn't fancy encountering somebody with a shotgun and no qualms about using it. To think Gordon seriously contemplated getting into that line of business just showed what a numbskull he had turned out to be.

Harvesting some surplus mollusks seemed like child's play compared to getting in league with people who polluted the woods and streams with their fertilizers and pesticides and posed a threat to the community.

Howsoever, the girl in front of him obviously experienced no such trepidation. She scurried through the undergrowth as nimble-footed as a blacktail doe.

Which reminded him of the fact that hunting season was on — and that his jeans and heather-gray T-shirt were far from being the brightly colored attire the Department of Forestry advised people to wear in the woods at this time of year.

Leif wiped the sweat off his forehead.

In these dry conditions, there was also the high risk of wildfires. His foot stepped on a dead branch and the bursting wood cried out.

He stumbled.

The girl stopped.

Leif managed to jump behind the nearest tree trunk just before her eyes could dart in his direction. Watch your feet, idiot! Do you want to let her know you're here? He groaned. What did he actually want? Not to get lost! Then don't follow her in the first place. Maybe she had damaged his brain with the racquet after all.

He peeked around the tree. Abalone had turned and resumed her journey. Hopefully she knew where she was heading. A place less sweltering and smelly would be nice, Leif thought. His damp T-shirt stuck to his skin, and the pungent odors made breathing unpleasant, resembling heated mold and a heap of rotting Christmas trees.

At least the mosquitoes stayed away from him. They never troubled him, contrary to his father, whom they usually feasted on like a swarm of piranhas.

Poison oak, though, was a different story. Leif hoped he didn't brush against any while slaloming through the redwoods; the wicked sap had given him bad rashes a couple of times in the past.

He frowned. With his grandpa, he had always felt safe in the woods. When he was in elementary school and his grandfather's heart still strong, the two of them used to go camping out at the Egg Take, the site at the Noyo River south fork where the Department of Fish & Game operated a collection station for salmon eggs.

Leif remembered it as great fun. They ate baked beans for breakfast, lunch and supper and pretended to be lumberjacks. A couple of times, his dad came too, although activities that didn't require a well-ironed dress shirt always seemed suspicious to him.

In the rainy fall season, when mushrooms sprouted all over the soggy forest floor, his grandpa showed Leif which ones could be eaten. "Only take what you can clearly identify," he had warned. "There are old mushroom hunters and there are bold mushroom hunters. But you won't find any old bold mushroom hunters."

Some of the fungi had funny names: pig's ear and sweet bread. His grandpa mostly looked out for small orange chanterelle and fat-stemmed porcini, and showed Leif how to distinguish the latter from death cap and destroying angel. Leif wasn't sure he would still know how to tell them apart.

But he remembered the creamy taste of the mixed mushroom stew his grandpa cooked every time they came back from the woods, cold and wet and hungry. At least his stomach was full now. His dry mouth longed for a drink of water though, but Leif didn't dare to stop and take a bottle out of the backpack.

Hopefully she would reach her destination soon. If she had one. Maybe his first guess had been right and she was mental. Was he following a crazy woman? What if she knew he was on her heels and planned to ambush him?

He could still see her in front of him, though, hair bouncing, dress waving. The path was almost unnoticeable now, covered with dry needles like the rest of the forest floor. She walked toward a massive tree stump, clearly old growth, the remnant of what must have been a giant once.

Leif tried to imagine how these woods had looked when the sailors of the Frolic saw them, long before the loggers wreaked havoc among its ancient inhabitants. Nourished by Pacific fog, the redwoods had grown to be the tallest plants on earth. To think these majestic creatures abounded everywhere in the coastal forests.

Abalone stopped dead in front of the stump. Its hauled-away top had left a clearing overhead. Sunbeams fell through it like a spotlight onto the motionless girl. Her straight and rigid posture suggested that this wasn't just a short break in her travels, but the end of her expedition.

Leif tiptoed to the cover of a wide tree trunk maybe twenty yards away from her, where he removed his backpack as slowly and noiselessly as he could, trying not to disturb the silence that hung between the redwoods.

Maybe it was too hot for any bird to feel like singing.

He pulled out the already opened water bottle and emptied the rest of its contents into his parched gullet — never taking his eyes off the girl, who stood petrified before the amputated foot of the tree that almost reached up to two times her height. Thankfully the liquid was still cool enough to refresh him. He decided against guzzling down the second one too. Who knew how much longer this strange outing would take and if they would find a stream somewhere or any human settlement.

Leif had just put the bottle away and shouldered the backpack, when Abalone came to life again. Reaching down, she pulled up her skirt, coiled it into knots on both sides of her hips — giving him full view of her very pretty legs — and started climbing the corrugated wood. Her fingers gripped into the gnarly bark. Her hiking boots found foothold after foothold. She mounted the slanted stump with the speed and elegance of a lizard. A red lizard girl gleaming in the sunlight falling through the lofty redwood crowns.

Standing on top of the stump as if it was an open-air stage made for the sole purpose of presenting her beauty, she took a rest, before she untied the fabric of her skirt and let it fall down. Leif gazed at the scene, wondering what would happen next: Wild beasts gathering around the stump to worship her? Birds descending through the branches to sit on her shoulders?

However, his romantic fantasies ended when Abalone threw her arms in the air and skipped all over the wooden platform like a kindergarten kid.

After a while, she began spinning, her body leaning back and both arms stretched out toward the middle of the stump as if an invisible person held them and was making her twirl around. She stopped and opened her mouth, like a fish gulping air. He guessed she was out of breath. But no. A tone appeared, crawling out of her throat, first muted and then increasing in volume and strength. A note. A long-drawn G.

He already had — painfully — learned last Friday that she wasn't mute when her high-pitched screams accompanied the racquet swooshing down on his head. But now her voice sounded flat and fragile, almost rusty. To his surprise, she started singing.

"A sailor went to sea, sea, sea,
to see what he could see, see, see."

Whatever he had imagined her to do in the woods, this was not it. To come all that way to dance on a tree stump and sing a silly song.

She looked earnest, though, and the more her voice improved, the more the children's rhyme sounded dark and sorrowful — a requiem rather than a happy whimsical tune. She stood still now, arms hanging limply at her sides, her head bent down: a mourner chanting in the sanctity of a green cathedral.

"And all that he could see, see, see,
was the bottom of the deep blue sea, sea, sea."

Repeating the words over and over, she started wiping her eyes with her sleeves. After a while, she slumped down in the middle of the stump and buried her face in her hands. The sailor went to sea no longer; her singing ceased as she was overtaken by violent sobs and moans.

"Flow my tears," Leif whispered, as he stared at the crying girl with a mixture of compassion and embarrassment, "fall from your springs." The first lines of John Dowland's masterpiece.

Mrs. Panetta had turned him on to the songs of the English Renaissance composer. They had been practicing a couple of his songs lately, still unsure of which one to pick for his pre-screening video. Leif had told her he considered the lyrics of 'Flow my Tears' a tad too depressing.

"Of course we do not expect a young person such as yourself to have tasted of such emotions," Mrs. Panetta had said.

The young person on the tree stump in front of him obviously had. The beautiful girl wept with a grief Leif didn't even know existed. Although, he had felt sad before, very sad. First when Hobo died. And only about a year ago, his grandpa passed away, leaving everybody heartbroken.

"But when you get older and experience life, you will develop a deeper understanding of these feelings," Mrs. Panetta had added. Was he supposed to find beauty in distress? Enjoy desperation? He wanted to comfort the girl. He pulled his head back a bit; his cheek grazed the bark. It felt unexpectedly smooth. Maybe the lovely tune would calm her down, or at least distract her from her overwhelming woe.

Be careful though that she doesn't discover where you are, he cautioned himself. Too late, though, for he noticed that he had already started singing,

"Flow, my tears,
fall from your springs!
Exiled forever, let me mourn."

The words flowed out of his mouth and got carried over to her by the hot air, as if resting on a velvet cushion.
"Where night's black bird her sad infamy sings,
there let me live forlorn."

She still cried while he continued with the second verse,

"Down vain lights, shine you no more!
No nights are dark enough for those
that in despair their last fortunes deplore.
Light doth but shame disclose."

It sounded awesome, but the lyrics were gloomy in the extreme. Didn't he plan on singing to give her consolation? Too late now.

However, at "Never may my woes be relieved," she lifted her face and started looking around.

Leif's voice reverberated through the towering trees, thrown back and forth between them, making it impossible to locate him behind his sequoia, where he stood leaning against the immense trunk, arms spread out around it, not caring about all the must-dos of the ideal singing posture like feet slightly apart, spine aligned, shoulders down and back. This moment was too special for technical nitpicking. Yet, he believed his voice had never sounded more brilliant or appealing as it did right now.

"Since pity is fled," he sung, but felt the greatest sympathy for the girl and couldn't remember a time when singing had filled him with such intense tenderness.

> "And tears and sighs and groans
> my weary days, my weary days,
> of all joys have deprived."

Contrary of the mournful words, an overwhelming euphoria took hold of him. To be part of this otherworldly experience...

By the time he started the forth verse, "From the highest spire of contentment," she stood upright on the remains of the giant tree with her arms stretched skyward as if to attract the wondrous bird that sang to her.

"Hark! you shadows that in darkness dwell," began the last verse, and the girl embraced herself, moved her body slowly and gracefully as if in a mystic dance, her head resting on her shoulder, as if the spirit of the ancient redwood had appeared to lament its fall. A dramatic scene, worthy of one of the great opera houses. But this was real life, not pretend emotion. True grief and suffering.

He remembered how Mrs. Panetta had reacted to his excitement when he spoke to her about his favorite arias.

"Of course the music is wonderful," she had said. "But we shouldn't forget that operas are really only fairy tales for adults. Don't be fooled, Leif. Redemption through love only happens in God's kingdom."

His song was coming to an end. He longed to bring the girl relief. And tell her how he felt.

"I saw my lady weep," he began. Studying Dowland proved to be an unexpected blessing after all.

> "And sorrow proud to be advanced so,
> in those fair eyes where all perfections keep.
> Her face was full of woe,
> but such a woe (believe me) as wins more hearts,
> than mirth can do with her enticing parts."

How every line shone with meaning.

> "Sorrow was there made fair."

Abalone sat on the edge of the stump, listening with an expression of rapture.

> "She made her sighs to sing,
> and all things with so sweet a sadness move,
> as made my heart at once both grieve and love."

She looked up and gazed toward the emerald roof high above her head.

> "O fairer than aught else the world can show,
> leave off in time to grieve.
> Enough, enough, your joyful looks excel."

Leif thought he detected a faint smile as her eyes wandered from crown to crown.

"Tears kill the heart, believe;
oh strive not to be excellent in woe,
which only breeds your beauty's overthrow."

He didn't want to stop now. What else could he sing? Something Italian? She wouldn't care that his pronunciation still needed major improvement. But no, he wanted her to understand the lyrics. The beautiful creature on the tree stump deserved something sweet — and honest.

"I will give my love an apple without e'er a core." Good choice, he thought. Lovely old folk song. "I will give my love a house without e'er a door. I will give my love a palace wherein she may be, but she may unlock it without e'er key."

The simple, slow melody seemed to melt in the sweltering air. He turned around and leaned his back against the tree trunk that concealed him.

"My head is the apple without e'er core," he sang, his eyes closed now. "My mind is the house without e'er door."

Here he stood, a minstrel in the woods, hiding behind a massive sequoia, singing to a girl who had just five days ago attempted to smash his skull with a racquetball racquet — serenading this very girl and actually meaning it.

"My heart is the palace wherein she may be, and she may unlock it without e'er key," he finished, prolonging the last note, making it linger until it finally evaporated, until nothing could be heard except the murmur of the mosquitoes and the sighing of twigs.

He opened his eyes.
Ocean blue and seaweed green glared at him.

# Twenty-Eight

## JEREMY
### WEDNESDAY AFTERNOON

Jeremy took the wooden band out of its hot bath and stuck his fingers into the holes of the core form. His hands remembered every move with ease, proof of how much he had loved making boxes.

After a dusty morning at the table saw and a couple of hours using noisy nail guns, he had longed to do something quiet and relaxing, when the battered steamer trunk, half-buried under a pile of fir planks, caught his eye. Locked up in there, together with the tools and forms, a couple of already prepped and cut swallowtails had waited for him. Why hadn't he taken them out in all those years?

To his surprise, the old wood didn't splinter.

Jeremy looked at the base and top band already drying on the worktable, soon to be a nice birthday present for Abbie.

As his hand started smoothing the hot tail around the core, warmth spread through his body. A feeling of peace, like coming home.

"Mr. Macklintock?" a female voice asked into the silence.

Jeremy frowned. He put the form down and placed the tail back in the water. Customers rarely showed up here. His T-shirt hung over the saw stand. He reached over, grabbed it and pulled it on.

Wiping his fingers on his jeans, he walked toward a small blonde woman, who stood just outside of the rolled-up workshop door. She looked at him with an expression of amusement, though maybe it was just the afternoon sun twinkling in her eyes. He wondered how long had she been watching him.

"Yes?"

She moved forward and extended her right hand. "Zoe Loomis." In her left hand she carried a semi-transparent plastic folder.

Jeremy made a bet with himself: ideas for a hideous walk-in-closet featuring lit-up display compartments for her handbag collection and eight hundred dollar shoes, or a compilation of magazine pages showing the latest gourmet kitchen makeovers.

"What can I do for you?" he said, pressing her hand briefly.

"Sorry for popping in unannounced," she said. "But I thought an informal visit might prove to you that I intend to approach things in a more relaxed way than Mrs.

Hotchkins. It seems to me your case has challenged her a bit."

Jeremy's eyes narrowed. "Are you trying to tell me you're from Children's Services?" So much for his intuition.

She tried to smile away his irritation. "I just got transferred. I've checked into the Sea Star Inn for now. It has a lovely atmosphere, and I've heard they don't have a ghost. That must be considered a plus."

Quite the chatty type, Jeremy thought, but compared to Mrs. Hotchkins's sharp to-the-pointness, this was possibly likewise a plus.

"Yes," he said, attempting a half-smile in return. "We have an unusual amount of haunted Bed & Breakfasts here. The Sea Star is not one of them. I refurbished all their cottages seven years ago and didn't have any supernatural encounters."

"I'm relieved to hear it," his visitor said and beamed at him. "I hope you can spare some time for me. I thought you might have finished your day by now."

Strange concept of working hours she had. It was barely four o'clock.

"Sure," Jeremy said. "We can talk right here, if you don't mind." He was not going to invite her into the house and let her snoop around there. He pointed to one of the two massive rocking chairs in the corner by the side door.

"These are very nice," she said, sitting down. "I love Mission style furniture." She started moving back and forth.

Even if she faked interest, at least she had some taste.

"My husband gave me an early Gustav Stickley desk a couple of years ago."

Jeremy leaned back in his chair, making it teeter. Mr. Loomis was obviously a man of means.

"It's only a small one," she said. "Not signed. A professor's salary has its limitations. And I guess I should use the term ex-husband." She frowned. "I've only had a month to adjust to it."

Why is she giving me her life story, Jeremy wondered, other than putting me at ease before she gets out the hammer?

She stroked the swaying armrest. Her fingers were pretty, straight and slender, but her short nails flaunted sky-blue paint. Ridiculous, she was certainly over thirty.

"You made these chairs, didn't you? The quality is awesome."

Flattery now. Stop the overture, lady, and bring it on.

"Mr. Macklintock." She stopped her chair.

I guess the laid-back part of the meeting is over, Jeremy assessed.

She leaned forward, folded her hands and rested them on her kneecaps. "You must be weary of people poking around in your private life." Ten silly blue fingertips fluttered while she spoke. "I would like us to be on the same page. Abalone will be fifteen tomorrow. All that matters is that she gets the help she needs. Please see my involvement as support. As far as I can tell from reviewing the files, you have done a good job under difficult circumstances."

"Until last Friday," Jeremy mumbled.

Nice spiel she was giving him. Building up confidence. Showing compassion.

Wolf in sheep's clothing.

Although, he liked her outfit: beige cotton slacks, Converse sneakers, and a light tunic with multicolored zigzag-stripes. Clothes for a fun day out. Casual, unofficial, non-threatening. The complete opposite to Mrs. Hotchkins. Nice try.

The big brown eyes — so honest, so trustworthy — searched for something in the file she held on to. Her left hand reached up to fix a pert strand of honey blonde in place.

The cut was much too short for Jeremy's taste, barely covering her ears. Not that they needed to be concealed, these delicate swirls of tissue.

She worked her hair, trying to contain the fleecy thickness, but it resisted her efforts and continued to spill over her temples.

He hadn't touched a woman's hair in a while. Seven almost celibate years, interrupted only by a fling with a cashier in Willits, and the one time pick-up of a hooker. And, of course, Tessa. Yet suddenly he was presented with Deidre yesterday, and now Mrs. Loomis.

He looked at her left hand: on her ring finger, a thin strip of whitish skin declared the absence of a wedding band, soft and pale as if ill at ease with its sudden exposure to the world.

"I've got a copy of the police report," Mrs. Loomis said, "with the explanation of last Friday's event." She still had one hand in her furry cap while the other flipped through the papers on her thighs.

Let me help you there, Jeremy felt like saying, and then shove his fingers into her hair and take out his frustration on poised Mrs. Loomis, who had barged into his workshop and privacy, thinking she knew all the answers. He winced, embarrassed by the violence of his thought.

"I understand Abalone had a very close relationship with her uncle?"

"You understand, do you?" Jeremy mumbled under his breath. Well, let me tell you, she had a very close relationship with her father too.

He just nodded.

"It is assumed that she saw — that she was a witness to whatever happened to her uncle and — to her mother?"

"That's all speculation!"

"Of course," she said and closed the file. "Would you mind introducing me to Abalone?"

"I guess I don't have a choice," he said, getting up. "I'll see if she's back yet." He stomped through the sawdust to the side entrance and slammed the door shut behind him.

He went into the house first, which was empty except for Gina, who had retired to her bedroom after making him a fruit salad for lunch. Jeremy exited through the sliding door of the kitchen and crossed the backyard to check the studio.

As expected, Abbie was not in yet. She had taken her bicycle in the morning, but by now, she was surely in the water.

Coming back, Jeremy stopped where Mrs. Loomis had stood before and no doubt watched him working. Sorry to pop in unannounced, her words echoed in his head with a mocking tinge. Now it was his turn to have a good look at her.

She still sat in the rocking chair, slowly swaying, and stared at her empty ring finger with an expression that contradicted the cheerfulness of her blouse.

The bulky chair made her look tiny, and somehow forlorn.

Jeremy rubbed his chin. She was only doing her job.

Well, she could have chosen a profession that didn't include meddling in other people's affairs.

However, she wanted to help.

Yeah, but what was to be expected from someone who couldn't keep up with her own life. All her great wisdom hadn't saved her marriage.

I'm well on my way to becoming a real jerk, Jeremy thought. Who was he to judge? He knew nothing about the reasons for her divorce, nor did he hold the monopoly on disappointment. Other people were privy to pain. Was he never going to let anybody close again? Trust nobody for the rest of his life?

He walked into the workshop. "Sorry, but Abalone is still out," he said, approaching the rockers.

Mrs. Loomis looked up and switched on her smile.

"Can I offer you something?" He stepped behind the chairs and opened the door of the old canning cupboard he had first restored and then re-purposed to hold his candy supply.

She turned her head and gasped at the display of his goods. "You're stocked like a 7-Eleven." She laughed. "Wow. Turtles! My favorites. And Teriyaki jerky."

"I also have refreshments." He pointed to a little fridge.

"But no hot drinks I'm afraid. The kitchen is closed." He pulled out the half-empty box of chocolate turtles.

"Abbie usually dives at this time of day, if the weather allows it." He paused, the candy suspended in midair. "Hey, would you like to see our famous sea glass site? We can wait there until she beaches."

"That would be great." Mrs. Loomis got up and placed her dossier on the chair. Blonde strands flopped over her forehead again. She rolled her eyes. "Please don't think I'm obsessed with my hair," she said, attempting to restore order. "It's just . . . I got it cut yesterday." Behind her, the still moving chair caused her papers to shift out of the file folder. "I regret it already," she added, not noticing the pages slipping through the opening in the rocker's backrest onto the dusty floor. "I used to wear it up in a bun. I guess I wanted to be dramatic."

Jeremy grabbed a plastic bag from the cupboard and packed turtles and jerky. "Let's have a little picnic," he said. "What would you like to drink?"

Forty minutes later, Jeremy sprawled on shimmering glass bits, in the company of Mrs. Loomis's shoes and no show socks.

Watching their owner wandering the waterline with rolled up pant legs, he found himself reflecting on the fact that Mr. Loomis had to be a first class moron. Why would anybody let go of such a charming creature? An attractive woman who appreciated quality craftsmanship and a good sugar high. Who loved beef jerky.

She looked over at him, holding up a turquoise marble. A rare marble. Either Mrs. Loomis was an exceedingly lucky girl, or somebody had thrown it there in an effort to seed the beach.

She still smiled.

Jeremy's fingers shoveled through the sparkle. And why not replenish? If it made people happy. Instead of spoiling everybody's fun and whining about the lost stuff. He smiled back and gave her a thumbs-up.

A pleasant dizziness permeated his brain. Maybe it was the sun, or the sweets. Or was it her smile? Looking at her, he wanted to forget the purpose of her visit, wished he could just sit and watch, not having to get up until her funny hair had grown over her shoulders down to her pretty multicolored waist.

He unpacked another turtle and decided to give himself leave. At least for the rest of the day. Leave to act like a man without burden. Leave to explore where this surprise encounter with Mrs. Hotchkins's enchanting replacement might lead.

Warm chocolate ran along his fingers; the Pacific swirled about Mrs. Loomis's ankles.

Had she mentioned her first name when she came in? Oh, yes. Zoe.

The sun shone through her blouse. Jeremy's tongue spread caramel onto his palate. Zoe.

A little boy holding a beach bucket showed her something in a tide pool. She talked to him. He pointed into the water with his green plastic rake. They laughed. The boy ran off and vanished through one of the passageways in the cliff. Zoe bent down to pick up another piece of glass from the glistening ground.

Jeremy hoped for his daughter to take her time and not disturb this moment, and wished for a sneaker wave to wash over Zoe and him, to carry them away to a place where the past didn't matter and second chances were real.

Yet, here he was, amidst a former dump site turned tourist attraction; maybe miracles did happen after all.

She smiled at him again, this time lifting up a disc of yellow glass. The light caught it and set it on fire.

Jeremy blinked. Blinked at Mrs. Zoe Loomis, who held the sun.

He would invite her to the Nautilus for supper. She looked like somebody who valued a scrumptious cioppino.

# Twenty-Nine

## GINA
### WEDNESDAY AFTERNOON

Punished — for not waiting. Punished — for choosing a man out of her realm. Life was not a fairy tale. There were no princes. You paid a price for your decisions.

"*Ha del barco!*" Señor Limón cawed as Gina rolled past the guest room. The traitor.

She had forgiven him, though. After all, he was just a dumb bird.

Gina turned the chair around and drove toward the cage.

"*Dichosos los ojos!*" the parrot announced as she opened the small metal door.

He hopped onto her lap. Absentmindedly, she let her fingertips twirl through the soft feathers on top of his head.

The memories of her wedding anniversary returned. There had been an increasing chill in the air as the afternoon progressed and the journey with the clipper neared its end, reminding everybody this was *not* the Caribbean. Haze swirled through the rigging of the ship. Fog lay in wait to shroud the evening.

Groups of guests, wrapped in sweaters and blankets, huddled together amidst big cushions on the foredeck, sipped coffee or hot chocolate and munched on cake pops, while one of the crew members told stories about the grim life of real pirates. Gina sat with Abbie and her grandmother Melody, listening to the tale of Anne Bonney and Mary Read, the most ferocious women pirates in history.

Though Abbie shivered, she refused to cover her naked shoulders. She would only wear the fuzzy mohair sweater she had brought, because it matched the turquoise of her tulle tail.

Gina looked around for Fern, to ask her where the stupid sweater could be, but she wasn't anywhere in the crowd. Jeremy and his father-in-law stood on the bridge, chatting with the captain.

Melody offered to search for it, concerned her granddaughter would catch a cold, but Gina knew in which of the cabins Ru had stowed their stuff in the morning. She got up and went down the wooden stairs into the belly of the ship, to quickly find the sweater and return to the deck for the end of the pirate story.

Thinking how much the interior reminded her of Jeremy's work in the Abyss, she walked through the tunnel of polished wood with the closed cabin doors on both sides.

Only the one she had come for was ajar. Approaching it, she heard the beating of wings.

"*Un beso, un beso,*" cawed Señor Limón from inside. Gina smiled. Her beautiful green bird had to have a sixth sense.

"You better obey your parrot," a woman's voice said.

Gina gasped and pressed her back against the wooden wall next to the door.

"Not here, Fern."

She flinched. Somewhere on its way up from her lungs, her breath got stuck.

"Come on." Fern's giggles sounded subdued as if her lips touched fabric — or skin. "Don't be so prissy."

"Fern, stop it." Ru, also muffled now and with less conviction.

"*Un beso, un beso,*" Señor Limón demanded again.

The door closed.

Gina exhaled. Succumbed to Fern's siren song. How could she have been so clueless?

So blind?

Their weekly diving tours. Fern 'helping out' with Abalone Adventures. It was not enough for her that all these guys drooled over her. No, she had to have Ru.

And were they not the perfect match? A sparkling pair. Now, they only had to rid themselves of their bland spouses and ride into the sunset.

Blazing heat pulsed through her body. How long had this been going on? Should she throw open the door and rush in? For a moment, she wished the old flintlock pistols hanging from her belt were loaded and she had some black powder handy. One bullet for Fern. One bullet for Ru.

None left for herself though.

What else could she do? Confront them? Shame them? Oh, Gina, this is not what it looks like. No? What is it then?

But where should she go from there? They still had at least half an hour of sailing before they reached the harbor. And she couldn't think of anything to say to them. They knew what they were doing, and did it anyway.

Upstairs, on the deck, Jeremy and Abbie still enjoyed the afternoon. Saturated with happiness. Just like she had been only moments ago.

No, she couldn't make a scene, couldn't bear the outrage, the scandalous ending of this blissful day. The shocked stares, the whispered questions, the gloating.

She would talk to Ru later. Privately. In the safety of their home. Maybe it had only been a moment of weakness. A recent development. Shallow. Trifling. Not worth destroying five lives over.

Somehow, her legs carried her into one of the washrooms. Cold water splashed onto her cheeks until their ashy color gave way to an agitated crimson. The nip in the air or the sun exposure would be a sufficient explanation for her flushed look. One of the ship's towels dried her face and hands.

The farewells took forever. Such a lovely day. Thank you so much. You're so lucky to have each other. Goodbye.

Presents had to be stowed in the trunk of their car. The clipper to be checked one more time for forgotten items. The crew to be thanked and seen off.

How about burgers? Ru was hungry again.

Her eyes watched him sinking his teeth into a meat patty.

Something wrong, honey?

Sorry, a slight headache. Too much sun.

Poor honey. Ru's arm gliding around her shoulders.

But hasn't it been great fun. Such a wonderful day.

The phone rang, jolting Gina back to the present. Señor Limón lifted his beak, ready to chime in, but changed his mind as if he understood that she would not give him the satisfaction of answering it.

If the phone had vocal cords, it would by now been hoarse from all the calling. Of course it was Elon, trying to reach her since Saturday afternoon.

Why did he, of all people, have to deliver the lost bracelet of her lost husband? Was there a message in that? Seven years she had mourned, secretly hoping for Ru to return and explain himself. But that had just added insult to injury.

And then to break down in front of the very man she had snubbed to marry Ru, and be swept up into a frenzy and lose her mind. Thank goodness Jeremy had interrupted them, who knew what would have happened. Gina sighed. She didn't want to think about these moments of confusion and helplessness.

Like that awful night, when she had gone to bed early claiming she felt sick — which she did, only for reasons other than she pretended — but couldn't say a word about her distressing secret. Ru brought her a cold cloth and Aspirin for her headache, was genuinely sweet and caring. Had she not been ear-witness to the scene on the clipper, she would have never believed it. He loved her.

How badly she wanted to forget what she had heard. She let him hold her hand before she fell asleep, a fact that still flabbergasted Gina to this day, and woke up to the squealing of hummingbirds around the feeder in the cork oak, with Ru's arm around her waist.

Eyes closed, her head still fuzzy from a string of blurred dreams, she listened to the droll voices of the tiny birds outside, her husband's body leaning against her back, warm and reassuring: the familiar dawning of a happy day.

Her last moment of felicity. Then Gina's eyes opened, and with the brightness of the early sunlight, reality whipped back into her mind. Ru and Fern together in the clipper's cabin. Un beso, un beso. The door closing in her face.

Gina slipped out from under Ru's arm and sat up. His body stirred. He didn't wake. She watched his long lashes flutter, the corners of his mouth twitching. A pleasant dream, no doubt.

Her throat started stinging; a series of hot flashes rushed through her flesh. Deceit. Betrayal. Adultery. The dreadful truth smothered the morning's innocence like scorching ash clouds flowing down the slopes of a volcano.

Gina ran to the washroom where she performed the icy splashing again until her face ached, before she subjected her naked body to the shock treatment of a cold shower.

However, coming out of the bathroom, she felt even less refreshed than when she had entered. Two cups of milk-and-sugar-free coffee later, Ru joined her in the kitchen, preened and smiling, endlessly jabbering about their marvelous festivity, and suggesting they should do just the same for their twentieth anniversary, while devouring two large bowls of muesli with blueberries.

Feeling like she would choke any second on the bite

of raisin scone she had managed to swallow down, Gina decided to speak to him in the evening.

They left for the Abyss, taking the cage with Señor Limón like they had done on so many days before. Ru disappeared into his office, and Gina stayed in the shop to deal with a delivery of wetsuits and serve a handful of customers. Yet, every time the doorbell rang and the big green bird emitted his cheerful *Ha del barco!*, she wanted to wrap her fingers around his neck and squeeze.

At lunchtime, Ru drove down to the Limpet to check on the engine oil and get pizza for them on the way back.

From the rack where she sorted the wetsuits, Gina said a casual, a cool goodbye as he walked out the door. Barely a nod, no hug, no kiss. She was collecting her strength to confront him.

Shortly after Ru had left, Fern bolted into the store. She claimed to have forgotten her beauty pouch on the clipper. Had somebody found it? Gina suspected the lost item to be a fabrication; her sister-in-law just wanted to see Ru. And indeed she left immediately after finding out he was not present.

Later, Gina would tell the police that Fern seemed on edge, fiddled about nervously with her car keys during the brief chat, and had worn a large straw sun hat covering the entire upper half of her face.

Gina spent the afternoon attaching price tags to neoprene, barely noticing her husband's prolonged absence, absorbed with the catastrophe of the day before and the preparation for a life-changing argument in the evening.

And then Jeremy had called.

Señor Limón flinched under Gina's fingers, bringing her back to reality. "*Ha del barco!*" he muttered just as Gina heard the entrance door opening and closing.

"Gina," Jeremy said, as he strolled into the guest room. "Are you feeling better?"

The sight of him surprised her. There was a tenderness in his features, a gleam in his eyes she hadn't seen in ages.

"Is it okay if I go to the Nautilus for supper?" he asked.

"Of course," Gina answered, relieved she didn't have to give an update of her own emotional condition. "Did Abbie have lunch?"

"I guess," Jeremy said. "I didn't see her."

"*Que pasa?*" Señor Limón fluttered up from Gina's lap and circled the room twice before landing on the desk. "*Que pasa?*"

"How's the parrot?" Jeremy asked and smiled. "I hope I haven't overfed him."

"As you can see he's fit as a fiddle," Gina said, attempting a smile herself. "Sorry for malfunctioning. I will take over my duties again now."

Jeremy bent down and kissed her forehead. "See you tonight," he said and left the room. She heard him walking down the hallway, and as the front door closed behind him, it sounded as if he was whistling.

"*Caramba!*" Señor Limón stated, perfectly conveying Gina's amazement. He shuffled through the glass on the desk, picked up a bean-shaped piece of cornflower blue, transported it over to the drill and dropped it in the bowl. Tilting his head, he looked at her with an inviting smirk.

Gina shook her head.

"*Lo siento*," she said, truly feeling sorry to disappoint her bird, but drilling was the last thing she wanted to do right now. But why not put him in his harness and bring him with her to the kitchen? Señor Limón had worn it last with Ru on the clipper, hopefully he would remember it and not resist. To Gina's surprise though, he let himself be tied with the little red straps as if he was a gentle pony used to daily bridling. She fastened the leash to her armrest, and Señor Limón perched on her shoulder, uttering unintelligible cackles, obviously welcoming the diversion to his daily monotony.

Heck, Gina thought as she entered the kitchen, I could use some diversion myself.

She realized right away Abalone did not have lunch. The food on the table was untouched. Gina looked at the fruit salad, made from the leftovers from Friday's delivery — a pretty appalling affair now, brown and mushy. Señor Limón cocked his head and eyed the contents of the glass bowl with obvious disgust.

Gina sighed. She had shamefully neglected her niece since Saturday. For supper she would prepare something special, if the remaining groceries in the house allowed it, and also lay out two fresh towels for Abbie's ritual evening bath. The large blue ones with the long fleecy fringes, Abbie really liked them.

Rolling toward the refrigerator, Gina's glance fell on the old calendar — tomorrow was Abbie's birthday.

Fifteen. She would drive back to the guest room later and wrap the new dress she had ordered a while ago so that she could give it to Abbie in the morning.

Señor Limón cawed and hopped from Gina's shoulder onto the armrest. The whiff of cold air emerging from the fridge must have startled him. The crisper contained just enough ingredients to throw together one acceptable meal. An online order for fresh fruits and veggies needed to be placed.

Gina moved over to her laptop that still sat on the counter by the blender. She hadn't been on it since Saturday morning when she confirmed the Hare Creek appointment. A quick check to see if anything important had come in during her time off might be a good idea.

Señor Limón returned to her shoulder and watched the changing pictures on the screen with great interest as Gina waited for her account to open.

The top email was from Pam, containing information about the Why Replenish Glass Beach PR event on location, scheduled for Thursday afternoon. If Gina wanted to attend, Pam could get somebody to carry her down the path. Wouldn't that be nice?

Yes, Gina thought, it actually would be. She hadn't been to the beach in years.

But there was more. Scattered among business emails and spam, she found seven messages from an unknown Yahoo account.

Elon, clogging up her inbox with emphatic one-liners.
Saturday evening: *"Georgie, please answer the phone!"*
Sunday morning: *"Talk to me!"*
Sunday afternoon: *"Sweetheart, I want to see you!"*
Monday, noon: *"At least we should try!"*
Tuesday evening: *"Let's forget the past and live NOW!"*

*"I love you."*

*"I'm coming by tomorrow at one."*

The two latter emails dated from today.

"*Caramba!*" Señor Limón declared again.

# Thirty

## ABALONE
### WEDNESDAY AFTERNOON

Speckles of sunlight touch the raven-black hair of the boy beside me. Beneath his long, dark lashes, his blue eyes shine with truth and purity. We sit next to each other on the edge of an old tree stump. The forest around us stands in awe, and the birds hold their breath. Every ear, every leaf, listens to the boy who sings for me. I hold his hand while his mouth forms beautiful tones, high and clear, like chiming bells of silver.

Who would have thought that he has the loveliest voice on earth and in the water? Hearing him makes my heart skip, and my skin tingles as if touched by a thousand feathers.

Did the little mermaid feel like this the day she first laid eyes on the prince? I have read the story so often; I know each paragraph, each sentence, each word.

I picture the little mermaid in the light of the setting sun as she raised her head above the waves and looked at the clouds tinted with crimson and gold. Through the glimmering twilight beamed the evening star in all its beauty.

A three-masted ship rested on the water, with only one sail set; for not a breeze stirred the mellow air. The sailors idled on deck and amongst the rigging, listening to the sound of flutes and harps and chanting voices that floated toward the sky.

As darkness fell, a multitude of lanterns lit up. The little mermaid swam close to the cabin windows, and now and then, as the waves lifted her, she could look through the clear glass and see a number of well-dressed people within. Among them was a fair young man wearing a vesture of silk and brocade; the others cheered and toasted, singing, "A merry birthday and long life to our beloved prince."

When the prince came out of the cabin, a hundred rockets rose into the air, making it as bright as day. Startled, the little mermaid dived under water, and when she stretched out her head again, it appeared as if all the stars of heaven were falling around her.

Great suns spurted blazing rays. Splendid fireflies flew into the dark-blue air. Light and sparks reflected in the sea. The ship and all the people on it, every detail, even the smallest rope, could be distinctly seen in this glorious illumination.

How handsome the young prince looked, as he pressed the hands of all present and smiled at them while the music resounded through the night.

The singing boy beside me is handsome too. His wonderful music resounds in the trees around us and in my heart. I had thought him just a Prop. Now I would feel sorry for hitting him if I had room for another feeling in my joy-filled chest.

"I love diving, like you do," he says and lifts my canteen to his lips. He is not afraid of the sea.

Every day, the little mermaid swam close to the shore, and her longing for the young prince grew stronger and stronger as she watched his nearby palace. Once, she went up a narrow channel leading her under a marble balcony where the prince stood and gazed at the stars, thinking himself alone with them. Many times, she peeped out from among the waves when he embarked on an evening sailing in a pleasant boat, with music playing for his entertainment.

She loved him greatly — enough to risk her own life to save him from drowning when his ship broke apart one night in the horrible storm that ended the merry-making.

The little mermaid dashed toward him, forgetting the scattered wreckage, the beams and planks that bounced and twirled on the water and threatened to crush her to pieces. She loved him so — yet he preferred the foreign princess. However, she never got angry with him over the rejection; although it cut her heart and hurt more than her bleeding feet when she danced for him.

What happens if you cannot make this other person love you best of all?

When your fondest hopes do not get fulfilled, will you become foam on the crest of waves? I feel my pain returning — it never goes away for long. I know now it springs from the memories and not from me walking among the Props. The past is my ever-present sorrow.

In desperation, the little mermaid's older sisters turned to the sea witch, who asked for their beautiful hair as payment for her help. She sheared their heads and gave them a knife. A knife with which to kill.

The little mermaid stood alone on the deck of the royal ship that carried the young couple and their wedding guests back to the prince's country. The on-board festivities had long ceased, and propelled by a favorable wind, the vessel glided smoothly over the ocean.

Leaning her white arms on the wooden railing, she searched the east for the first blush of morning. She knew her fate. The prince, the man for whom she had forsaken her kindred and her home, had married another, and the first ray of dawn would bring her death. In the twilight, she saw her sisters rising out of the water, as pale as herself. The shine of the moon reflected on their scalps.

"When the warm blood falls upon your feet they will grow together again, and form into a fish's tail, and you will be once more a mermaid," the sisters cried and hurled a knife onto the planks of the ship.

"Haste," they shouted, "he or you must die before sunrise." And their tears mingled with the sea as they sank beneath the waves.

Her fingers clasping the sharp weapon, the little mermaid drew back the crimson curtain and entered the velvet tent where the prince lay sleeping next to his bride, her fair head resting on his breast.

In the sky, the rosy dawn grew brighter and brighter. The little mermaid bent down and kissed the prince's brow.

His lips quivered and he whispered a name. The name of his bride.

All his love was fixed upon her; his right hand had been placed in hers, and he had promised to be true to her, here and hereafter. The beautiful princess reigned over his thoughts and in his dreams.

The knife trembled in the hand of the little mermaid. But her love for the prince was stronger, she could not plunge the blade into his heart.

Holding a knife is one thing, using it is another. Just because someone lifts a weapon doesn't mean her intention is to kill. The little mermaid flung it far away into the waves and the water turned a crimson color as it sank. Drops spurted up, red as blood. She looked at the prince once more and threw herself into the sea. Once she had saved him from drowning; now she spared his life, but not her own.

Yet, it is all wrong. It hasn't turned out that way. The weapon got cast into the waves — after it was used.

The old tree stump we sit on is the place where I last sang with Mommy. Where we were happy.

I press the hand I hold in mine. Another one, please, my eyes say to the boy, soothe my pain with your wonderful voice.

# Thirty-One

## JEREMY
### WEDNESDAY EVENING

*E*arly evening, and all seats on the deck of the Nautilus were taken now. Jeremy leaned back in his chair.

Charlotte had welcomed Mrs. Loomis and him, disguising her surprise at seeing her favorite lone-wolf customer showing up in female company with a shower of professional attention. She had given them the small table shielded by rectangular planters with tall hedgelike grasses.

The green wall muffled the voices of the other patrons and blended them with the noises of the harbor: the rumbling of the incoming boats, the shouts and hoots of the people canoeing, the swishing vehicles on the bridge, the occasional yell of a seagull.

"Great idea. I love cioppino," Zoe said in reply to his meal recommendation and closed the menu. She gazed toward the ocean.

"This is a nice place."

A breeze floated over from the wide spotless blue, embraced by the rocky arms of cliffs and jetties. The towering bridge, guardian of the harbor, allowed the salty whiff to pass through between its lofty pillars, as it proved too gentle to stir the river mouth's surface or disquiet the trees and bushes growing on the opposite bank. Arriving at the deck, it tried in vain to dishevel Zoe's hair, now kept in place by elegant, expensive-looking sunglasses. All it could do was ruffle the edges of the paper napkins and murmur in the high grasses like it had secrets to tell if only someone would listen.

"So serene," Zoe said.

"Looks are deceiving," Jeremy said, surveying the familiar view. "Our harbor entrance is one of the most dangerous on the West Coast. Only eighty-two feet wide. The swell comes in directly; there's nothing to block it. Crossing the bar can be quite a challenge."

He glanced back at Zoe. "Many boats have capsized."

"Hard to believe looking at it now," she said. "It's picture-perfect. Of course, I'm familiar with rough weather, being a West Coast girl. But we are more sheltered in Seattle."

During the exchange of their most memorable storm experiences, food was ordered and drinks arrived.

The conversation flowed, Zoe having the larger share, and Jeremy marveling at the fact that them being together had all the allure of a first date without its awkwardness, as much as he was able to remember from his own primeval days of rendezvousing.

Since they had left the workshop, Zoe hadn't tried once to steer the conversation toward the reason she paid him a visit in the first place. Just as if she had forgotten all about it. As if they had met as strangers searching the shore for treasures.

Her cute blue fingertips played with the pieces she had collected in the afternoon, which were now lying next to her wine glass. "Your beach is truly spectacular," she said. "I got some pretty souvenirs. Although the marble doesn't look like it has been there for longer than a couple of weeks."

"You can tell?"

"To be honest, I'm a bit of an expert," she said and took the first sip of her second glass of white wine, a Chardonnay from the Anderson Valley she declared to be excellent. Jeremy was on his second ale, enjoying himself and the relaxed approach of Mrs. Zoe Loomis. It seemed to him he had never felt better in the company of a social worker, or indeed any female of whatever profession.

After she had accepted his dinner invitation with the condition that there would be two bills, they first agreed to go with one car and then decided to take a cab so they could have a couple of drinks.

"I'm not trying to schmooze you. But I grew up in Davenport, where we have some of the fanciest stuff you will ever find. Like sea glass mushrooms, eyes, and star rods. And have you ever heard of peacock sea glass?"

"No, what's that?" Jeremy asked and leaned forward, although of course he knew the whole story already, having attended the festival in nearby Santa Cruz for several years. Coming from her lips though, it would gain new, enchanting aspects.

She pulled at the long polished necklace that hung around her neck. The silver shone like a moonbeam. At the end of the chain, a large oval of glass emerged out of the zigzag fabric's depths.

"This is the highlight of my collection. Set in platinum. I never leave the house without it."

The pendant dangled in front of Zoe's chest, shard-of-the-year award-worthy: a magnificent paperweight shrunk to pebble size. Iridescent colors swirled through the glass. From its inside emanated a golden glow. A unique piece, deserving of the precious metal it was paired with. The delicate setting was masterly done, forming a narrow border of tiny shells, sea stars, and anemones. He bent closer and touched the pendant, thinking of where it had snuggled just moments ago.

"It originates from an art-glass manufacturer in Davenport," Zoe said, close to his face. Her breath smelled of apricot. "After a rainstorm in the early Seventies, the San Vicente Creek overflowed. The glassblowers used to store their discarded trimmings in bins in the backyard. The water came and flushed them downstream. All these multicolored bits ended up at the shore, where they have been tumbling in the sand ever since."

Rustling behind them, Charlotte appeared with their order.

Zoe let the pendant slip back into her blouse and placed a napkin on her lap. "You should take your daughter down there," she said, when they were alone again, and picked up her spoon. "I could show her the best spots."

"That would be great." Jeremy nodded and took another swig of ale. However, he didn't want to think of Abalone right know. He dreamed of traveling south to hunt peacock glass with the lovely woman who sat across from him and fished scallops out of her lazy man's cioppino.

"This is good," she said, chewing on tender mollusks. The tomato sauce had colored her lips. She sipped on the Chardonnay, and a pink hue spread on her cheeks. Was it the wine, or the evening sun?

Or looking into his eyes and guessing his thoughts?

"Mom and Dad have my collection at home together with their own. My sister took hers to Denver. Our family has a fun and fierce competition. We usually go glassing in wetsuits. I don't want to brag, but it can be quite extreme, particularly in winter. It's not for cowards. People get badly bruised, but it's the best time for 'slaying nuggets'. You have to fight the waves while digging with a shovel . . ."

Sharing her insider tips while savoring her meal, she glowed like the pendant hidden on her body. Jeremy imagined her standing in the surf wearing only the zigzag tunic. Every time she bent down to fish for sea jewels, the tips of her long sun-bleached hair touched the spume.

"Our glass is rare, not as plentiful as at your Xanadu beaches. A lot of perseverance is needed to find these beauties."

But one of them has washed ashore right in front of me, Jeremy thought.

She tilted her head.

"By the way, what were you working on when I interrupted you?" Oops, she had caught on to him. You can't just sit there and watch me perform, her smiling eyes seemed to say.

"A wooden bandbox," he blurted and put his spoon down.

"My father used to make them. He taught me when I was very young. I used to spend hours in his workshop. How he was able to get this hard wood to bend intrigued my little mind. I never found out where he learned it. We didn't talk much. I don't think he was a happy man, but when he made boxes, he seemed content. He died early." Jeremy sincerely hoped he didn't sound like a bumbling fool.

The smile vanished from Zoe's face.

"I'm sorry to hear that," she said. Her right index finger started moving the marble back and forth on the white tablecloth. "Isn't it sad how much of what we feel remains unexpressed? We're so afraid to get hurt. And then we're forever grieved by the missed opportunities."

Jeremy stared at her. What was she communicating? Did she think they had an opportunity that shouldn't be missed? He felt tempted to express himself in a way she might find surprising.

"When you came to the workshop, did you watch me?" he asked instead.

A cute smirk spread on her face. So, he had been right.

"Yes, I admit it," she said. "I didn't want to pry, but — you weren't like I had imagined." She dabbed her lips with the napkin. "I mean from reading the file."

Jeremy was able to camouflage his flinching by taking a bite of aioli baguette. No doubt, Mrs. Hotchkins hadn't found many praiseworthy qualities in him, probably painted him as some kind of antagonistic maniac.

"You looked so engrossed, so at ease. I had the impression whatever you were doing was special to you." Zoe leaned forward and whispered, "Those moments are precious."

Jeremy swallowed down the bread. Her face was close again. "They are," he said. The chocolate brown of her pupils posed such a contrast to Fern's pools of blue. A blue that never seemed to be moved, never really engaged, like the color of faraway mountains, the seam of the horizon, distant and unreachable.

Zoe's eyes offered insights with every flicker of the lids, changing from curiosity to excitement, from wonder to delight. He hoped she would see these mirrored in his eyes, and above all, understand the sincerity of his feelings before she discovered the desire building up in him.

Whatever it was, though, she must have liked because she threw back her head and giggled.

"On top of that, you had no shirt on," she said. "So you must pardon me for gawking."

Was this for real?

She couldn't be drunk; she had only nipped on her second glass. Had the stars aligned? Was this the reward for his endurance and restraint? He knew love at first sight existed; he had suffered from it for years. But that it struck two people simultaneously only happened in schmaltzy movies and cheap novels.

Or didn't it?

"I'll have to forgive you then," he said and took his glass. "To special moments."

"To special moments," Zoe said, and the rim of her wine glass nudged his pint with a silvery clink. "May they abound."

They finished their cioppinos, ordered apple pie and espresso, paid their separate bills and contributed equally to the generous tip for Charlotte, who discreetly ignored the fact that he and Zoe beamed like seven-year-olds visiting a fun fair.

Sitting next to Zoe in the backseat of the cab, Jeremy wondered what Charlotte had said on the phone when she ordered it. The professional distance she had displayed extended to the whole duration of the taxi ride and would have fooled everybody into thinking the man behind the steering wheel — Pete Maynard, known as the town's most jovial chatterbox — was in reality an introvert suffering from a pitiable shortness of words.

Yet, this reflection did not employ more than a couple of Jeremy's brain cells since the others were taking pleasure in the closeness of Zoe's body and the warmth of her thigh as it lightly rubbed against his.

Their driver turned on the radio.

"Build me up, Buttercup, baby," the front speakers pleaded.

Jeremy frowned. He hadn't heard the song in a long time. In grade twelve, Steve and he had experienced a serious Motown addiction and loved The Foundations, even though they were a British band imitating the sound.

"Buttercup, don't break my heart."

Right now, he didn't want to be reminded of one-sided love stories. People being messed around. Lifted up, just to be dropped again.

Next to him, Zoe's body moved to the rhythm. Her shoulder softly bumped into his upper arm. This time, there would be no disappointments.

Although he only had water after his second beer, he felt besotted, lightheaded. Drunk on Zoe's presence. On anticipation. Suspense. Another nudge from her shoulder sent heat from fiber to fiber, from cell to cell. His body seemed to have morphed into one giant receptor.

Unfortunately, it was also sensitive to the assaulting reek of the pineapple-shaped cardboard dangling from the rear view mirror. He longed to get out and smell Zoe instead of the Hubba Bubba odor sticking to the car seats. And he couldn't wait to hear her voice again. But mute Pete was far from being deaf, so Jeremy kept quiet, too. He didn't want Zoe to start life in town as tongue fodder. She followed his example, still gently swaying, her eyes fixed on the road in front of them and the bobbing dashboard figurine — a blue shark dressed as a hula girl.

Two shallow pop songs and a brisk run up Main Street later, the taxi stopped at the end of Elm Street.

"Let's get out at my place. I'll walk you to the inn. It's not even a mile," Jeremy had suggested when they waited for the cab in the parking lot of the Nautilus. "This is one of these rare evenings without fog. Usually, we are socked in by this time. Your first day here and you will be able to stand on the Pudding Creek trestle and watch the sun set."

"Yeah, let's do that," she had answered. *Pudding Creek.* Sounds like a place I want to see."

They shared the fare, just like they had done on the way down to the harbor.

Now, the natural understanding between them showed in the speed with which they coupled their bills in the driver's hand and fled the car.

"Don't you wonder if these scent designers have ever come across a real fruit?" Zoe asked when Pete and his smelly vehicle had left. She lifted her right arm to her nose and snuffled at the fabric of her tunic.

"I think they deserve to be pummeled with a truck load of pineapples," Jeremy said.

Zoe laughed and unlocked her car. She pulled a thin cream-white cardigan from the backseat. "Let's go and air ourselves out," she said and stuffed it in her purse.

"Absolutely, just give me a second." Jeremy jogged over to the workshop to fetch his sweater. He thought briefly about checking on Gina, but he didn't feel like dealing with her regenerated grief right now.

A short peek through the side window revealed an empty kitchen. Surely Gina and Abbie had already eaten supper, and everybody was back in their private territory.

Jeremy glanced over at the small woman who stood by her car, waiting for him, not far away from the spot in which he had seen her for the first time, only hours ago. How funny to have mistaken her for a customer. His initial shock to find out she was from family services. To think his rudeness could have frightened her away. One day, he would tell her about it, and they would both laugh.

"Ready," he said, joining her.

They strolled down Old Haul Road, the only people on the long straight band of pavement, running parallel to the cliffs on the left.

From the adjoining backyards to their right, sounds of happiness reached their ears. The chortles of children jumping on a garden trampoline. The excited yelps of a tiny dog. In one of the houses, somebody played a clarinet.

What a change had taken place here. From 1916 on, timber had traveled this way, first transported by train coming from the Ten Mile River drainage area. Then, twenty some years before Jeremy's birth, the tracks got ripped out and the road built. As a child, Jeremy often came to watch the truck monsters with their ten-foot wheel span, rattling over the bridge and down the street, delivering giant logs to the ever-hungry saws. Now, all these memories were fading away, erased by the present and so much more pleasant use of the area: cycling and jogging, and walking with your sweetheart.

The street lamps flickered and slowly lit up as if the departing sun transferred its glow to them. Zoe's hair glimmered like gold thread. Who would have thought an old utility road could be that romantic?

The woman by his side had been silent for quite a while now, gazing over the open meadows on her left toward the ocean. A million pennies for her thoughts at this moment. How could he make her talk again? Jeremy wondered, craving for the intimacy of their dinner conversation.

He sniffed the air. "There's a tropical breeze tonight," he said. "I still smell pineapple."

She turned her head and gifted him one of her broad smiles.

"We probably have it etched forever into the inside of our nostrils."

*We. Forever.* Beautiful words coming from her lips.

"Oh, I could do without that," Jeremy said, lightheartedly. It sounded wrong. But not without you, he wanted to add.

She looked away from him, toward the colorful evening show at the horizon.

"So, how come you have decided to move to this little village?" he asked, eager to have her engage with him again. "I'm sure it doesn't compare to Seattle."

"Well, things have been, kind of, disagreeable there for me lately," she said. "It's a great place to live — but, as I've told you, I got divorced recently. Prof. Van —."

Zoe coughed.

"Sorry. My husband thought it wise to knock up one of his students. I might not have been as upset as I was, after all I was his student once. However, he has proclaimed for the last ten years that he didn't want any more children. And I tried so hard to change his mind."

She snorted. "You can imagine my surprise to find out, not only did he have an affair with a twenty-four-year-old, but she was pregnant and he the most delighted father to be. A man who declared himself too old, and content with the two kids from his previous marriage."

Crushed hopes. Her emotions connected with his. He felt the pain and anger, the disillusionment, like an echo of his own misfortune. Should he take her in his arms? Hesitant, he winced instead.

"Oh, please don't assume," Zoe muttered and stopped.

"Oh, I did not," he hurried to say.

"Hendrik was already separated when I met him." She continued walking. "Or at least that's what he led me to believe. To think he's one of these creeps who exchange their wives on a regular basis. I'm just mad at myself for having wasted all this time with him."

A whiff of cold blew over from the water. Zoe stopped and pulled out her cardigan. She wrapped her small figure in its softness and threw the shawl-like front parts over her shoulders.

Now everything about her was bright: Her hair, her skin, her woolen top, her pant legs. She's aglow, Jeremy thought. Illuminated by the streetlamps and the big reddish-golden spotlight in the sky preparing to call it a day.

On her face, though, he saw the traces of forlornness again, just for a moment, mixed with embarrassment — and regret. He had never been able to read somebody like he read her.

"I hope I haven't startled you with my rant," Zoe said, looking down. "Did I even answer your question?"

She walked on, and he followed.

"When I got the call from Mr. Wes —, um, got the offer to come here, I thought I could help somebody and also have the opportunity to think about my future. But I shouldn't have told you all this."

"I'm glad you confided in me," Jeremy said, feeling inclined to open up himself, to let her know how deeply he understood.

"Thank you," she said and swallowed. "You are kind. Believe me; I wasn't prepared for something like this."

"Me neither," Jeremy said, ready to take her into his arms.

A vehicle, parked in the turning circle at the end of the road, started, and its engine howled.

The headlights flicked on, two white laser beams aiming at Zoe and him.

They continued walking. The car sped past.

A short time later, the asphalt under their soles changed to redwood. In front of them extended the trestle, spanning creek and beach, connecting the cliffs. Only five hundred twenty-seven feet forth, on the other end of its lumber walkway, the inn waited for Zoe.

Far in the west, the bottom of the golden disk dipped into the sea and melted.

Zoe leaned over the bridge's wooden railing and pointed at the sandy expanse below. "Do we still have enough light to go down to the beach?" she asked.

Jeremy checked out the area beneath them. The tide hadn't reached the trestle's wooden legs yet.

"Come with me," he said.

Soon, they climbed down a small path in the cliff. The rock became sand. Through the dark beam structure of the trestle, they watched the setting sun deliver a flawless spectacle, vanishing in a splash of orange and pink.

"The posts look like people holding hands with each other," Zoe said.

Jeremy reached over and took hers. "If I kissed you, would that compromise your professionalism?" he asked, pulling her toward him.

"Sometimes one's priorities require adjustment," she said, her face close to his.

Kissing a social worker under the Pudding Creek trestle. In all the years dealing with Mrs. Hotchkins, he would have never guessed anything remotely close could ever happen.

Right now he felt he could forgive her, could forgive everybody as long as this kiss lasted and another would follow and another.

Zoe leaned back.

"I have to tell you something important about myself before we continue this," she whispered, "although, maybe you won't want to have anything to do with me when you know."

"I don't think that could ever happen, baby," Jeremy mumbled into the collar of her blouse. "But this is not the time to talk. Tell me later." The tip of his tongue licked upward along the side of her neck. "Mmm, you taste fruity, pineapple girl."

She laughed, and he silenced her with his lips.

The fingers of his left hand dug into the silken tufts on her head. His right arm encircled her cashmere waist.

Only in the brief moments they took to catch a breath, he heard the faint sound of voices from the direction of the inn. Sometimes, wood creaked overhead. Water licked sand.

Out of the corner of his eye, Jeremy saw the moon hanging above the ocean, the silver smile in the sky — clearly amused to observe Zoe and him kissing against every single one of the trestle's thirty-four uprights that didn't stand in the creek.

She sighed and detached her mouth from his. "I think my feet are getting wet."

"Mine too," he said, determined to continue what they were doing even if it meant going under.

"I haven't asked anybody to come up for a coffee since I was in university," she whispered. "And I don't even have coffee, and the cottage is single-story. Would you come anyway?"

The kiss she got as an answer left her in no doubt about his intentions.

## Thirty-Two

### LEIF
#### WEDNESDAY EVENING

If somebody had asked him beforehand how many songs he could remember, Leif would never have guessed such a large number. The nearby stream gurgled in the dark as if trying to suggest an amount. Leif shook his head. The blades of the grass he lay on stroked his cheeks.

He looked at the girl resting next to him. The riverbank meadow was their bed, the night their velvet blanket. What a finish to an extraordinary day. He felt exhausted and charged at the same time.

In his left hand he held his phone, ready to be used as a makeshift flashlight should there be any disturbance in the thick darkness.

The woods on both sides of the river allowed no view of their interior, black curtains concealing the secrets of the nightly forest.

Leif couldn't see the moon, only its light tickling the treetops far above. In the indigo band of sky meandering between them twinkled tiny dots of brightness. He counted them. Definitely fewer than the songs he had performed.

"Singers are not concerned about their voices before they go on stage. They worry about forgetting the lyrics," Mrs. Panetta had said to him once.

Yet this afternoon, he had recalled, in trance-like enchantment, word for word with ease and precision. When he ran out of current repertoire, he switched first to the gospels then to the hymns he had learned in the church choir, which didn't seem out of place at all among the tree columns of this natural cathedral, where a boy sang and a girl listened to praises for their creator's abundant, never-ending love. Through the small blue opening above their heads, sitting like a stained glass window in a dark cupola, golden light fell onto this special offering.

Leif felt blessed. To be able to perform for someone other than Mrs. Panetta and himself, someone so graceful and grateful in equal measure, who urged him on, stimulated him in a way no drug on earth could ever do.

Now his true self had been set free, like a powerful scent, and released into the world, it could never be caught or contained again.

After a while, he started to repeat his favorite songs, not wanting the experience to end, refusing to stop sharing his passion with the girl beside him, who listened not only with her ears but seemed to absorb each note he sang with her eyes. He didn't care if he ruined his vocal cords in this marathon, to have possessed his gift for this special moment in time was all that mattered, to make her forget her grief, to see the expression of delight on her face and feel the touch of her soft hand holding his. To put it to use here, for this memory that he could cherish for the rest of his existence. Even if it meant becoming a lawyer and getting buried by divorce settlements for the next fifty years, it would have been worth it.

From time to time, he moistened his throat until his second bottle was empty, and the contents of her canteen equally exhausted.

"I wish we had more water," he said and wiped the sweat from his forehead with the back of his free hand.

Abalone let go of his other hand and stretched her legs.

Don't move, he wanted to say, I'll gladly die of thirst as long as I can sing for you, but she had already glided down the side of the stump.

She walked a couple of meters and, with her back to him, straightened herself, moving her body like a tender redwood stem in a gust of wind.

Stupid wimp, you've blown it, Leif thought, now she's going to leave. But instead, she turned around and beckoned to him.

"Come," she whispered. It sent a shiver down his spine: the first word she had spoken to him. He scrambled up and slipped down the wrinkled wood.

Every time, she took him by surprise. Just like before, when he had stood behind the tree, opening his eyes to see her in front of him, feeling his racing heartbeat, expecting to be hit for the audacity to shadow her. His astonishment and joy as she reached out and took his hand.

He followed her through the woods again, this time close, at arm's length, staring at the glossy red waves flowing in front of him — instead of observing the ground he walked on, which caused him to stumble over dead branches twice.

A good while later, Abalone guided him across train tracks (they weren't as lost as he thought) and soon they reached a placid stream. Of course, the railway wound through the Noyo River Canyon.

Here by the water the air was less stifling. They knelt down on the grassy embankment and dipped their containers into the cool flow. Leif lifted his bottle: the contents looked clear in the transparent plastic.

He decided not to worry about any possible reasons for pollution. Who cares, he thought, it's only for today. The animals around here drink it. He took a sip. It tasted great, fresh and cold. He emptied the bottle and filled it once more before he bent over the water and splashed his face and neck.

When he looked up again, Abalone stood next to him, pulling her dress over her head, revealing the small black bathing suit he had seen her wearing on Saturday, from his hiding place, when she jumped over the sofa.

Leif tried to unscramble his thoughts, to find her, only a moment later, swimming in the middle of the river. He took off his jeans and T-shirt, decided to keep on his undies, and plunged into the water.

In the twilight, they had supper.

His phone lay between them, emitting its greenish gleam, like an alien substitute for a campfire. Both of them pulled nuts out of their bags, which caused a laugh. She went over to the water and washed the fruits she had surprised him with. He cut each in half with his pocket knife: A crisp apple and a soft-fleshed peach.

After they had eaten, he texted his mother, stating he would sleep over at a friend's place, and hoped nobody would come back for specifics. *"Enjoy yourself"*, was the brief reply.

He asked Abalone if she wanted him to send her father a message to say that she was safe — which would have been, of course, a ludicrous exaggeration — but she shook her head.

"Sing again," she said. Her voice sounded smoother now. "Please."

He was the one who made her speak again. His singing had awoken her out of her silent world. Overwhelmed with joy and pride, he filled the evening air with yet another song.

Now, Leif listened to the forest playing its own kind of music. With the cool of the night, noises had appeared: Faint rustling, muffled growls, hushed shrieks. Furry flanks brushing against bushes, small paws breaking twigs. Surely, the dusky-footed woodrat or some other rodent scuttled around, gnawing and rummaging on a search for food or adventure. A couple of times, Leif heard splashing in the river, maybe deer having a drink.

At the first startling hoot, he had jumped. High up, a giant shadow crossed the water.

He braced himself for the screams of nocturnal birds hunting overhead.

Nearby, he found a heavy stick. As he lay down again next to her, Abalone had reached over and taken his hand.

The wooden weapon waited by his feet, just in case a predator should make an appearance. He wouldn't get up, though, for anything less than a cougar or a bear — he didn't want to embarrass himself by trying to protect Abalone from a flying squirrel.

So far everything was peaceful, and the girl next to him seemed completely at ease. In the shimmer of the stars, he could see her eyes, looking upward.

He gazed at the black profile of her face, traced the curve of her nose, the outline of her full lips. Her hair lay coiled under her head like a pillow.

Trying to align his breath with hers, Leif watched her chest rise and fall.

She still held his hand in hers. Its warmth entered through his palm — gushed through his body, driven by the knowledge that only the thin fabric of her dress covered hers.

The bathing suit hung over a willow branch, next to Leif's boxer shorts, where they had been placed to dry after their owners came out of the water. Not wanting to take any chances of frightening Abalone away, Leif had grabbed his clothes and dashed into the woods to get dressed.

He didn't need to see her naked. The pictures in his mind already overwhelmed him, her body moving underwater, the white skin gleaming; her clear eyes wide open, while he struggled to see, being used to wearing a diving mask.

He lifted his eyes to the sky, feeling like somebody was staring down at him: tiny radiant pupils giving him *the look*. Of course, he wouldn't dare touch her. He was content just being close.

He had started out stalking Abalone, and now he lay beside her under the stars. He smiled, remembering how he had scolded himself for thinking they would go home together. Never in a million years could he have guessed this outcome. A true gift. He felt like singing. In the future he would not suppress this urge again. No more lies, no more sneaking around. His lips spread into a wide smile. Apparently, Abalone had beaten some sense into him on Friday. He had already decided to give up poaching. Tomorrow he would come clean, tell his parents about the plans for his future. Then ask Mrs. Panetta if he could sing a solo on Sunday.

In seven or eight hours, the sun would rise again, to the dawn of a new day — and a new Leif.

## Thirty-Three

### GINA
#### WEDNESDAY EVENING

*G*ina placed the last two garment bags in her lap and drove over to the bed where she added them to the ones already piling up there. She pulled the zipper of the bag on top, feeling a bit like a child on Christmas morning.

Powder-blue roses came to light, printed all over smooth white silk. The bag beneath it contained mauve organza. The next: coral-red taffeta with white polka dots, followed by sleeveless black satin with a bateau neckline, a design very similar to the one Audrey Hepburn wore in Sabrina.

Gina smiled.

Mrs. Yelland had never failed to mention this particular detail.

Her neighbor had enjoyed a few years at the periphery of Hollywood after falling in love with some producer assistant's assistant of the movie company that came to town for outdoor shots in the late forties. The finished black-and-white drama had a happy ending and won an Oscar; Mrs. Yelland's marriage, on the other hand, didn't. She returned home divorced and worked as a switchboard operator for the sawmill, without ever getting another shot at romance or glamor.

Gina stroked her palm over the ruffles of the petticoat peeking out of the next bag. Once these beautiful dresses had been Mrs. Yelland's darlings. Gina still remembered the day she saw them for the first time.

"I wish I had something chic to wear," she had said and squirted more Windex out of her bottle. "Elon Wagner has asked me if I want to learn to dance."

"That's nice of him, sweetie," Mrs. Yelland said, breathing smoke into the living room air. She sat in her burgundy leather recliner with a well-thumbed copy of Vogue magazine on her knees.

Next to her ashtray, on the end table, ticked an old Sunbeam kitchen timer with a picture of Mickey Mouse dressed as a cook.

Mrs. Yelland always baked a marbled Bundt cake when Gina came over to tidy up. But right now, the smells of burning cigarette paper and pungent window cleaner overpowered the sweet aroma coming in from the hallway.

"His parents run the studio on Franklin Street, don't they?"

"Yeah. He has invited me to a beginners' class for ballroom standards. Don't you think that's stuffy?" Gina asked, wiping her rag over the coffee table's glass top.

"No, sweetie!" Mrs. Yelland shook her head. Her white-blonde hair was coiffed in a puffy Monroe style that reminded Gina of cotton candy.

"It's very elegant," Mrs. Yelland added, and her cigarette-holding hand waved through the air, leaving a thin trail of smoke. "And sophisticated."

"Maybe. I don't think I will do it, though. My baggy pullover dresses look awful. And Dad says he doesn't have any money to spend on nonsense."

"I wish he would remember that next time he goes to a bar," Mrs. Yelland mumbled to herself, but Gina's attentive fifteen-year-old ears heard it nonetheless.

The timer went off, startling both of them. Mrs. Yelland got up and rubbed her right hip. It had never properly healed after the operation. She grabbed her cane and walked out of the room to deal with the cake.

Later, after the cleaning, when Gina joined her neighbor in the kitchen for coffee, a large flat cardboard box was sitting on one of the chrome chairs by the Formica table.

"I don't have much occasion to wear it anymore," Mrs. Yelland said, as Gina stood in front of her, speechless, holding sage-green duchesse satin to her chest. "Although it still fits me, of course. But I guess there comes a time when you have to let things go."

Gina put her head through the halterneck and fluffed up the voluminous skirt.

Mrs. Yelland nodded and smiled. "The color suits you very well, sweetie. I'm sure your friend will make googly eyes."

This remark turned out to be an utter understatement.

"I thought he was going to keel over," Gina reported to Mrs. Yelland after her first evening class, and then she showed her the Viennese Waltz she had learned. Over the following weeks and months, Foxtrot and Cha Cha, Mambo and Swing were performed in Mrs. Yelland's kitchen, and more dresses made their way into Gina's closet.

Wasn't it strange, Gina thought, as she caressed the two-toned chiffon emerging from the next bag, that both Ru and Elon had fallen in love with her while she wore the clothes of other women. She looked at the dresses lying on her bed, still so pretty.

With their new owner being away in San Francisco, they had bided their time in storage, not suspecting for a moment they would never dance again. When Gina moved back with Ru, she had them dry-cleaned. Then, they got sealed in black vinyl and cached in the rearmost corners of her closet.

She unzipped the last bag.

A cocktail dress of midnight-blue silk. Gina lifted one of its long sleeves to her nose and sniffed at the cuff. Behind the musty odor lingered something else.

A flowery smell. She closed her eyes. An ocean of white blossoms. *Eternity.*

Elon had given her a bottle for her twentieth birthday — together with the tree. She glanced toward the windowsill. Her ginkgo still held his little green head up high. It had been a sweet present. A great romantic gesture. But what good was symbolism if no action followed?

Still holding the silk to her nose, Gina inhaled again. Was the scent really there or did she just imagine it?

She had loved the seductive black-and-white commercial with the young couple on the beach. The dark rocks and bright sand reminded her so much of her favorite places. Elon was visiting, and they roamed the shoreline, happy to be together again after the long absence. Tender, loving, passionate.

Gina was bursting with anticipation.

Imagining her life continuing now like in the magazine ad for her wonderful perfume.

*What begins here never ends*, it said under the picture of another beautiful young couple playing with their small children, smiling in a moment of perfect marital bliss.

However, the three weeks together neared the end. Would Elon go away again without a change in the status of their relationship? Gina lay awake at night. Should she propose to him? These were the nineties. Modern times for modern girls. She worked on her bookkeeping certificate, and her cooking skills would get her hired in any humble diner across the country. She was an asset, not a liability.

But she couldn't imagine going down on a knee in front of Elon, offering herself to him. How did men whip up the courage?

Except at her job, she wore the perfume everywhere; the scent made her feel special, and it let her forget the smell of heated fat that permeated most of her days. She tried to imagine her kitchen work as a dance performance, quickstepping between the fryer and the stove.

But every time she saw her sweaty face in one of the stainless steel surfaces, she wondered how graceful Ginger Rogers would have looked between slicing potatoes, breading cod, and straining the lard.

Sometimes in the morning when she was the first to come in to prepare the day's food, she tried to emulate Fred Astaire's number from A Damsel in Distress, tapping the kitchen's base cabinets with her feet like they were drums. "The only work that truly brings enjoyment," she sang and banged the pots and pans with wooden spatulas.

How the significance of the lyrics got lost on Elon, she couldn't understand. They had seen the movie countless times. Elon couldn't be that thick. What was wrong with him?

He didn't fancy her as much as she did him — that was the explanation she came up with.

Elon's parents invited her to join the advanced classes after he had left again, but after a couple of evenings Gina excused herself. The upcoming exam served as a credible pretext. Without Elon, she felt awkward there, watching his parents jive through their life perfectly in tune, and she always had to fight against the thoughts of him twirling around, holding somebody else.

I love you, his email said. Could it be true? Supposedly, old love never died. His kisses had tasted lively enough on Saturday.

Could there really be a chance for them — after all this time? What did she have to lose? He knew her waltzing days were over. If he could content himself with what was left . . .

Gina pulled her prom dress from the garment bag. She lifted herself out of the chair onto the bed, took off her T-shirt and slid the organza over her naked skin.

Amazingly the zipper in the side closed all the way. The bodice squeezed a bit at the waist but not as much as she had anticipated. She shook out the skirt. Its ballerina-length covered her battered calves nicely.

Tomorrow she would put on this dress for Elon, and then he'd better say the words she had expected from him twenty-five years ago.

ABALONE'S BIRTHDAY

# Thirty-Four

## JEREMY
### THURSDAY MORNING

*A* screeching fanfare pierced the morning, a sound only pleasing to seagull ears. Jeremy suspected the source to be overhead, hearing big webbed feet waddle on the roof shingles while their owner deluded itself into thinking it was a songbird.

You're neither a lark nor a nightingale. Go somewhere else, rowdy, and find yourself a juicy clam for breakfast. Jeremy pressed his head into the pillow and tried to wish the seagull away, but it remained in place and increased the noise level as if using a megaphone. What was so important that it had to be bawled into the newborn day? An outrageous announcement no doubt.

Perhaps these birds were privy to human secrets, sharing them with each other to have a good chuckle.

Hear, hear: Jeremy Macklintock just had a night to remember! He's in love with a woman he only met yesterday if you can believe it.

Jeremy smiled and opened his eyes. Close to his face lay a hand. He moved his head forward and placed a kiss on each of the fingernails — although he couldn't see the paint in the twilight, he had a clear picture in his mind. Cerulean blue, the color of a perfect sky.

Zoe moaned and attached herself to his side. Her cheek slid onto his chest. Jeremy felt the soft gusts of her breath blowing over his skin. She was still asleep. He lay motionless, listening to two heartbeats playing ping-pong.

With the increasing brightness entering the room through the thin window coverings, its furnishings and decorations became visible.

The weathered light gray of walls and floor, the golden ecru of the textiles, the white of furniture and panel mouldings. He had designed the interior together with Fern. 'Driftwood, sand, and clouds' had been their theme.

Jeremy felt an itch in his breast, right under Zoe's cheek, but refused to twitch, not wanting to disturb her. He looked over at the giant canvas that dominated the wall over the sideboard next to the bathroom door.

Lovesick and broken, he had worked here, in the weeks after Fern's death. Lost in a cloud of intense mourning, he sought to find comfort in building a memorial to the woman who had planned to leave him — creating a stage for the over-sized art prints of Fern's stunning tide pool series, featuring bulging starfish, voluptuous sea anemones and hairy urchins on a bed of lush algae, painted in a subdued color scheme. Romantic — and astonishingly sensual.

He flinched: the itch had reappeared.

Uncanny that, with the variety of hotel rooms available in town, he had to wake up, after this surprising night of pleasure, under one of his dead wife's paintings. When he entered the cottage with Zoe, the woman in his arms was all he could think of, see, smell and taste. They didn't waste time turning on lamps; the soft yellow gleam in the sheer curtains, coming from the round solar lights that marked the footpath between the cottages, was all they needed to find the bed and each other.

Overpowered by the sensations her presence supplied, the interior of the place and the pictures in it stayed far from his mind.

Now the awareness of where he was felt like a cold, wet sponge shoved in his face. The picture over the sideboard showed two purple sea stars, their fleshy extremities entwined in an almost lascivious manner.

Jeremy didn't have to look up to know which painting presided over the bed. Above the padded headboard hung *Tide Pool Dwellers*, number two in the series of seven, forty-three by seventy-three inches, Giclée on cotton canvas, stretched with mirrored edges. He had put it there himself.

Living, his wife had wanted to leave him; deceased, he seemed to be stuck with her. Now, Fern's eerie presence seemed to deride him, to emphasize the fact that he had spent hours making love to a stranger. What did he know about Mrs. Zoe Loomis?

Nothing, and everything. Enough to want to wake up next to her for the rest of his life.

He buried his face in Zoe's hair, inhaled its lovely warm smell — pie crust, puff pastry. Not pineapple.

He smiled. Their joking had continued throughout the night, with talk about fruity body parts, leading to allusions of apples and pinecone sizes.

No bad memory was allowed to overshadow this experience. He would explain the problem and ask her to move to a different hotel. Charlotte's mother ran a nice bed and breakfast.

Zoe stirred.

"I need to tell you something very important," she muttered and peeked through the mess of hair covering her eyes.

Jeremy brushed back her savage curls with his hand. "And I really want to know," he whispered and kissed her temple. "But I should get going now. This is a very small town. I will be back at ten and take you out for breakfast. Okay?"

"Sounds great," she purred.

After a long embrace and a kiss that would have led to him staying had they been in any other bed in town, he got dressed and sneaked out of the cottage.

The sun rose over the woods in the east. Its light reached the quiet ocean, making it shine like wet sea glass. A morning without fog. Rare and remarkable. He breathed in the crisp air. It tasted of change. A sense of tranquility swept over him. Whistling, he crossed the trestle, this giant friendly millipede, its wooden feet dug into the sand of Pudding Creek Beach, now forever connected with an endearing memory. Jeremy started to jog.

A short while later, he entered his workshop to finish the oval bandbox. His hands performed the moves they knew by heart while Jeremy's thoughts returned to the woman waiting for him at the Sea Star Inn. The finished box was, he realized, one of the nicest he had ever done. The cherry wood glowed — just like Zoe. It would make a wonderful present for her. He would fill it with Turtles.

Jeremy went to the house and into the kitchen, more out of habit than by intention.

He didn't feel like making coffee; he would have a cup with Zoe. Or tea, or whatever she drank in the morning. All these wonderful things waiting to be found out. So much to discover.

He was thirsty though, for a drink of water or juice. Walking over to the refrigerator, Jeremy frowned at the assortment of mementos on its door. Away with this morbid collection. Under the sink, he found a plastic bag. Photos and keepsakes got dumped, sealed with a double knot and buried under a pile of old receipts in the junk drawer. He took his coffee mug from the counter and filled it with ice-cold orange juice.

"To new ways," he said and toasted the quiet fridge. Its engine came on with a jolt, startling Jeremy into a laugh. Even his appliance was happy to see the stuff gone.

He drank half of the OJ and felt his stomach gurgling. A little snack couldn't do any harm. Jeremy reached past the open door into the cold and picked a soft white cap with a green topping from a china plate covered with Saran wrap.

This recipe had long become a supper standard for Abbie and Gina. Usually, he participated in their meals with reluctance and clandestine disgust.

Now, for the first time in years, it actually looked appetizing to him. And it was: fresh and chewy, with nice pesto inside, not bad at all. Behind the mushrooms sat a jar of pickled bull kelp.

He opened it and lifted one of the ginger-colored loops with two fingers. It smelled of onion and garlic. New ways indeed, Jeremy thought as his tongue received the crispy piece: sweet and sour, with an interesting coppery tang — yum. He took another one. Satisfied, he screwed the lid back onto the jar and put it away. That would bridge the time until the breakfast with Zoe. He downed the rest of the juice and rinsed his mug.

As he passed the black-and-white portrait of Abbie and her mother in the hallway, Jeremy almost expected Fern to turn her giant head and give him a look, but she didn't. Nothing happened as he took the canvas off the hooks and leaned it against the wall, the other way round. The spell was broken. This picture had to go, her paintings too — he would take down all things Fern. Her parents could have them.

He opened the door of his daughter's bedroom. How could she ever get over the past with this huge reminder on the wall? Why not paint over the mural and make this place his and Abbie's? And create space for a new woman in his life. Maybe he should have done this a long time ago. It had been a haunted house all these years, with the paralyzing presence of Fern's ghost.

It was barely eight o'clock. Painting these three walls would take him not more than an hour. Four gallons of Whitecaps semi-gloss were stored in the workshop. Two coats and the mural would be gone, leaving a clean slate. He could do it and still have enough time to shower and dress and drive by the only convenience store in town that carried Turtles year round to purchase a package and put it into the present for Zoe.

Ninety minutes later, Jeremy walked through the hallway again, this time coming from his bedroom. Fern's paintings and the large photo of her and Abbie were stored out of sight in the back of his closet. He would give his parents-in-law a call on the weekend and tell them to get the stuff. Exhilarated by his new-found radicalism, he started whistling.

Passing Gina's door, a smile crept over his face. What would his sister say when she saw all this? He would give her a call after breakfast. A last glance into Abbie's bedroom: the fresh white walls beamed at him. Well done, they whispered. Well done.

Still whistling, Jeremy left the house, went into the workshop and picked up the box for Zoe. The polished cherry wood shone in the morning sun. In the middle of the lid, he had glued on a decoration, the silhouette of a tiny turtle cut with his jigsaw out of a leftover piece of dark-stained walnut veneer.

Simple, but pretty. Maybe he could start making boxes again and approach a few gift shops. The two wood colors worked so well together, reminding him of chocolate on a doughnut.

He smiled: time for food.

Jeremy got into the van, backed out of the driveway and rolled past Zoe's silver BMW with the Washington license plates. The Evergreen State. Pretty snazzy car for a social worker, he thought, but probably another gift from her well-off ex, and it was not a brand-new model as far as he could tell.

She would have to adjust to less extravagant offerings. Jeremy glanced at the box on the passenger seat, not doubting for a moment that she would gladly do it. When was the last time he had felt like he could burst with joy?

The van hummed along Elm Street, toward the convenience store.

Fifteen minutes later, he pulled off Main and stopped in the parking lot of the Sea Star Inn.

Jeremy opened the package of Turtles and placed the chocolates into the little wooden container. Getting out of the van, he checked his appearance in the side view mirror. Shaven and groomed. "You clean up nicely," Fern used to say. He didn't care a whit for her opinion anymore.

The light-gray linen blazer and striped cotton shirt went well with his best pair of jeans, and thankfully didn't smell as musty as he would have expected them to do after being ignored in the closet for years. He had almost forgotten how it felt to dress up for a girl.

Although yesterday, Zoe hadn't minded being seen with him in public wearing a T-shirt and worn work jeans. He smiled and locked the van.

The cottages basked in the sun. Through the gaps between them, Jeremy could see the meadows on the cliff top and the ocean, and the lonely group of tall cypress trees sitting on the edge of the bluff by the trestle, their slender stems and feathery windswept crowns leaning close to each other for support.

Just a few yards more and he could take Zoe into his arms again. His feet moved faster, around the corner onto the stone path that led to the small houses at the rear end of the inn's property.

A familiar figure stood in front of the Pink Barnacle, holding a garden hose. Deidre was soaking the roots of a lavish hydrangea. Its marshmallow blossoms matched the cottage's name.

Jeremy frowned. There was no other route to take. Surely she had already spotted him. Why her of all people? Could he not have bumped into her co-owner, Catherine Bartlett, instead or one of the cleaning staff, who would have let him pass by with a friendly nod? He should have walked down the haul road and sneaked in from the back.

Sunrays tickled his cheeks. Great, now he was blushing like a sixteen-year-old on top of it. Good thing he had decided against buying Zoe a bunch of flowers.

"Hi, Deidre," he said and gave her a casual smile.

"Nice to see you, Jeremy," Deidre said, wiggling the water hose. "I'm filling in for the gardener today." Her eyes fixated on the wooden box in his hands. "Were you looking for me?"

"Ahem, no," Jeremy mumbled, glancing down at the polished oval container. He didn't long for Deidre's refreshment anymore. Zoe's soft rain had fallen on his thirsty soil, soaked his withered grounds, flooded his desert plains.

He cleared his throat. "I was on my way to Mrs. Loomis's cottage."

"Mrs. Loomis?" Deidre asked and yanked at the hose. She moved closer to him and administered liquid to the plant next in line.

"Yes, she's staying in the Fantasea. Checked in yesterday."

Deidre's nose curled. "I think you got that wrong," she said. "Dr. Van Mellen is in the Fantasea. I rented it to her myself around noon."

Where had he heard this name before?

"Dr. Van Mellen?"

"Yes," Deidre nodded. "Small, shapely, mid-thirty, blonde mop. Good-looking."

"Brown eyes, slacks, blouse with zigzag stripes," Jeremy continued her list, "blue nail polish."

"That's her. From Seattle. Staying for two weeks."

Jeremy flinched. "Gina must have mixed up the names," he muttered, trying hard to remember which face muscles to employ for a businesslike expression. "I'll give her a call — oh, and your closet quote is in the mail. Thanks, Deidre."

He turned and walked away. The sound of water spilling out of the garden hose mocked him all the way back to the parking lot.

The rain had been a mirage, and after seeing it, the drought suddenly became unbearable.

Jeremy got in the van and put his key in the ignition. But he didn't start the engine; instead he called a mobile number in Sacramento.

"Westfield."

"Hi, Melody, how's it going?"

"Jeremy! Nice to hear your voice." His mother-in-law was always genuinely pleased when he phoned. It happened seldom enough.

"I just wanted to thank you for sending over Dr. Van Mellen," Jeremy said.

"So she told you. Wonderful," Melody cooed. "I'm so relieved you're getting along. We saw her on Monday. I liked her. But I wasn't sure if it was a good idea to send her 'undercover' as Chester called it. We really do hope she will be able to help Abalone."

Jeremy ended the call after a couple of additional pleasantries.

He switched the phone's power off, feeling he wouldn't be able to speak to anybody for a while. Or drive anywhere. So he just sat there, the phone in his hands, staring at the turtle box on the dashboard.

Deceived again. One weak moment and he managed to get his heart broken by a shrink masquerading as a social worker — go figure. Although it was a surprise he had any heart left to injure. Well, she had pulverized the shards.

His weak moments, able to ignite chain reactions. What would happen now? Something huge no doubt. Like the series of events that ensued from him slapping Fern in the face.

The outburst of feelings after years of bottling them up and pretending to himself and the world he could live with their arrangement. Her supposed visits to her parents' place in Sacramento, when in reality she was screwing a banker in the Mission District or some wannabe Picasso in Gualala.

"I've never felt before like I do now." She had stood in the middle of the living room, telling him that their marriage was over with the calm and patience of somebody explaining something fairly obvious to a developmentally challenged child.

"I really liked you Jeremy, but this is bigger — it's overwhelming. So intense, so burning and alive."

He felt his face flushing with the color of the Red Hot Poker that grew outside all over the backyard.

What did she think he had felt all these years for *her*?

"You're such a slut, Fern!" he screamed. "Do you have to destroy everything we have?"

"We have nothing, Jeremy," Fern snapped. "I will go to San Francisco with Ruben."

This was the moment when Jeremy noticed the eyes in the small opening between living room door and doorframe.

"Abbie!" he hollered. "Come in and hear from your mother that you're nothing!"

"Don't do that," Fern hissed. "And you're not getting her. I'll take her with me." She stepped toward him and whispered, "Abbie's not yours anyway."

He lashed out.

Fern spun and fell, theatrically, but didn't notice the coffee table and grazed her face on the corner. Abbie came flying into the room, flung herself over her mother and started crying.

Of course, it was partly true. Fifty percent chance a paternity test would rob him of his daughter.

He left the house without another look at them and locked himself in the workshop, where he senselessly sawed for the next few hours — an activity that did not provide him with an alibi.

He heard Fern leave in her Cayenne, the latest bombastic birthday present from her parents, thinking she had taken Abbie with her.

Only later, when the little pink bicycle was found somewhere behind the boathouse, Jeremy learned that Fern had left without Abbie and driven to the Abyss. Where she only met Gina. At least Fern had the mercy to depart without notifying his sister as well.

Jeremy didn't have the nerve to tell her either. First the shock of seeing his lifeless wife on the stretcher after they had fished her out of the harbor, then the fears about his daughter's disappearance. Abbie was discovered after a night of frenzy and dread. But it remained a mystery what had happened to Ru. The police expected his body to wash ashore somewhere; after all, the blood on the deck of the *Limpid* was not Fern's. The coroner deemed the cause of her death to be drowning, but they treated the case as suspicious due to the wound on her forehead.

Jeremy proclaimed to know nothing about it. The fight with Fern became marginal in his mind. Nobody ever noticed the slight discoloration in the wood of the coffee table's corner. He had mended it secretly, on the first night after Abbie was found, sanded and polished and replaced the tiny pieces of abalone inlay that had come off when Fern's forehead banged against it.

Two seniors exited the cottage next to the parking lot and strolled toward Jeremy. He pretended to be texting. They reminded him of the Harstroms. A sweet old couple.

Still fond of each other, he could tell from the way they walked side by side, their arms locked. How does it feel to grow old with someone you love? Jeremy wondered. Well, he would never know.

The pair got into the Buick next to him and left.

Jeremy hurled his phone onto the rear seat and rolled down the passenger window; it was getting hot in the van.

After miraculously being found and brought home, his daughter became very quiet and walked around the house in a daze. Like everybody else, he waited for her to talk about what she had seen, but she did not open up about the events of the fateful day, including the scene she had observed at home. When they were alone, he had tried to explain it to her. "It was an accident, baby. I did not want to hurt your mother. Please tell me what happened on the boat."

At no time did he receive an answer. Silently, she slipped away from him.

Of course, telling people about the argument and its root cause would have put him in the top spot of the list of suspects.

He was the guy with the compelling motive. Crime of passion. Double murder caused by jealousy. But then, nobody else seemed to know about their affair, and Ru and Fern had been seen leaving the harbor together on the *Limpet*. For their final hypothesis, the police settled with surprising a gang of poachers or encountering a great white.

Both would account for Ru's disappearance. Yet Fern had drowned, and her body showed only one injury, caused by her own coffee table.

A DNA comparison with the Fuertes family confirmed the small quantity of blood on the deck of the *Limpet* to be Ru's. It was possible he had hurt himself with a diving knife or speargun arrow. A shark might have smelled the blood in the water and attacked them.

The poacher theory had its merits. But never for a moment did Jeremy believe Fern would have gone diving with a fresh head wound, nor would Ru have allowed it. Or gone with her. And nobody ever explained why she was wearing a wetsuit two sizes too large.

As for the town gossip — Jeremy didn't see why his brother-in-law should have killed Fern. She had made it clear that they intended to be together. It must have been some kind of accident. And where did Ru go afterward? The *Limpet* was found empty. Abbie adrift in the dinghy by herself. His car parked at the boathouse. How could he have escaped swimming or on foot?

The only possible witness remained silent. And her father decided to do the same.

Through the open side window, Jeremy could still hear the sound of water gushing out of the garden hose.

He looked up.

Deidre worked in front of the Red Snapper cottage now with her back toward him.

Jeremy moaned.

It had taken a while for the rumors to subside, but eventually the police closed the case, and people found other topics to feed on than the mysterious and scandalous stories surrounding the *True Limpet*.

He had tried to protect Abbie and himself.

And keeping the secret about their spouses' infidelity granted Gina an untarnished memory of her husband. Why burden her with additional pain? The possession of hidden knowledge was no pleasure, as Jeremy knew, being the guardian of Fern's closet skeletons.

And a ghastly bunch they were.

Her escape to New York, shortly after graduating, where she got rid of Bryant Cranmore's baby.

The unsavory story of an affair with one of her art professors, who had left his wife for her and tried to shoot himself when Fern broke up with him.

Of course, Jeremy would learn all that later. Later, long after the wedding. Learned that Fern had breezed back into town and resumed the relationship with her former boyfriend, regardless of his marital status and the three little Cranmores born during her time in New York. A relationship that continued for some months, even after she had started fooling around with Jeremy.

Still, this knowledge could not make him love her less.

He had absorbed every drop of her attention, relished each morsel of affection.

Even discovering why she agreed to marry him didn't break the spell. One afternoon, walking on the beach together, watching a tiny Abbie scurry around on the shimmering bits of glass, his mother-in-law had blurted, "Oh, how thankful I am that she lives," or something pathetic along that line. Jeremy didn't relent until he had dug out the ugly facts. Chester had made it clear to his daughter that he would cut off all financial support if she got a second abortion.

At least his parents-in-law hadn't been aware of his unverified fatherhood. Jeremy was certain they would have tried to get custody immediately.

His stomach growled. Surely indigestion caused by the strange items he had eaten at home in his dopey euphoria.

Now he should already be sitting at a nice table outside of the Bean and Bagel, enjoying an omelet, bacon and tater tots with the lovely Zoe. Who waited for him only forty yards away in the Fantasea. Wild horses couldn't drag him there. Nothing but a fantasy this had been. He would never speak to her again. One deceitful witch in his life had been enough. Jeremy took the wooden box off the dashboard and opened the lid. Inside their little plastic wrappers, the Turtles were getting squishy.

He loved melted chocolate, but the discovery of Mrs. Loomis's true identity had spoiled his appetite. He put the lid back on and tossed the box onto the seat behind him, where it opened and scattered its contents over the phone.

Three years ago, he had caved in to his doubts. He had sneaked into the studio and collected hairs from the sofa on which Abbie slept (hoping the root follicles were intact for testing) and send them to a laboratory he found on the internet, together with a cheek swab sample of himself. He had never spent a more worthwhile hundred and fifty dollars.

Liquid splashed onto asphalt. Deidre was coming close to the parking lot with her hose now. Hadn't she heard about the water emergency? The severe drought?

Jeremy started the van. He wasn't in the mood for further embarrassment.

# Thirty-Five

## GINA
### THURSDAY NOON

Gina's fingers touched the bulging mass of fabric covering her legs. She let out a sigh. How could she have fallen asleep in this puff of rosy organza — surrounded by black plastic that reminded her strangely of body bags?

What a horrible thought to have first thing in the morning. Particularly on this very morning. She sat up and pushed the garment bags onto the floor. Why hadn't she put them away last night? At least the other dresses hung side by side on the rolling clothes rack in the corner, where she left them to air out; neat and orderly, as if just delivered.

She glanced at the alarm clock. 10:43. Good grief — she hadn't slept that long in ages.

In a little more than two hours Elon would stand in front of her door. And to be late on Abbie's birthday. Of course, there wouldn't be much of a celebration, no cake or balloons, no teenage friends coming over to party. Birthdays used to tiptoe through this house, putting on a sober and subdued demeanor as if ashamed of their boisterous nature. Still, Gina had wanted to get up and have breakfast with her niece, give her the dress she had wrapped yesterday before playing for hours with Mrs. Yelland's heirlooms — dreaming of the past, and the possible future.

Gina's nostrils tingled. She sniffed at her pillow: slightly musty. The cover had to be changed. Although, this was not the piercing odor she smelled. It reminded her of fresh paint. Jeremy had to be working on something in the driveway. Yet, would the fumes travel into the house from there? She listened. All was quiet. Strange. Gina bent down, picked up her braces and started fastening them to her legs. At least she had managed to take them off last night before falling into what turned out to be a coma-like sleep.

She pulled the wheelchair close to the bed and moved her body into it. The petticoat billowed. She squashed it down with both hands, no sense in taking the dress off now. Her plan had been to put it on anyway.

She sniffed again. Not to receive Elon smelling like a quart of paint, though. Oh for a couple of drops of Eternity to dab onto her neck. Wondering if there was any old perfume left in the bathroom closet, Gina rolled into the hallway. The odor intensified: it seemed to be coming from Abbie's room. She pushed against the door.

The scene inside made her feel thankful for already

being sitting down, as it would have caused her knees to buckle even before her injuries. The mural was gone! The choir of purple starfish, the palace among emerald kelp, the little mermaid in her floating shell, the seahorses and dolphins, all replaced by bright-white emptiness. Judging by the strong fumes, it had just been painted over this morning. The structure of the abalone shards forming the shell carriage was still visible, as well as the small white bumps of the sea glass that had adorned the mermaid's hair and neck. Although it wasn't there anymore, Gina could still see the girl's sweet face. The picture seemed burnt onto her retinas. And she remembered the story. On her fifteenth birthday, the little mermaid swam to the surface, to the shore, and looked at the land and its inhabitants for the first time in her life. Was Abbie's fifteenth birthday a magical date too? Painting the walls a cleansing? A weird rite of passage? Had the incident from last Friday triggered this? Could it be a sign that her niece would be able to let go of the past now?

Gina reversed her chair and returned to the hall — the naked hall. She glanced up and down the long corridor. Through the band of skylights, the high-standing sun emphasized the bareness of the walls. What had happened to Fern's paintings? And the photo?

"Curiouser and curiouser," Gina whispered, entering the bathroom.

One of the blue towels hung over the chrome rail, used, with a couple of paint smudges on it. Abbie must have had her bath this morning. Normally, she never washed before going to the ocean, but hey, Gina thought, if new customs were to be introduced to this house, she would be the first to wholeheartedly welcome them all.

A faint odor of shaving cream hovered in the air. Did Jeremy help Abbie paint and put the pictures away? He had seemed so strange when she saw him last, smiling and whistling. What was going on?

Gina decided in favor of a birdbath and grabbed her washcloth. After cleaning, and brushing her teeth and hair, she applied some clumpy mascara leftovers from a dried-out tube. All other cosmetics in the vanity looked equally ancient and unappealing. Elon would have to put up with her *au naturel* — but what about the perfume? Gina opened the small closet behind the door. The inside reeked of Fern. It still contained her sister-in-law's flacon collection with expensive French designer fragrances.

Gina frowned. She would rather smell of Benjamin Moore. How could she have lived all these years with reminders of the woman who destroyed her happiness? Why not get rid of the stuff now? There's no time like the present, Gina thought and picked up the small wicker basket at the bottom of the closet.

Thankfully, no neighbors walked or drove by as she made her way out of the entrance door, onto the even-level path connecting the house and the workshop.

Nobody beheld the over-dressed woman in the wheelchair at the side fence hurling perfumes into the empty dumpster.

One of the glass bottles broke as it hit the metal. She smiled; the garbage men would be pleased. Trash smelling of Chanel No. 5.

Returning, she frowned at the shiny black BMW with the license plate from Washington that was parked at the end of the driveway. Jeremy's van was gone; had he taken a client somewhere?

Back in the house, Gina opened every window she could reach to let the beautiful sea breeze blow away the paint fumes. She fed Señor Limón a couple of apple slices and a few grapes, before she collected her crutches, and the little ginkgo from the windowsill in her bedroom, which she relocated to the living room, where Elon would hopefully spot it right away.

She rinsed her hands under the tap in the kitchen. The bunch of lavender she had cut yesterday and arranged in a vase on the dining table gave off its sweet balsamic scent. Gina inhaled deeply. What a diverse olfactory start to her day. Yet, she noticed the absence of one familiar smell. Jeremy's single cup pour-over brewer stood unused next to the blender. For the last few years, Gina had been greeted by the aroma of Classic Roast and the presence of filter and coffee grounds in the sink every morning. Jeremy's mug sat in the dish drying rack. Abbie, on the other hand, had not used anything, neither a glass nor a plate. However, much more perplexing than these minor variations of the breakfast ritual was the empty door of the refrigerator: Abalone had taken off the memento collection! The matte silvery surface warily reflected the unaccustomed view of the kitchen. Gina peeked inside the fridge. Obviously, Abbie had nibbled on the mushrooms.

The doorbell rang. Gina glanced at the stove clock. Too early for Elon. She sped to the entrance.

On the doormat stood the Harvest Market delivery driver, trying to hide his bewilderment at her unusual attire behind a box of fresh produce.

"Hi, Artie," Gina said, smiling while moving her chair back to make room for him. "Could you please take it to the kitchen for me?" She ran her hands over her skirt. "I don't want to ruin my dress."

After Arthur had brought in the new grocery box and left with the old one, Gina covered her splendid outfit with an old pinafore and prepared spinach salad with white beans and a zucchini marinata for lunch. She would invite Elon to eat with Abbie and her.

But where was the birthday girl? Gina checked the clock again. It had been unusual for her niece not to come to the house last night to have supper. As little as she ate, she was always rather punctual for the mealtimes, her courtesy being another way of letting her aunt know she appreciated the effort. Gina sighed; since the weekend, everything must have been pretty chaotic for Abbie. Taking three china plates out of the cupboard, Gina wondered when she had seen Abbie last. For sure yesterday morning, packing an apple and a peach in her sling bag and then filling a container with nuts. Thinking about it, it had not been the small container she usually took but a larger one. By Abbie's standards, that amounted to food for three meals.

Gina placed the plates on the table. If Abbie hadn't been in the house this morning, who had painted the walls and removed the pictures from the hallway and the stuff from the refrigerator door? Could it have been Jeremy?

But why?

He loved the mural so much, and the fridge collection was his untouchable shrine. Hard to believe he had eaten stuffed mushrooms for breakfast.

Gina pulled the phone out of the chair's side pocket and called her brother's number. Voice mail.

Had he taken off together with Abbie? Something was wrong here. Gina glanced down at her braced legs coming out from under the puffy organza. A grotesque outfit — she looked like a monster doll.

She wheeled herself through the open patio door onto the deck. "Abbie," she shouted toward the studio. "Abbie, please come out for a moment!"

The studio stood quiet and secretive in the dry grass.

"Abbie," Gina yelled. "Are you there?" She heard the sound of a car stopping at the side of the house. Jeremy, thank heavens. He could run down to the beach to see if the dinghy was gone. "Jeremy!"

"Georgie?" Elon strode into the backyard, carrying a brown paper bag. He was all dressed up in a khaki cotton suit, with a white shirt and tie. "What's wrong?" he asked, his voice concerned, yet his face unable to hide the pleasure of recognizing her dress.

"I haven't seen Abbie since yesterday morning. I have a strange feeling."

Elon put the paper bag down on the deck and took her hand. "Sweetheart, please don't worry. I'm sure there is a perfectly harmless explanation."

"Please, could you check the studio? And I want to know if she has taken the boat out. She stores it in an opening in the cliff face, by the path."

"I know where," Elon said, carefully placing her hand back in her lap.

Gina felt his fingers brushing over the skirt, lingering, relishing it — she knew that of all the splendid Yelland gowns, he had loved this one best. Elon touching organza. Gina felt her face flushing; the fireworks of memories his short gesture sparked. The feel of the picnic blanket spread out on the soft sand, the rhythm of the waves meeting the rocks, the burst of heat despite the Pacific's nightly chill.

Luckily, Elon didn't see her reaction as he had stepped off the deck and now jogged across the lawn to the studio door. He knocked.

"Abalone, please open up."

No reaction. He tried the handle and it allowed him to enter. He vanished for a moment and, coming out, shook his head in Gina's direction before straddling over the back fence. He was still in great shape and light on his feet; she wondered if he danced these days. Gina squeezed her fingers around the armrests of her chair. What was she thinking? They had to find Abbie!

"The boat is there," Elon said, joining her on the deck after a short while, sweat on his forehead. "And I couldn't make out Abalone on the beach or in the water."

"What about her bicycle? Was it leaning against the fence? She took it yesterday morning."

"I didn't see it."

"Maybe Abbie had an accident. Or has she run away? Today is her fifteenth birthday. I'm almost convinced she hasn't been home since yesterday morning. And Jeremy was so very strange."

Gina noticed the panicky tone of her voice but couldn't stop the outbreak of words. "He whistled. I haven't heard him whistle in years. This morning he whitewashed the mural and took the stuff off the fridge. I don't know what to think. And there is that black car from Washington State sitting in our driveway."

"Calm down, sweetheart," Elon got down on his knees by her side. Gina turned toward his suit jacket. This was nice, their height difference now like it had been when they were young.

"Have you tried to phone him?"

"Of course. Five times. I only get his voice mail."

"He might be out on a job." He was near enough for her to smell his breath. Pleasant, familiar.

"No, Elon. He *never* turns his phone off. He calls me *all the time.*"

"Georgie, I promise we will find both of them. Let's go inside. I'll make a couple of calls." He leaned on the armrest to get up, but Gina was faster and grabbed his shoulders.

"Thank you for being here," she said, pulling him close. "I'm so sorry to wreck this moment with my family problems."

"Sweetheart," Elon whispered, his lips touching her ear, "your problems are my problems."

# Thirty-Six

## ABALONE
### THURSDAY, NOON

This is a place of peace. I float on my back in the river. The sun twinkles through the leaves above me. Golden dots dance on the water, highlighting the tips of my toes. I never see them when I dive; they stay hidden in my fin. I wonder how the little mermaid felt when she looked at hers. I have disliked my toes for a long time: the small white worms that they are; pale sprouts — ugly like the tentacles of the polypy.

The little mermaid had wanted feet so badly, yet they gave her so much pain. I wish for the tail she renounced. Over the years, I've drawn countless pictures of the one I hope to receive, and I know exactly how the ideal tail would look:

elegantly streamlined and silver blue; some scales sparkle with crimson like rockfish fins, dotted with the Coho salmons' small black freckles, ending in a perfect fluke similar to the gray whale's, shaped like two hands holding a heart. So infinitely preferred over the ungainly chunks of flesh at the end of my *legs*.

As soon as I'm back on land, I will conceal them in my boots. I don't know if the little mermaid used to wear shoes. It is mentioned that her soles bled on several occasions, though nobody around her ever seemed to be aware.

When she climbed with the prince to the tops of high mountains, it was so bad that even her steps were marked; yet she only laughed, and followed him till they could see the clouds beneath them. So even the prince, who truly cared about her, never noticed it. How could he not see the red footprints on the palace floor when the little mermaid danced for him? Surely blood would be bright on white marble. It is on white skin. And on tanned skin. He didn't love her enough.

I think about consequences these days. What if something you wanted with all your heart, and have lived toward, proves to be an error? What if the desired place is not how you expect it?

I must prepare myself to deal with unpleasant surprises. The little mermaid knew what awaited her. She had to make the prince love and marry her. The sea witch was a credible source and her warning unmistakable: "Every step on land will hurt as if sharp blades cut your flesh. And if the prince gets betrothed to another, you will turn into foam on the crest of the waves."

Can I really believe what the book shows me; the underwater world and its beautiful, friendly people? Will they welcome me? What if they think I'm not their kind and reject me? What if they saw me when I was younger? I didn't mind fishing with a speargun then. Shooting arrows. Piercing living creatures. When they lay on the wooden planks, I stroked them. My fingertips ran over their silvery skin. They flinched and struggled, and their life seeped out of them onto the deck of the boat. We brought them home, and I'm ashamed now I ever ate them. I hope they have forgiven me.

The boy is standing behind the blackberry bushes thinking I don't see him. I wonder if it is a coincidence that his hair is raven black and his eyes as blue as the prettiest cornflower.

I have enjoyed being with him, walking together through the sweet-scented woods, where the green boughs touched our shoulders, and the little birds sang among the fresh leaves.

He told me his name is spelled *L e i f*, but it sounds like *leave* — fitting for my last day among the Props. *Take Leave*. I wish he would sing again.

I remember the little mermaid swam up the river to the prince's balcony, where he stood and watched the stars. He would have been very surprised if she had made a sound or shouted. It could have startled him; maybe he would have dropped the crystal cup he was sipping red wine from, or maybe he would have been so perplexed to see her that he stumbled and fell over the marble balustrade to his death. These things happen.

However, she kept silent and later she couldn't say how much she loved him, that she had rescued him and given up everything for him, because her tongue was gone. She had decided to leave her world, and there was only pain and regret — and no return.

At night, when the prince and his court were asleep, she went to the palace's broad staircase that reached into the sea. She sat down on the marble steps, bathed her burning feet in the chilly water and thought of all those she had left in the deep.

Yet, in the end, there was a way back: killing the prince.

# Thirty-Seven

## LEIF
### THURSDAY, NOON

Through the blackberry hedge, Leif watched the green, shimmering pool. A little left of the bushes, the riverbank curved into the stream as if trying to embrace it. There, the water rested, taking a last break before continuing the journey to the river mouth and losing itself forever in the vastness of the Pacific Ocean.

Leif picked some more berries and tossed them in his mouth. The juice stained his fingers the color of Abalone's dress, which was spread out on the soft grass of the riverbank, patiently waiting for its owner, who lay in the small cove, looking like she slept on the water. Carefully, he collected another handful of fruit, only the largest and ripest, and put them one by one in his water bottle, which was now almost filled, as a surprise for Abalone. She would thank him with a mesmerizing gaze; he longed to look into her eyes again. His enchantment over their sudden companionship was undiminished, despite the increasing grumble of his stomach, caused by the meager breakfast of leftover nuts and river water.

Leif tensed up. From the middle of the stream, a shadow approached Abalone. About ten feet away from her, a small furry head poked out of the water. The river otter stopped and peered at the bathing girl (who either hadn't noticed its appearance or didn't mind) as if it, too, was bewitched by Abalone's presence.

The sudden howl of a car engine rang through the woods. The otter flinched and dove out of sight. Leif turned around. A Jeep sped out of the trees and stopped by a pile of rusty metal chains next to the rails running through the small clearing. He waved to the driver, thankful Gordon not only owned a boat but also an off-road vehicle. Of course, his friend showing up was not entirely an act of Good Samaritism, as Leif had messaged him about going for a dive in the afternoon to possibly retrieve the lost bags or fill some new ones if necessary. Max had been pissed, and Gordon eager to get into his good books again.

"Hi, Gord," Leif greeted.

"Dude, what are you doing here?" his friend hollered and jumped out of the dusty Suzuki. "Did they throw you off the train?"

"I was camping."

Gordon stomped toward him, peering at the slack

backpack that squatted next to Leif's feet and the blackberry bottle in his right hand.

"Without equipment? Do you plan to audition for Survivor? Shoddy story, bro." He turned back toward his Jeep. "Let's get going."

"No, wait. I'm not alone."

As if she had heard her cue, Abalone appeared in the opening between the hedges that shielded the stream, walked out of the water in her bathing suit and picked up her dress. The expression on Gordon's face was priceless.

"Don't tell me you spent the night out here — with her." His voice oscillated between disbelief and envy. It wasn't hard to figure out in which direction his thoughts were taking off.

"None of your business."

"A tryst with a sassy wood nymph." Gordon chortled. "And here I'd thought you wouldn't fancy another spanking."

"You might want to switch to your best manners," Leif hissed, annoyed that when it came to teasing him, Gordon could display such untypical rapier wit.

"If you can remember where you have misplaced them. Abalone is neither mute nor deaf."

"Yeah, and she's pretty hot," Gordon said under his breath, still staring at Abalone, who stood at the river edge, now in her dress, wringing out her hair. "You can't blame me for wondering, bro, given the force of your last encounter."

"Keep your imagination in check. This isn't what you think."

"Puppy love?" Gordon elbowed him in the side. "Come on." He went over to the Jeep.

"Anyway, I trust you've tamed her, and she's not going to throw a tantrum while I'm driving."

Leif rolled his eyes, thinking it was time for him to get new friends, and followed Gordon to his vehicle. "You're safe, don't worry," he said, realizing that the rear bench was taken out and he would have to sit on the floor. "Safer than I'll be," he mumbled to himself. At least the hardtop would give him some protection. "By the way, we'll need another wetsuit," he added for Gordon to hear.

"You recruited her?" Again his friend's face contorted into a grimace of surprise. "Respect, man. But you're paying her out of your part, right?"

Leif looked to the ground. No more lies, he had promised — but this was a white one, to make Gordon believe he was going to harvest mollusks for Max this afternoon when in fact he wanted to show Abalone where he had found the bracelet. After waking up and having another swim together, he had told her outright that he hadn't found it at the beach.

"I know," she had whispered, peering at him with her two-color eyes.

"Do you want me to show you where?" he had asked her, and she nodded.

Leif had checked Google maps for the nearest road, and then they had walked along the train tracks to the first stop where a car would be able to pick them up.

Gordon still stood in front of him, awaiting the answer to who would remunerate the unexpected addition to their poaching party.

"Don't worry, Gord," Leif said. "I'll handle that."

"Okay. Fine with me. If she's as good at diving as everybody says, we should be able to double our productivity." He slammed his hand on Leif's shoulder. "Good job, bro."

Leif felt a pang of remorse for unduly exciting Gordon's anticipation, but he preferred to have him in a positive mood for now. "Do you have the goodies?" he asked. During their early morning phone call, he had given Gordon detailed instructions about the route to find them and the lunch to bring.

"I sure do," his friend answered, and opened the passenger door.

Leif tried to ignore the smell of weed wafting out of the Jeep. Gordon grabbed the plastic shopping bag waiting in the foot room and handed it to Leif. "A salmon panini, two banana nut muffins, a pint of cherry tomatoes, and pumpkin seeds." He picked up a cardboard drink tray. "An extra-large coke, and a spinach smoothie." He glanced at Abalone. "Which now makes sense."

Leif sat down on a small stack of logs and dumped the bag's contents onto the wood beside him. With any luck, the food would air out quickly, and they could have lunch right here before driving back to town. "Anyway, thanks for getting this. I'm totally famished," he said, sniffing at the fish sandwich, but Gordon didn't offer a reply because his attention was taken by Abalone coming closer. The white shells stood out against her wet dark-red hair. The sea glass strings sparkled around her neck. Light shone through her dress which was damp from soaking the moisture off her skin. And if it was possible to walk elegantly in hiking boots, she had mastered the art. She seemed to float.

Gordon stood motionless, holding the tray of beverages like a waiter who had forgotten which table ordered them. Leif grinned and, hoping his friend's dumbfoundedness would last for a while, he jumped up to present Abalone with the blackberries.

# Thirty-Eight

## DAN
THURSDAY AFTERNOON

Dan yawned. The long shot of the town hall meeting room was rather dull. He took a swig of Vitaminwater. Why hadn't he tried a more unconventional angle? The mayor and the council members, each sitting at small tables arranged in a row, looked like clerks behind airline counters ready to weigh your baggage.

At least, the large Star-Spangled Banner in the corner provided some fresh color among the browns and grays of the room's interior.

Such a pity he didn't have the camera with him last Friday when he had seen Abalone Macklintock dance in the sparkling surf.

What a great opening shot it would have made, and he could have used short clips in between this mediocre material.

First, the director of the Community Development Committee had read the staff report dissing the preposterous idea, and now the chairwoman of the local business association was going to highlight all the advantages. Why did his boss think that any national channel would pick up this non-issue? It was quirky, to be sure. Maybe fit for a humorous kicker story at the end of the news, but not for a forty-minute feature length.

"Listen," the close-up of Pam Fowley on his monitor said, as if addressing him directly, "we have collected 1,347 signatures so far. The citizens of this town love Glass Beach, and they want it to remain an attraction for our guests. Questions have been raised about the ecological effects of our proposal. We are not the uncaring, greedy capitalists we have been portrayed as over the last months. This is neither drilling nor fracking. The welfare of our environment is of the utmost importance to us — as is the welfare of the people living in it. To put the concerns regarding a possible pollution of our coastline with waste glass to rest, we have turned to a renowned scientist in the field."

Dan yawned again.

At least she was pleasing to look at, her low-cut top the redeeming feature of her presentation so far.

Maybe your expert will have an idea on how I could transform the footage of this snoozefest into a riveting documentary, he thought, chuckling. Hopefully she would wear something hot again this afternoon, and he could get some nice shots on location at the business association's PR event.

"Professor Oliver Mulroy from the Department of Geosciences at the Florida Atlantic University will speak to us in a couple of moments via Skype about the biological and chemical research he conducted to determine if recycled glass could be used as fill material for eroding beaches." On the video screen over the heads of the council appeared a face with well-tanned wrinkles.

"Good evening, Professor Mulroy," Pam Fowley said, nodding in the direction of the screen. "Thank you for joining us at such a late hour. It must be almost twelve in Boca Raton."

"Good evening, ladies and gentlemen," the large face answered. "It's indeed late, Mrs. Fowley, but I'm more than happy to burn the midnight oil and acquaint you all with the results of our recent research." The professor moved back a little in his chair, allowing a view of a crammed bookshelf and a stretch of wall with a poster showing an aerial shot of the Everglades.

"All over planet Earth, critically eroded beaches pose a myriad of social and environmental challenges, prompting an effort to explore alternatives to more traditional sand sources. One alternative involves the use of recycled glass cullet as coastal beach fill in erosional shoreline hot-spots. Studies have shown that it possesses the same physical and chemical characteristics as native quartz beach sand found throughout the world's beaches." Papers got shuffled close to the microphone, and the professor held up a photo of three large plastic buckets.

"Here you see containers with 100% cullet. Crabs, mollusks, urchins, and other marine life were introduced to each bioassay and analyzed through scientific observations."

Dan couldn't control his mouth's movements anymore; it opened wide frequently on its own account. The combination of the two Quarter Pounders in his stomach and Professor Mulroy's monologue proved positively sleep-inducing.

"After a prolonged exposure to recycled glass cullet matrices, it was determined that an artificial cullet substrate does not adversely affect macrofauna habitation or microfauna colonization. This study clearly demonstrates that recycled glass is a biologically safe alternative when used in marine applications."

Herewith, the professor had finished his exposition, obviously expecting applause. The audience duly employed their hands, the members of Pam Fowley's entourage most emphatically.

Dan gulped down the rest of his warm Vitaminwater. The woman had done her homework.

From behind his table, the mayor cast a long, somewhat irritated look at his ex-wife, who appeared genuinely pleased with the professor and herself.

"Thank you, Professor Mulroy," she said toward the screen, "for the enlightening facts you have presented to us. All the best for your future research."

The professor wished everybody a good night, and the screen went blank.

"We now have scientific proof that supplementing our fantastic beaches with pre-tumbled waste glass would not have any negative effects on the ecosystem. Our Glass Beach has a special geographic design. Nothing gets washed away; it's a big natural tumbler. Whatever we put there will stay and not spread into the marine environment at large. Please look at this photo."

A picture appeared on the screen.

"Most of you might think it's showing a collection of particularly fancy pieces from our famous beaches. In reality, though, what you see here is common sand under a microscope, magnified three hundred times. We are proposing nothing more than throwing large grains of sand among smaller grains of sand." Mrs. Fowley was radiating confidence now, triumph almost palpable.

"In fact, not only should we replenish, but also encourage our local glass blowers to garnish the beach with their leftovers. All over the world, bottle factories and glassware producers used to tip their end-of-the-day waste over the cliffs, to the delight of present-day collectors." The screen behind her showed a picture sequence of rounded glass bits in fantastic color combinations.

"Murano, Italy; Barcelona, Spain; and the small town of Seaham on the east coast of England are only a few examples." More pictures of translucent pieces looking as if modern artists had embellished them with tiny abstract paintings. "This move might also bring the detractors on board who claim the refined tastes of connoisseurs would not be met by glass that's insufficiently rare or antique."

"Dan, stop whatever you're doing!" Charlie Lentman stood in the doorway with all the authority of his two hundred fifty pounds.

"I just got a call from the police. A teenager is missing. They want us to put it on the website and send an emergency newsletter to our subscribers. Let's tweet it, too."

"Who is it?"

"The girl who was involved in the wacky incident last Friday. Jeremy Macklintock's daughter. Didn't you say you saw her just before it happened?"

"Yes, at Glass Beach."

"They don't have a current photo of her, so we are to use one of the photos that were posted on Facebook. Please do it ASAP before you head out to the shooting. This is the description her aunt gave the police." Charlie dropped a scrap of paper on his desk and disappeared.

Dan picked up the note and read it over. The poor girl. He sincerely hoped nothing bad had happened to her. He logged into the MENDO Live website and started typing a new post:

*The Mendocino County Police is asking for the public's assistance in locating a missing 15-year-old female. Abalone Macklintock was last seen yesterday, at 8:00 a.m. at her place of residence on Elm Street. She is wearing an ankle-length burgundy-colored dress and is possibly riding a pink children's bicycle. Abalone is described as 5'9" and around 130 lbs., with long and wavy dark-red hair. Her eyes are of different colors: the right one blue, the left one green. If you have any information, please call . . .*

# Thirty-Nine

## JEREMY
### THURSDAY AFTERNOON

Hoofs clomped on asphalt. Jeremy turned his head to the left. A white horse pulled a shiny carriage around the corner of 2nd Street onto M Street, past the wooden bench he had been sitting on for the last twenty minutes.

"This is the Pink Lady, one of the highlights of Eureka's Old Town," the coachman announced to the beaming young couple in the back of his carriage, who approvingly beheld the ornate Queen Anne house behind Jeremy's bench. "It was built as a wedding present," the coachman added, and his enchanted passengers emitted synchronized sighs.

Jeremy winced, feeling like a bride abandoned at the altar. What had possessed him to come to this place named after an exclamation of joy, and torture himself by watching happy pairs being chauffeured through this manifestation of a romantic dream?

He was, obviously, out of his mind. After driving up the coast for almost three hours, trying to figure out the latest disaster in his love life, he had remembered the time when his father had taken them here to see the famous Carson Mansion in its eclectic glory. A family trip, one of the few good days of his childhood.

He gazed at the large building across the street, again feeling the wonder of his eleven-year-old self, at the astounding woodwork in the gables, turrets, cupolas, porches and pillars. It hadn't changed in all these years. An architectural gem. The most photographed Victorian house in America. An exquisite relic of the Gilded Age with a magical blend of eighteen century styles. The mansion rested in the midst of the lush, meticulous grounds like Sleeping Beauty. Untouchable, unattainable. A private club owned it, making it accessible only for a select few.

You can peer at it from the outside, but you will never be admitted, Jeremy thought. Wasn't that exactly his fate with love? He could never get in. The people he loved most refused to return the feeling on a permanent basis.

For Fern, he had barely been more than the flavor of the month. Abbie's affection had lasted for eight precious years before it got revoked. Mrs. Loomis's interest was a lie in the first place — yet so utterly convincing. He could still taste the sweetness of her kisses. What a talented actress. The only mutual love in his life existed between him and Gina.

And her he had let down.

He should have addressed Fern's escapades right away.

Jeremy stared at the fairy tale mansion, which stood tall against the blue noon sky. In his present mood, the lively roofscape reminded him of a giant perching bat — boasting its gloomy splendor, tainted by haughtiness and egotism. Hard to believe now that he actually had, once, been inside. On a late August day, about twelve months before his mother left, it had opened its doors for him and his family. An acquaintance of his father worked in the building as a custodian and treated them to a private tour. Open-mouthed, face flushed with excitement, Jeremy had wandered behind the adults as if he had been taken to visit Disneyland, overwhelmed by the work of master craftsmen from Europe. In addition to the amply used indigenous sequoia, Mr. Carson had imported ninety-seven thousand feet of *primavera*, a white mahogany from South America, along with other exotic woods from the Philippines, East India, and Mexico. More than once, Jeremy had lagged behind, on purpose, to trace the intricate carvings with his index finger. A smile crept over his face. Sitting here, on the bench at the corner of 2nd and M Street, Jeremy realized he truly loved what he did for a living and that, thankfully, it loved him back. It was the thing he could hold on to, now that the past was erased and the future blank.

In front of his inner eye, the paint roller went up and down over Abbie's face, gradually covering her lovely features, the only part of the job that had bothered him. The faint smile still recognizable through the first coat of Whitecaps semigloss. A new life was what he wanted, a new Abbie, or the old Abbie he had known.

What would she say when she saw her freshly painted room? Say. He could only wish she would actually *say* something. He should have stayed, to explain, to deal with her reaction.

Jeremy got up and walked back to the marina where he had parked the van. He had just fumbled the key out of his pocket, opened the door and sat down when a police cruiser stopped in front of him. He glanced over at the meter; his time had expired.

A female officer approached the van. "Are you Jeremy Macklintock?" she asked through the open window.

She was young, barely thirty. Her chin-length bob haircut had Zoe's light-golden hue, but the dark roots betrayed its falseness. Deceit lurked everywhere around him.

"Yes, ma'am," Jeremy said, his driver's license suspended in the air between them. How did she already know his name?

"I don't need to see that," she said, her facial expression friendly but serious. "We got notified by our colleagues in Mendocino County. There is some problem with your family. Please call your sister immediately. Do you have a phone with you?"

Abalone. Jeremy struggled to breathe. Again, he pictured her face vanishing behind white paint. She had seen what he did and flipped out. Had attacked Gina. Done harm to herself.

"Mr. Macklintock?"

"Yes, ma'am." Jeremy turned around in his seat and fished for the phone hiding under the chocolates. The Turtles had liquefied in their wrappers. "I'll call right away."

# Forty

## GINA
### THURSDAY AFTERNOON

The ginkgo twins on the coffee table waved their little green fans to the rhythm of the music. Or was it her lightheadedness causing the illusion? In any case, Gina had to beam at them. Standing on Elon's slow-moving feet while he held her, she felt as if she were fifteen again, getting shown the Foxtrot steps for beginners. Her hand lay on his shoulder, and the diamond on her ring finger twinkled in the afternoon sun.

"Let's do it right, this time," he had said, pulling a small box out of his jacket. They found the clip on You Tube: Fred Astaire and Ginger Rogers dancing 'Cheek to Cheek', and now Gina's laptop belted out the familiar tune.

Elon had already hit replay twice, and the ginkgos were not getting tired of it.

"You still have your tree!" he had blurted out when they entered the living room. Gina had turned her chair to see him opening his paper bag and taking out a bonsai, shaped almost exactly like the one he had offered years ago, only the glazed terracotta holding it was a red oval instead of a blue square.

"Well, it's the symbol of longevity," Gina said, and shortly after, they clasped each other, lying on the sofa again, picking up where they had left matters unfinished the Saturday before. Once in a while, a voice from the guest room demanded *un beso*, and Gina gladly complied.

Elon had persuaded her that she couldn't improve the situation by worrying. The police searched for Abbie. There were no reported accidents involving her; the hospitals in Mendocino County hadn't admitted any patients fitting her description. With a couple of additional calls, Elon found out that Jeremy's phone was presently located within the city borders of Eureka, which caused Gina to exclaim, "What the hell is he doing in Eureka?"

"Work?"

Gina shook her head.

Elon contacted the police in Humboldt County with the van's license plate information, and only fifteen minutes later, Jeremy's number flashed in the house phone's display. Now he was on the way home.

Over the last beats of the music, the door bell rang out, merrily echoed by Señor Limón.

"Jeremy?" Elon asked.

"He has a key," Gina answered.

"Maybe he wants to give us a heads up so that we can make ourselves presentable." Elon directed his feet toward the living room door. "Let's surprise him," he added and grabbed her tighter, giving Gina no chance to object that with Abbie missing Jeremy would certainly not be in the mood for jokes. Yet she couldn't bear to wreck the moment.

"This is the start of our life together," Elon said, as if guessing her thoughts, while he transported her backward through the hallway. "I will not allow anything or anyone to spoil it." He sounded so convincing, and the support of his arms made her feel light and secure. Gina decided to believe him, to take his love and pull it over herself like a feather comforter and let it drown out the world.

When the entrance door opened, astonishment was equally shared by all five persons present.

Pam stood on the doormat, behind her the owners of Petersen's Delicatessen and Carmichael's Tackle & Sport, groomed and dressed up as if ready to attend Sunday school.

"Hello," Pam exclaimed, eyeing up Gina's attire before addressing Elon. "Sheriff, what a pleasant surprise." Her hand gestured toward the deli's delivery bicycle parked in the driveway. "We've come to take Gina to the beach."

## Forty-One

### LEIF
THURSDAY AFTERNOON

She perched next to him on the port gunwale of the *Wave Runner*, smelling of apple blossoms. Leif grinned — he did too. Today even Gordon's awful wetsuit lubricant was enjoyable.

Abalone gathered her hair around her hand and, pressing it against the back of her head, pulled her hood over it. The sky blue and olive of its camouflage design matched her eyes perfectly (Gordon had picked up one of the high-end open-cell spearfishing wetsuits and a monofin at the Abyss on the way to the marina, obviously under the influence of her gaze). A few red strands escaped and curled over Abalone's temples and along her neck.

Of course, she couldn't enter the cold water without protection, but he loved seeing her hair flow. Soon they would immerse together. He had decided to go without scuba gear, so there would be no disturbance, no load on his back, and he could fully concentrate on the surreal beauty of his companion. Her presence would transform these familiar surroundings, like a blue light changes the scenery on a night dive, bringing out the fluorescence of the creatures living in the deep. Gordon's father had shown him videos of his Fluo dives in Australia and Thailand. Coral reefs lit up like Times Square at 10 p.m. Green, orange and crimson, as if somebody had cracked a gazillion glow sticks.

Leif glanced over at Gordon, who handed Abalone two mesh bags with the bow of a servant. She took them, her face unperturbed, not for an instant disclosing her knowledge. He had told her everything, revealed all his secrets while they trudged side by side along the train tracks. The poaching, the singing lessons, the now jeopardized money in the bank account in Richmond meant to pay for his tuition fees, how much he missed his grandpa and that he could never find the right moment let alone the words to tell his parents about his dreams. He even was candid about following her around since Monday, and having slighted Eleanor.

Leif fastened the second strap of his leg wrap and made sure the knife was secured.

Abalone had nodded as if she perfectly understood.

The ocean was still calm, although a light wind had sprung up. The *Wave Runner* cut through the water, passing a crowded Glass Beach on starboard.

They had almost reached their destination. Soon, Gordon would leave to take the boat back to the marina and then deposit their shoes and Leif's backpack holding their clothes by the cliff path at Glass Beach.

Leif gazed across the softly rippling sea. He was pretty sure he would recognize the location the bracelet had lain. A spot with large underwater rock formations full of mysterious holes and crevices, hiding places for snails.

Abalone put on her fin. They were ready for the backward roll. Leif placed one hand over his mask to prevent it from dislodging when he entered the water. Abalone grabbed onto the gunwale and raised her legs, moving them up and down. The aqua-colored fiberglass monofin Gordon had chosen for her fluttered through the air. Together with the blue-greens of her wetsuit, it looked almost like a mermaid's tail.

As Leif fell off the boat into the icy Pacific, a cascade of pictures flooded his mind, like a time-lapse video, showing the unbelievable, exceptional happenings of the last twenty-four hours.

Somersaulting in the water, he found Abalone waiting for him. Through his diving mask, he had a perfect view of her submerged eyes: the black dots of her pupils, swimming in clear brightness; a captivating, piercing stare. And once in a while, tiny bubbles escaped her mouth and nose as if she breathed out diamonds. How wonderful to be here with her. The crowning glory of their time together.

Abalone flung her body around, moving downward, and as Leif followed her to the rocky ocean floor below, a feeling of uncertainty took hold of him.

He knew why he wanted to dive with her. But what were her motives? What was she hoping to find there?

# Forty-Two

## ABALONE
THURSDAY AFTERNOON

He swims with ease and elegance. We glide together through the turquoise haze, going to the surface. He can hold his breath long but not as long as I. If we had the time, I would show him my favorite places, the secret caverns full of shiny glass, the sheltered spot among the kelp stems where peace takes hold of your heart.

But now that the fog veiling my memories has lifted, I know I have to complete one task before I leave, pay the debt I owe. He has talked a lot on our morning walk, about making things right, about coming clean.

I didn't remember for such a long time — all I knew was my desire to live at the bottom of the ocean.

We rise to the surface, arms spread out wide, the air in our lungs lifting us towards the light. Our faces emerge at the same time. His cheeks are alive with color from the water's chill and the physical effort. On my lips, I taste the salty flavor of sea and tears. We are alone now. He has told the boat to drive away. The rocky coast is close enough to swim to, my beach only a little south-east from here. Sun rays pierce the water like shiny arrows. A few dolphin kicks later, we are on the ocean floor again. It has been many years since I have seen a mask close to me. I had forgotten the excitement of diving with somebody who's not a seal. It's like a foretaste of being with the merpeople. Bodies moving in the same rhythm, fins touching — under-water smiles. Drifting side by side through a world of wonder.

However, today I cannot pause to enjoy its attractions: the colorful stars, big and small; the colonies of spiky balls; the curious creatures whose name I bear, sitting everywhere like scared turtles hiding in their shells; the delicate structures of corals and anemones; the large lingcods with their light and dark body patterns, mimicking the rock surface; the bull kelp saplings, waving their hair; no time to play with the seal pups in the seagrass meadows.

Today I have a purpose that is grave and gloomy.

He points and nods. This is the spot. I trust his memory has not tricked him. A shoal of ocean perch lingers above, as if monitoring us. Rifts and holes gape between the rocks, gateways leading to unknown realms. I turn to inspect the crevice to my right. My palms roam over the scaly crust of living beings that makes everything look alike, resembling scab on a wound. Sediment spreads easily down here.

Algae grow fast. Creatures feed. Creatures settle. Fabric disintegrates, but nylon rope doesn't. Metal stays metal. Bone remains bone.

The water whispers as one of the perch vanishes in an opening to my left. Is the fish trying to show me something?

I grab onto the protruding stone edge and slip sideways into the mouth-like gap. Sheltered from the light coming from above, the colors change. The rock is dabbed with splotches like a painter's palette, burnt orange and umber, and the Cadmium dark red of dried blood.

I twist my shoulders and enter deeper into the hollow. My hands wander over its shadowy ground. Small things come to life under my palms. Some spongy, some rough. Abalones abound here. My fingertips run over the row of respiratory holes in one of the carapaces. The foot is attached to a hard, flat triangle.

I exit and beckon to Leif, who's waiting in front of the rock formation with a curious face. He swims near. I reach out and touch his thigh where he carries the knife. I press the release button and slide the blade out of the sheath. He flinches back, startled. I have frightened him. Don't worry my eyes say as my hand seizes his shoulder and my mouth touches his. I think of the little mermaid kissing the statue of the prince in her underwater garden. His lips feel cool but soft, not like marble, and they push onto mine.

I withdraw and turn, smiling while I glide back into the twilight of the hole, Leif behind me, his body half in, half out, trying to see what's going on. The knife edge scrapes off the coating that limpets and barnacles have created and reveals a smooth metal surface: the steel fluke of an anchor.

I drop the knife, grab the metal with both hands and yank. It's shoved deep into a rock fissure.

I wince as a head bumps into my hip. A long snakelike body slides past my thigh. I have disturbed a wolf eel. The water gurgles as Leif moves behind me, surely to make room for the eel and its ferocious grimace. Strangely appropriate that one should live right here. Despite its fierce exterior though, it is not dangerous. I will need air soon. I yank and yank until the anchor comes loose. I feel the chain attached to the slip-lock shank, and the rope attached to the chain.

I need air now. I dash into the open. The wolf eel is gone, and so is Leif.

I look up: his dark body floats high above me. He does not paddle.

I ascend toward him.

He does not move at all. His face points down. Small dark clouds are coming off the side of his head. He must have bumped it against the cave wall when the eel dashed toward him.

He's unconscious — like the young prince when his noble ship sank in the storm, groaning and creaking; the thick planks giving way under the lashing of the sea as it broke over the deck, the mainmast snapping asunder like a reed; the ship lying on her side, the water rushing in. The little mermaid saw the prince sink into the deep waves, and rejoiced, for now he would be with her, before she remembered that human beings could not live in the water. By the time he got down to her father's palace, he would be quite dead.

But he must not die.

So she swam among the beams and planks that were strewn across the surface of the sea, forgetting they could crush her to pieces. She dove, rising and falling with the waves, till she managed to reach the prince. His limbs were failing him. His beautiful eyes were closed.

I whip the water with my fin, dart to Leif and turn him around.

I slide my right arm around his chest and rest his head against my neck. My hood comes off, and my hair starts whirling like hers did.

I couldn't go into the water without a wetsuit; I was too small and the land far away, the sea rough. She had told me to stay. But I should have tried. I should have tried. I knew how to do it. Uncuru had taught me the cross-chest carry.

I should have jumped overboard and grabbed Mommy's head, put it on my shoulder and swam toward the coast. We should have died together. Instead, I held her hand until it was ice cold. But not this time. I will bring him ashore.

I tighten my grip and kick against the water.

He must not die!

# Forty-Three

## DAN
### THURSDAY AFTERNOON

Dan let his camcorder pan across the glass at knee height. The frog perspective delivered a spectacular view of the beach, the ambient light making the most of its colorful topping.

The scattered rocks stood out sharply against the cloudless sky. The ocean murmured around them, reflecting the sun.

He now had about enough material in terms of landscape cinematography. A few more close-ups of the sea glass, in dry conditions, and splashed by the surf, and they could start the main part of the afternoon shooting.

A bunch of tourists shuffled through the glass in the distance, one eye on Pam Fowley giving her entourage a final prep-talk in the middle of the beach, and even a local VIP graced them with his presence: on one of the logs by the cliff sat the county sheriff (obviously off-duty as he wore a suit instead of a uniform) together with Gina Fuertes, who seemed a bit overdressed for the occasion.

Dan shouldered the camcorder and slipped his hand into the support strap on the zoom lens. Looking through the viewfinder, he focused on Mrs. Fowley, who had positioned herself in front of an all-male backdrop — eight members of the business association (dressed in black, probably to set off her scarlet mini-skirt suit) forming a half circle behind her. They looked like a choir ready to perform, except they didn't hold song sheets but two-gallon Ziploc bags bulging with glass.

"Ready when you are," their leader stated, both her thumbs pointing skyward.

Dan responded with one of his. "And action," he shouted, pressing the record button.

"We are here today," she began, and eight smiling faces nodded, "because we care."

Her sidekicks changed to a more solemn demeanor.

"Our beloved Glass Beach is facing a crisis..."

While she went on to praise the advantages of her recommended solution, repeating the arguments he had heard from her already, Dan felt his own opinion finally settling. He saw the whole thing as a kind of nature's performance art, an ephemeral event. Junk turned jewels. Beautiful but fleeting. The same way it was created it would vanish, the surf grinding it to tiny specks, blending into the sand. They all could count themselves fortunate that the environment had dealt admirably with the initial abuse, unaided by the progeny of the perpetrators. It should be enjoyed while it lasted, not be turned into a circus.

Pam Fowley's mouth still moved.

"This is a magical place," she now said, voice and hands raised. "Let's keep the sparkle!" Sure of their approval, her sweeping gestures included the sea glass collectors standing at and on the cliff, watching her performance. "Replenishment means prosperity," she concluded.

Dan stepped back.

They would now disperse and empty their bags of glass on the beach.

However, Jordan Longdale turned his head as Greg Young and Caleb Petersen both pointed out to sea while Ben Carmichael dropped his glass and ripped off his suit jacket and shoes. The camera panned between Pam Fowley's perplexed face and the eight men dashing into the water.

Dan flinched as Sheriff Wagner sprinted past him, hollering back toward the cliff, "Georgie, take the phone out of my jacket and phone 911!"

# Forty-Four

## JEREMY
THURSDAY AFTERNOON

On Jeremy's right, the Sea Star Inn flew by, the very place that had hosted one of the most heady nights of his life — and one of the most sobering awakenings. Briefly, he wondered what Zoe was doing right now. She must have clued in that her cover was blown. They hadn't thought of exchanging phone numbers. Of course she could find Macklintock Carpentry in the business directory; the answering machine in the workshop would take care of that.

And hopefully she had the decency not to phone his home and involve Gina in her despicable charade. Jeremy dug his fingernails into the vinyl wrap of the steering wheel.

How could he even waste a thought on the little bitch while being without information as to the whereabouts of his only daughter?

Gina had phoned twenty minutes ago to tell him she and Elon would be at Glass Beach for the next hour. Saturday's smooching had obviously resulted in reconciliation, and of course he was happy for both of them. At any other time, he would have rejoiced and congratulated her; however, Gina finding love and purpose the very moment he was faced with losing it all seemed like cruel mockery. Had Abbie really not been home since Wednesday morning? Yesterday afternoon, he had wished for her to stay away. Last night, he had looked into the dark kitchen only caring about following a stranger to her hotel room. And yet, it had felt so right. So genuine. So lovely.

The van closed in on the intersection at Main and Elm. The Denny's sign on the corner reminded Jeremy of the missed breakfast and the lunch he didn't have. As he switched into the right turn lane, he heard a siren. The traffic came to a stop. From the opposite direction, an ambulance rushed down Main and turned left into Elm Street; he sneaked in behind it, following the blaring horn all the way to the dirt track of Glass Beach Trail, his palms getting sweaty on the steering wheel. Please, not Abbie. The ambulance stopped about fifteen yards before the cliff.

Jeremy parked a little ways from it, dashed out of the van, cut in front of the paramedics and their stretcher, and ran.

Small groups of people lined the cliff edge. Talking. Pointing down. How well he knew this scene.

Please, not Abbie.

He should have never agreed to this diving nonsense in the first place. Mrs. Hotchkins was right all along. Gross negligence on his part. And now the ocean had finally claimed his daughter too.

He stumbled down the path, almost slipping as the beach came into full view.

This location was surreal to begin with, but the present sight outright bizarre. Black suit jackets were scattered all over the multicolored ground like sunbathing crows. Sea glass collectors gathered on both sides of the beach, gawking at its middle, where Dan Hanson, video journalist at MENDO Live, filmed a group of men in sopping dress shirts and pants, huddling around a slim body in dark rubber lying on the ground. A pair of feet with diving fins reached into the water.

Two fins, not one. In between the forest of wet pant legs, Jeremy could make out the hair: black and short, not long and red. Elon knelt on one side of the body, Deidre on the other, bent over the neoprene chest, weeping. Pam Fowley stood behind her, together with a small blonde woman in beige cotton slacks.

Jeremy ignored the zigzag-clad arm waving to him and sprinted toward his sister, who sat in the shiny glass, looking like a pincushion doll, wearing (if he remembered correctly) her high school prom dress.

"Gina, what's going on here?" He slumped down next to her, disregarding Zoe staring in his direction. "Where's Abbie?"

At the waterline, everybody stepped back as the paramedics arrived and took over.

"I'm so sorry; I was about to phone you," Gina answered. Her cheeks flushed. "Abbie's fine."

Jeremy gasped; relief washed over him like a sneaker wave. Water shot into his eyes.

"She has rescued Leif Saunders. They must have been diving together," Gina added. "She was here just a couple of minutes ago. She gave me a hug."

"Jeremy, could I have a word with you?" Zoe stood in front of him, looking as sweet as yesterday, the sun peeking through her thin tunic. What a difference a day made.

"I don't think there is anything I care to hear from you, Dr. Van Mellen," Jeremy answered, not sounding as sharp as he had intended while turning away to mop his shirt sleeve over his cheeks.

Gina glanced at him, then at Zoe, and back at him.

"Please. I waited. I tried to contact you." Zoe's left sneaker dug its rubber tip into the glass.

"I was asking Mrs. Saunders if she knew your mobile number when somebody came and told her that her son had an accident. I drove her here in her car."

"Bravo. Your good deed for the day," Jeremy replied, managing to increase the iciness in his voice. "You can leave now." Next to him, Gina pretended not to overhear their exchange by staring hard at the paramedics, who carried the stretcher with Leif toward the cliff path, followed by Pam Fowley, Deidre, and eight drenched men wearing their retrieved jackets — in an unintended spoof version of a funeral procession.

"Please, let me explain." Zoe reached for his shoulder with her blue claws.

Jeremy jumped up. "Don't touch me, Doctor." He stomped away to spare his sister further awkwardness.

Zoe followed.

"There's nothing to explain," he said, turning to face her. "You deceived me. You said you're Mrs. Hotchkins's replacement."

"I said nothing of the sort!" blurted Zoe.

A couple of yards away, Elon walked past, politely ignoring their dispute.

"But you let me believe you were from Social Services."

"Would you have talked to me otherwise?"

"Of course not," Jeremy said, watching Elon stand in front of Gina, helping her to get up and pulling her toward him, which sparked the unwelcome memory of Zoe being so close that he could feel her peacock glass pendant poking into his chest.

"Well, there you go," she snapped.

"You used a false name," Jeremy hissed.

"No, I didn't! Loomis is my maiden name, and I'm switching back to it. But all my credit cards are still under Van Mellen. And I hadn't planned on inviting you to my room."

"Please don't remind me that I've slept with one of Chester Westfield's cronies." As if he needed a reminder. "How much has he paid you?"

Elon walked past them again, this time with Gina in a fireman's carry. Her rosy dress billowed like a spinnaker sail.

She peeked around Elon's upper arm and smirked at Jeremy.

"We're heading home. See you later."

Zoe swallowed. "Your father-in-law is concerned about his granddaughter."

"He can't wait to get her in his clutches so he can turn her into a spoiled brat like her mother."

"Do you think she's better off now? Mute and isolated?"

"At least she doesn't think the world revolves around her."

"And how do you know she doesn't? Have you talked to her lately?

"No, have you?"

Zoe was so close. He could smell her hair.

"The last thing I'm going to say to you, Dr. Van Mellen," Jeremy said, remembering the words she had used introducing herself to him, "I enjoyed your relaxed approach."

Zoe flinched. "Jeremy, I have been as surprised by this as you."

How did she deliver her lies so convincingly? He had to shove his fists in his pants pockets to hinder his arms from reaching for her. "Oh, really?" he said, his voice a bit squeaky. "Hands-on is not your usual M.O.? Or do you call it foreplay therapy?"

"Jeremy . . . I understand your anger . . ." Her soft tone evoked another gush of recollections: her skin on his, her fingers, her lips. He had to get away from her now, or make her leave.

"Spare me your psychobabble. I must admit though, you're a specialist. Dr. Van Mellen's full-body treatment. I'm sure you only have satisfied clients!"

"I wanted to tell you last night . . ." Her voice quavered.

"And this morning, but you said let's talk later."

"Sure, it's my fault."

"I came to help your daughter."

"Why don't you help yourself first? You seem pretty unbalanced to me. I will move and take Abbie with me. You and your ilk will not get her."

Jeremy looked around. The beach was empty. The sea glass collectors had called it a day. Dan Hanson and his camera sat on a rock while he smoked a joint.

"Hey, Dan, did you see where my daughter went?"

"Sorry, man. No idea. One moment she knelt by the boy, the next she was gone."

"Thanks, Dan." Jeremy marched past Zoe. "There, are you happy, Dr. Van Mellen? Because of your interference, I have to search for my daughter again."

He arrived on top of the cliff, breathless; a short distance away, Elon rode down Glass Beach Trail on a delivery bicycle with Gina waving from the rear cargo box. The afternoon had acquired a comical note Jeremy wasn't in the mood to fully appreciate yet. He spun around for a last inspection of beach and water, only to find Zoe coming up the path.

"Don't follow me," he yelled.

"I can go where I please. This is a public place."

Her watery eyes contradicted her snotty tone. She was hurt. He hadn't fooled himself about being able to read her emotions. *She* was hurt? Pathetic. Bawl if you need to but look for consolation elsewhere, Jeremy thought and jogged toward his van.

The ambulance had not yet left.

He peeked into the open back, where Leif's head was being bandaged. Deidre sat next to her son, holding his hand. Pieces of black material hung down over the edges of the stretcher like fruit peels; they must have cut the wetsuit off his body. The large fins on Leif's feet moved slightly back and forth. Funny that nobody had removed them.

The second paramedic appeared at the rear end of the vehicle.

"How's the patient?" Jeremy asked.

"He's conscious and stable," the paramedic answered and shut the back door. "His head needs stitches, and they'll probably keep him in the hospital to check out his lungs."

"Good news," Jeremy said, noticing Zoe creep past them. "Take care." He walked toward his vehicle, fingering for his keys in his pants pocket.

A convertible raced along Glass Beach Trail, distributing dirt in all directions, and swerved to a stop in the dry grass next to the van.

"Macklintock! What's your daughter doing with my son?" shouted Kent Saunders and bolted out of his Audi, entirely lacking his usual composure. A wild boar in a business suit. Jeremy had a brief moment to reflect on the smart decision to stay away from his wife before the man's red face came dangerously close to his own.

"It looks like she saved him from drowning," Zoe said, and stepped toward Leif's father, thus diverting his attention. "I'm Dr. Van Mellen." She took him by the elbow. "Would you like to see your son? Your wife is here too."

She led him to the back of the ambulance; the paramedic opened the door for him, and Kent climbed in obediently.

Zoe winked at Jeremy. Surely proud of herself to have rescued him from the boar. Did she think that he wasn't man enough to handle the situation? If she now expected gratitude from him, she needed her own head examined. Jeremy frowned; all this was a delay to prevent him from checking on Abbie. He decided to get the van later, ran down the path toward his backyard and climbed over the fence.

The sun reflected in the window front of the studio. Something looked different. He stepped close and peeked through the glass. New drawings covered the back wall. He rushed inside. Abbie had taken down all jewelry sketches and replaced them with a row of tabloid-size Bristol boards: the events on the *True Limpet*, presented like a graphic novel. His eyes hurried from picture to picture. To his left, Zoe entered the studio, but he didn't have the strength to tell her this wasn't a public place and throw her out. Side by side they stood, studying the drawings, both reaching the last sheet at the same time.

"Good Lord," Zoe whispered.

Jeremy dashed to Abbie's collector's chest and pulled out the drawers: every single piece of her sea glass jewelry was gone.

In a flash, he jumped over the fence and stormed back down to the water.

Abalone had drawn herself swimming into a cavern in the rocks. Passing through it, she was welcomed there by a group of fish-tailed men and women, whom she handed pieces of jewelry as gifts. Abalone with a fishtail, merpeople surrounding her, dancing in a palace under the sea.

A cake decorated with shells forming the number fifteen. Merpeople singing 'Happy Birthday'.

The beach was deserted except for Dan Hanson filming the increasing wave action.

"Abbie!" Jeremy yelled, pacing over the glass. "Abbie!" He couldn't make out anything in the water. The kelp bulbs looked like a hundred bobbing heads.

Dan turned, the camera still on his shoulder. "I saw her swimming out there five minutes ago." He smiled. "I hope she comes back soon. The light is awesome right now. It will be a great final shot."

"Get out of my way," Jeremy screamed, pushing him aside. The surf soaked his shoes and pants as he stumbled into the waves. "Abalone! Please don't go!"

FIVE YEARS LATER

# Forty-Five

## GINA

From the door to the auditorium, Gina peeked down at the lobby and the droves of stylish big-city folk mingling, chatting, and trying to get a quick glass of champagne. Elon and Kent had made it almost to the front of the bustling line-up. They both looked smashing in their tuxedos. Elon a bit slimmer, of course, Gina smirked, but maybe Kent was just bloated with fatherly pride. Since a year ago, when he had given up hoping Leif would come around to admitting his mistake, he was thoroughly invested in supporting his son's career. Through the throng in front of the washrooms sailed Deidre, flawlessly draped in floor-length chiffon and no less proud.

Next to her beamed Catherine Panetta, still high on the deserved praise for having fostered Leif's talent. Her hands caressed the lace on her new gown, a last-minute gift purchased by Gina in the hotel boutique after seeing the Laura Ashley-esque nightmare with all-over pansy print Cathy intended to wear. Finally, it had been her turn to be the fairy godmother supplying a splendid outfit.

Gina smiled as she watched her black orthopedic boots taking her safely back to her seat on the east balcony. The wide-cut silk pants mostly covered them — not being able to wear a dress in public was a small sacrifice for using her legs again. However, she still had to be economical with her strength and didn't want to tire herself out by standing around needlessly. This morning, at the Guggenheim Museum, she had used a complimentary wheelchair to drive down the ramp because her plan was to have a dance with Elon (albeit a slow one) if there should be any opportunity after the dinner.

As she sat down, her eyes glanced across the theater's bright-red rows of backrests toward the empty stage. They all had enjoyed the performances of the young musicians so far but couldn't wait for Leif to appear.

Gina reached for the concert program lying on Elon's chair. The cover showed blurry treble clefs in different shades of aqua and turquoise whirling behind the words 'Dreams come true', the motto of the event. A rather hackneyed phrase, to be sure, and yet tonight, it struck Gina as wonderfully appropriate, profound and touching. Dreams come true, indeed.

She opened the program. Next, after the intermission,

would be a singer and lute player from Japan: Umi Arai performing 'Always With Me' from the animated feature *Spirited Away* in her native language. The black-and-white photo next to the name showed a beautiful young woman holding a bulbous string instrument with a bent neck. After that, she would accompany countertenor Leif Saunders singing 'Flow My Tears' by a Renaissance composer named John Dowland.

Leif's portrait picture was new, black and white as well, probably taken for the concert program. Wearing a light-colored turtleneck sweater with chunky knit pattern, his dark curls tousled, he looked sideways into the camera, confident and masculine. Somehow more mature than at Winter Break when he had been home for Christmas. Of course, they all would have preferred if he had finished his Bachelor of Music in San Francisco.

His second song tonight, a duet with the Japanese girl, would be the aria 'Bist Du Bei Mir' by a German composer named Stoelzel, which was, according to the program, a hit from the Baroque period.

'When You Are With Me'. Sweet title.

Today she had walked down Broadway with her husband of four-and-a-half years. Thanks to two successful operations, paid for out of the insurance benefits. 1.5 million — too much for one person.

Gina glanced at Leif's picture again. She had been able to assist this gifted young man in making his dream come true.

The next page provided the English translation of the song:

'When you are with me, I go with joy,
to death and to my rest.
O how joyous would my end be
if your fair hands would close my faithful eyes.'

Gina frowned and closed the program, wishing she hadn't read it. All she wanted now was to love and live. Later, she would tell Elon about it, in their hotel room, after the dinner, while they undressed.

"Who makes kids sing such morbid stuff?" Elon would ask, pulling her onto the bed.

"I know," she would answer, her cheek nestling against his chest. "But they looked like they enjoyed it a lot." The sentence would stay with her for a long time after.

# Forty-Six

## LEIF

His supporters had seats in the east gallery, way back. Leif couldn't make them out from where he hid in the wing. Thankfully they wouldn't be able to spot him either. Although right now, they surely were as transfixed by Umi's rendition of 'Itsumo Nando Demo' as he was. She performed alone on the vast wooden platform of the Symphony Space's largest theater, in front of the black grand piano positioned center stage, and it seemed the straight glossy hair flowing over her bare shoulders and down her back extended behind her, giving the instrument its shiny finish. Her silky gown's crimson skirt fell over the chair she sat on like the petals of a giant blossom.

In her lap, she cradled a honey-colored lute, plucking it with tender touches, making it chirp, crisp and bright, while her smooth lyric contralto formed foreign words, mysterious, alluring — an incantation to breathe life and joy into everything around her. The huge brick wall at the back of the stage seemed to push forward to listen; the dark curtains on both sides trembled as if attached to the lute's strings; the people in the auditorium glided to the edges of their seats to be closer. Umi's song permeated the place, and everything became part of it. Long ago he had dreamed of falling in love while at music school, just to have it happen when he had no need for it anymore.

His eyes searched the bewitched audience, and now he recognized his mother's cobalt-blue sleeves next to Mrs. Wagner's elegant pearl-gray suit jacket. Leif poked two fingers into the space between his neck and his collar — the shirt was suddenly poised to choke him. He knew he should be happy to have his people here. His mother and Gina Wagner had organized the trip four weeks ago posthaste when it transpired that Magnus Berson would not be able to participate due to nodules on his vocal cords. Umi suggested Leif as a substitute (they had already practiced together for several weeks by then), although he wasn't a foreign student, his voice charmed the organizing committee, and together with the time constraints made for a quick decision.

As a surprise for Leif and a sign of appreciation for her, his parents had invited Mrs. Panetta, which was, of course, terribly kind of them. A weekend in New York, tickets for the Yukimura Foundation's benefit gala for foreign students' scholarships, and the black tie dinner at The Tent at Lincoln Center immediately following the performance.

When he picked them up at the airport in the minivan his father had booked for the weekend, nobody noticed Leif's forced excitement at meeting them all.

Since the day he had nearly drowned, after being spooked by the darn eel and smashing his head against the cave ceiling, his life had been an open book, and Leif felt as if he had received general pardon for his bygone misdeeds. Yet, as he shook the sheriff's hand, Leif almost blushed at the memory of the morning at the dining table five years ago when he had been interrogated by him. Leif quickly turned to the sheriff's wife and hugged her, and it wasn't a fake gesture at all; he was genuinely thankful for her generous help. After all, she had made it possible for him to have his own place. It wasn't as nice as the one he had had in San Francisco, no extra bedroom for overnight visitors here, but compared to the cramped shared lodgings many of his fellow students had to endure, it was heaven. Gina Wagner had been adamant about the importance of having one's own space when you're away from home.

Out on stage, Umi started purring. This part of the song still gave him goosebumps; similar to those he had gotten hearing her for the first time four and a half months ago. Hurrying toward his reserved practice room, he couldn't help but stop and listen. She sat on the floor at the end of a side corridor, playing hushed and absorbed. Then she started singing, and immediately Leif wished for Odysseus's smarts, for beeswax to seal his ears, or a rope to tie himself down somewhere soundproof.

This was how sirens called, the closest he ever came to being hypnotized. He sneaked up and down the hallway trying to get glimpses of the singer, her black fringe, the small ivory face, her eyes (which were focused on her fingers dancing on the fifteen strings of the renaissance lute she held), finding himself spellbound by the silvery whispers of her instrument and the astonishingly rich, deep voice.

He forgot about his booked practice room, forgot about swiping his ID card. The room was gone, together with his peace of mind.

Naturally, he tried to avoid Umi afterward, but she always popped up, as if pursuing him. Dark and delicate, with an air of boldness.

Singing 'Always With Me', it seemed she had used magic to ensnare him and left him no other choice than to follow her, even if he would drown, or be turned into a pig.

"The English translation of the lyrics is rather clumsy," Umi had said once, between two bites of sashimi. "It's only scraping the surface of the true meaning."

And Leif nodded, tapping the chopsticks onto his plate to even them out. How well he understood; he had only splashed around in the shallow waters of love so far. Now he was ready to delve into its fathomless depths.

They often feasted together on the *Omakase* menu in one of her favorite sushi bars. "It means 'I'll leave it up to you'," Umi explained to him. "You trust the chef to create something truly special for you."

*Omakase* became their private joke, their code word, their substitute for vows of love. "*Omakase*," she said before inserting her mouthpiece when he taught her how to scuba dive at the Y.M.C.A. pool on the Upper West Side (even though she grew up in Sakai, a port city with great beaches, she had never ventured out into the sea).

"*Omakase,*" they whispered to each other before their exams. "*Omakase,*" he breathed into her ear in the twilight of his bedroom, as she unbuttoned his shirt, thrilled to find him a novice — and a quick learner.

In two days, they would drive to the Hamptons. He had rented a small beach house in Culloden Shores, affordable by the standards of the area but still an arm and a leg. Thankfully he had the means.

After the accident, Max had proved to be softhearted and given him sole access to the bank account in Richmond, a secret stash of money Leif had barely tapped into so far.

Umi and he would be able to sing together, swim together, live like a couple for a full week, before she would fly to Japan for the summer and he was supposed to hop on a plane bound for San Francisco International Airport.

According to Google, from there it was only twelve hours more to Osaka. A non-stop flight, the round trip for way under two thousand dollars. Then a mere taxi ride to Sakai, where she lived with her parents. Maybe he could invent an audition to delay his homecoming for a couple of weeks.

Umi began the last verse; soon, it would be his turn. Leif took his eyes off the singing girl, remembering the audience, by far the largest he had ever performed for. Yet he felt no tension. She would be there, accompanying him on the lute when he sang. He wasn't anxious about forgetting the lyrics. It was 'Flow My Tears'.

He yanked at his bow tie again; why hadn't he picked the adjustable one?

'Flow My Tears,' of all songs. But Umi loved Dowland. She relished the emotional experience of his compositions, in spite of her character being the exact opposite.

Cheerful and optimistic, she could crack up at the silliest things. And she plunged into Dowland's depression like a bungee jumper, knowing that she would safely bounce back since nothing in her life was giving her any cause for grief. Initially, he had felt uneasy about performing the song with her. Memories of a certain day insisted on being acknowledged. Singing between sequoias. Two-colored eyes. He pushed the thought away.

A last sigh from Umi's lute, and her song was over. The audience snapped out of its trance and exploded into cheers. Umi stood up and bowed. The spotlights above showered her with brilliance. Leif let go of his collar and straightened his shoulders. She came toward him, beaming.

"You were marvelous," he whispered and stooped to meet her offered lips.

"*Omakase*," she replied as they went out on stage together.

# Forty-Seven

## JEREMY

The sunlight hit the sea like silver rain, setting off Zoe's silhouette. Her hair was long now, bleached by the sun and windblown, as he had imagined it. She stood in the water with naked feet, her jeans pulled up, next to her the twins, Liam and Quinn, their small legs a bit shaky on the soaked ground. Every so often, the gently incoming surf reached their pudgy knees. They held little nets in their fists, as if they were out to catch butterflies. Their mother showed them how to rake the mesh through the wet sand. Davenport Beach had become a favorite spot for his family when they were down here for their regular visits with Zoe's parents.

The vast sandy strand, the high cliffs, the single triangular rock poking out of the sea, almost shaped like the one in nearby Shark Tooth Cove; how fond he had grown of this view.

Jeremy squinted. Maybe twenty yards in front of Zoe and the boys, the water stirred and a large black tail fin broke the surface. Liam pointed toward it with his net and chortled. The fin slapped the sparkling ripples and disappeared.

"Abbie," Quinn shouted. "Abbie!"

Jeremy closed his eyes. He still wasn't able to see his daughter emerge from the sea without having flashbacks of the crazy afternoon five years ago.

MENDO Live could not have wished for a better shot: Abalone standing in the surf, dressed in bright-blue like an incarnation of the sea, her left arm raised, holding a skull. The footage got nationwide exposure: teenagers find missing man's skeleton on bottom of NorCal coast. The one minute clip included Leif being dragged onto the sparkling shore, a short interview at his hospital bed, with Abbie and Gina by his side, and underwater pictures of the coast guard divers recovering the rest of Ru's body (they also retrieved the bag of jewelry Abalone had deposited there).

No recording existed of Jeremy and Zoe hugging (she had arrived next to him the second Abbie's head popped up in between the kelp) because Dan Hanson's zoom lens focused on the waves and the approaching girl. Neither was there any of them kissing, or of Zoe apologizing and promising she would never lie to him again for the rest of their lives. So far she had kept her word.

Jeremy opened his eyes to see Abbie in the water that reached up to her waist, taking off her monofin. Zoe turned her head and gave Jeremy a smile. She knew it still affected him. They often talked about the moment when they had stared together at the drawings pinned to the studio wall, at the mosaic of pictures on each page, stark black and white; a slow-motion narrative, unbearably expanding time.

Abbie hiding under a tarpaulin in the dinghy, her widened pupils peeking through one of its eyelets.

Fern and Ru at the stern of the *True Limpet*, arguing. The text in the speech bubble above Ru's large, angry face reading, "I don't care what you've told him."

Fern grabbing his sleeves. Shaking him. Her bubble shouting: "I want us to be together!"

Abbie's fingers pulling rope.

The *Limpet*'s hull coming close.

Above, bubbles against the cloudy sky.

"You're too used to getting your way."

"But I love you!"

Abbie crawling out from under the tarpaulin.

Abbie standing up in the dinghy.

Her hands on the ladder of the *Limpet*. Her eyes over the gunwale.

Ru pushing Fern back. "Get it: I don't want you!"

Fern bending down.

Ru half turning to enter the cabin. "I've told you before I will never leave her!"

Fern holding a speargun, the grip against her chest. A close-up of the arrow sitting in the barrel.

Ru laughing. Raising his hand. "Put it down!"

Fern's upper body bending as she's pulling the elastics of the speargun with both hands toward the notch. Her bubble: "You're not doing this to me."

"Fern, leave the rubbers alone. Don't be an idiot!"

The cable clicking into the spear notch.

Abbie propping her hands on the gunwale, yelling, "Mommy, no!"

Fern's head turning toward Abbie, shock distorting her features.

The speargun dropping. The handle falling onto the deck. The arrow flying. Forward. Upward.

Ru holding his neck, collapsing.

Fern screaming.

Abbie scrambling into the stern of the *Limpet*.

Ru lying lifeless in Fern's arms, blood all over his white polo shirt (here Abbie had used red oil paint, creating a startling effect). Abbie clinging to Fern's shoulder, sobbing.

Abbie and Fern hugging and crying, their faces becoming one.

Ru on the deck, tied up with nylon ropes. Fern and Abbie pushing him overboard together.

Fern hauling the spare anchor into the water. Ru's body flinching and rushing into the deep.

Fern putting on Ru's wetsuit. Kneeling in front of Abbie, kissing her. "Stay here, I'll be back soon."

Close-up of her monofin in the water. Abbie at the *Limpet*'s gunwale, searching the sea for her mother.

Fern's head in the water, the Band-Aid gone, a deep bright-red cut across her forehead (again oil-paint).

Her face exhausted.

Her eyes desperate.

Her arms moving slower and slower.

Abbie entering the dinghy, paddling toward her mother, trying in vain to pull her into the boat; their faces blending into one ugly distorted grimace.

With the knowledge of the drawings, Zoe and he had been able to convince Abbie that she had no blame, that it was an accident and her mother's fault to have picked up the speargun in the first place.

Having saved Leif's life and been able to retrieve her uncle's remains, Abbie said she had received forgiveness. And she also forgave.

Jeremy blinked into the sun again, seeing Abbie wave to him with her fin.

"Dad, I've got some multis and a mushroom," she shouted and bent down to show her finds to her brothers.

Zoe touched Abalone's arm. They all turned around and started skipping through the sand toward him.

At this moment, Jeremy realized, even if he had found the shard of the century, he could not have been happier.

# EPILOGUE

*H*ere in the cave, the water is still and brilliant, as if it has turned into sea glass and captured me like an amber fossil. Jewels are littered all over the floor. The sun beams enter at the right angle to make them shine. Some things never seem to change.

To my right, rockweed pats the gleaming ground like greedy fingers, willing to stuff gems into the air bladders on their leathery leaves. I pick up two fair-sized reds and a pink stopper stem lying close to a batch of spiky sea urchins. Each piece is well-rounded and perfectly symmetrical, as if the rare glass has chosen to congregate in this spot.

A tiny hermit crab tries to take off with a bean-shaped bit of orange, but I don't mind; my pouch is already bursting with treasures.

An ochre sea star digs its fleshy arms into the sand under the glittering glass.

I swim forward, past two foot-long chitons ready to roll into balls should I care to investigate what they hide below their armored bodies. A huge lingcod shoots forth from the back of the cave, like the protector of the place, trusting in its scowl to deter me from robbing the secret vault.

This is such a fantastical scene; no wonder I have believed a fairy tale. The lingcod stares at me with sad eyes. I sneak a turquoise oval into my pouch before I retreat from its territory and swim into the kelp.

Gone are the times when I was convinced I would meet fish creatures down here having human faces. No merpeople were ever waiting for me. They are the invention of an author, part of his made-up story — with a silly ending attached to it: 'Daughters of the air' earning immortal souls by watching over children, whose conduct will determine their fate. Everybody wants a happily ever after, but in my opinion, the little mermaid should have turned into sea foam when she threw herself overboard. It would have been truer to life.

I'm embarrassed to have believed this nonsense. But trauma does that, Zoe says.

Think of it as an invisible injury. You were a child trying to cope with witnessing violence and death. You experienced guilt and grief. It leaves you powerless, anxious. Yet, I have felt stronger when I had no recollection. My life had a purpose then. I'm weaker now. And somehow, though I still love being submerged, diving seems less satisfying these days. However, I'm glad I did not leave. I would have never met my sweet brothers and witnessed the joy they have brought to our home. Zoe has become a good friend. We talk a lot. Many things are still painful to remember.

My lungs need air; I kick my legs and ascend into brightness. Taking a deep breath, I look across the shiny sheet of water toward the land. The glass-covered shore spreads out in front of me. I never grow tired of its beauty and the message it conveys. All these glittering bits were shards, hurled over the cliff, lying there for years with the memories of being broken, their edges raw and damaged. Yet, time and surf smoothed and frosted them; looking at them now, I know healing will come.

It could all have been much worse. I'm glad I didn't sacrifice my legs, or tongue — or cut short my time. I also have retained my skills. I still like to draw and make jewelry, which is a good thing.

Dad thinks I should study design at an art school. But I have not yet decided what to do.

I have a hard time letting go of the ocean. This is why I couldn't fly to New York. I'm not ready to travel that far. I would have loved to see Leif on a big stage. Aunt Gina said he sounded better than ever. His voice is more refined, sophisticated. Except he will never be as good as on that day in the forest when he sang for me alone.

I can't wait until he comes home for the summer.

His new school is so far away. During the years in San Francisco, we were together every weekend. Soon he will return, although not as soon as I had hoped.

He has to stay for something important.

It is just a small delay.

I know he has to practice his voice with excellent teachers. When he is back, he will only sing for me.

I move my fin and start swimming toward the beach.

Before long, he will be here again. When we dive together, I feel I have the best of two worlds. He knows it was me who saved him. No foreign princess will ever come between us. And I don't have to win his heart because I already own it.

Just as he does mine.

Dear Reader,

If you have enjoyed this book,

please give it a rating or post a review

at Goodreads

or your favorite online retailer.

Thank you very much!

## ACKNOWLEDGEMENTS

Many thanks to Stacey, Jill and Janelle for beta-reading the manuscript, and to Debra Ann for weeding out the last mistakes.
A huge thank you to all review chain readers — your feedback and support have been wonderful! Amanda deserves a special mention for spotting the twelve fingertips.
I'm indebted to the members of the Facebook group 'Seaglasslovers', who fueled my sea glass obsession with their amazing photos and invaluable knowledge.

## ABOUT THE AUTHOR

Silke Stein is a graphic designer and the author of *Trina Bell's Humming Summer* and *Sleep, Merel, Sleep*.

Silke currently lives on the west coast of Canada, where she combs the shores of the Pacific Ocean and tends to her ever-growing sea glass collection.

When she is not at the beach, or writing, or helping her husband playtest his latest board game invention, she designs book covers for fellow authors.

To keep up-to-date about Silke's news, latest releases and giveaways, please visit:

**www.silkestein.jimdo.com**

# Who wants to be awake forever?

Life has changed for eight-year-old Merel. Since the birth of her sick baby brother, her parents seem to have forgotten she exists. But when she finds a tiny silver violin in her bedroom rug, things take a turn for the worse. Merel learns that her sleep has abandoned her and that she must embark on a perilous journey to recover it or stay awake forever. Together with her devoted toy sheep, Roger, tired Merel sets out in search of Lullaby Grove and, before long, is haunted by a scary stranger.

Follow Merel into a surreal world. Meet a sleepy king with an obsession for feathers and a transparent old man on a night train going nowhere. Discover why the moonfish cry, why you should never walk across the Great Yawns, and whether Merel can escape her pursuer, win back her sleep, and realize what matters most.

*"I thoroughly love this storybook and believe adults, as well as children, will be reading this one for years to come."*
—Lori, book blogger and former library supervisor

*"One of the most adorable middle-grade stories I've ever read!"*
—Ivana, book blogger, *diaryofdifference.com*

*"A lovely children's book filled with lots of nonsense and silliness. Underneath all that is an important message about family and love and treasuring those closest to you."*
—Janine Atkin, book blogger, *@unashamed_bookhoarder*

*"I can't even begin to describe how wonderful this book is."*
—FallingLeaves, Goodreads reviewer

# "An amazing coming-of-age story."

Twelve-year-old Trina Bell has finally had enough. Why should she spend another dull summer watching Great-Aunt Roswinda lawn bowl and nibble cucumber sandwiches while her estranged father has all the fun? This year, she won't let him get away with his usual excuses. To her surprise, she succeeds. Her dad, the famous wildlife photographer, agrees to take her with him to the Canadian rainforest.

Trina's triumph is short-lived, however; soon she finds herself alone on Vancouver Island, in a strange apartment building that may not be what it seems.

But when she befriends Moss, the three-legged dog living across the street, and becomes involved in a puzzling case of vanishing hummingbirds, events take an astonishing turn.

Will Trina be able to solve the mystery, and win the love of the father she longs for?

"This is one of the most enjoyable books I have read in a long time! It is both magical and real at the same time."
—**Joanne**, children's librarian, USA

""Trina Bell's Humming Summer is a fabulous, original story."
—**Suze Lavender**, book blogger, *withloveforbooks.com*

"I absolutely loved the story. It was exciting and sweet. I especially liked the father/daughter relationship. It's easy to relate to and really tugs at your heart strings."
—**Amanda**, Goodreads reviewer

"The imagery that Silke Stein uses is amazing. The plot is VERY unique. I had a hard time putting it down."
—**April Gilly**, *Readers' Favorite*

CPSIA information can be obtained
at www.ICGtesting.com
Printed in the USA
LVHW092349150121
676619LV00001BA/84